A SECRET HISTORY OF TIME TO
COME

He pushed his way through the dense and
endless forest, a tall young man, tough
and brown, in homespun breeches and
rough leather boots. In his hand was a
folded paper, yellow and brittle. Some
words could still be read – ESSO ROAD
MAP: NORTH CENTRAL STATES.

He had been travelling northwards for
nine days and believed that soon
he would unravel the mystery of the
Old Ones, the people who had Been
Before . . .

Robie Macauley is the author of *The Disguises of Love,* a novel; *The End of Pity*, a collection of short stories; and, with George Lanning, *Technique in Fiction*, a book of criticism. He studied under Ford Madox Ford and, at Kenyon College, under John Crowe Ransom. After four years in the United States Army Counterintelligence Corps, he taught at various colleges and universities, was the editor of *The Kenyon Review* from 1959 to 1966, and was the fiction editor of *Playboy* from 1966 to 1977. He has held Rockefeller and Guggenheim fellowships as well as a Fulbright Research Fellowship at the University of London. Stories of his have won the *Furioso* fiction prize, a Benjamin Franklin magazine award for fiction, and have been reprinted in *The Best American Short Stories* and *O. Henry Prize Stories* volumes. He has contributed to *The New Republic, Playboy, The Irish University Review, Esquire, The Partisan Review, Cosmopolitan, TriQuarterly, The New York Times Book Review*, and other periodicals.

A SECRET HISTORY OF TIME TO COME

Robie Macauley

CORGI BOOKS

A SECRET HISTORY OF TIME TO COME

A CORGI BOOK 0 552 99032 9

First publication in Great Britian

PRINTING HISTORY
Corgi edition published 1983

This book is set in 10/11 Plantin

Corgi Books are published by
Transworld Publishers Ltd.,
Century House, 61–63 Uxbridge Road,
Ealing, London W5 5SA

Made and printed in Great Britain by
Cox & Wymans Ltd, Reading, Berks.

To Cameron
and Paula

In regard to the age of this desolate city, I shall not at present offer any conjecture. Some idea might perhaps be formed from the accumulations of earth and the gigantic trees growing on top of the ruined structures, but it would be uncertain and unsatisfactory. Nor shall I at this moment offer any conjecture in regard to the people who built it or to the time when or the means by which it was depopulated, and became a desolation and a ruin; whether it fell by the sword or famine or pestilence. The trees which shroud it may have sprung from the blood of its slaughtered inhabitants; they may have perished howling with hunger; or pestilence, like the cholera, may have piled its streets with dead, and driven forever the feeble remnants from their homes; of which dire calamities to other cities we have authentic accounts, in eras both prior and subsequent to the discovery of the country by the Spaniards. One thing I believe, that its history is graven on its monuments. . . . Who shall read them?

—JOHN LLOYD STEPHENS, *1841*

1

Day of portents, day when the skin crawls suddenly, day of soundless thunder enough to deafen you, the day when Caesar's statue in the forum begins to bleed mysteriously. This is a personal record, note-in-a-bottle, one fingerprint of my own left on earth—and so I go back to that day when it all began to happen.

It may be that everyone felt it, but at the time, I seemed all alone with the sense of awful beginning. In our lives, first days are almost never recognized, until we go back in memory and put a mark on them.

It had rained in the night and more rain was forecast for the morning. In the city, people arose, ate breakfast and scanned the headlines that had gone one tick more ominous. Public transportation may have seemed a little slower than yesterday and they may have had to wait an extra twenty minutes for the bus or the subway train; but they were used to that. If they tried to make a long-distance call, they had trouble getting through, or didn't get through at all. But the day began more or less as usual in offices, factories and schools. The dogs go on with their doggy life and the torturer's horse scratches its inno-cent behind on a tree. I had a dentist appointment at 55 Washington Street that morning.

But, if I remember my University of Chicago Latin, *auspicium meum verum intellegat,* as a Roman would say: my guts told me. I was shaving in the dull, habitual way in front of the bathroom mirror when my hand began to tremble as if it held a live wire. Nausea, shock, a quick panic in muscles drawn so taut they hurt. An absence of all sound, in which there was a slow bell tolling silently. I put the razor down with a weight of mortality I'd never felt before. It all lasted, probably, about ten seconds.

March 14 was one of those days when the wind drives off the

Western plains in one great sweep from the Dakotas to your apartment windows to spill an airy sea of water on this city. The streets were like an ocean floor, Atlantis of the Loop, with the buildings watery-wavery through the rain, among them a few people and cars swimming like lost fish to find their holes in the reef. My raincoat (it says 'water-resistant' on the label) gave up after a block and began to bleed inside. Because there were no taxis, I sloshed on toward the *Sun-Times* office, where I kept a warm-up suit and gym shoes in a box. I'd put them on until my clothes dried. And then the feeling hit again.

I remember stopping dead still on the sidewalk, almost dizzy, my muscles convulsing again, my ears ringing. I don't believe in omens, presentiments, ghostly things like that, never did. At first, I thought I was having a heart attack, but my heart seemed perfectly normal.

'Flee at once, all is discovered. Doyle.' Once I read that Sir Arthur Conan Doyle made a bet with a friend that he could send that telegram to twenty of the most famous and reputable men in England and most of them would get out of the country by nightfall. Oddly, I remembered that story at the moment I stood on the sidewalk, trying to straighten up. As if God had reached down and laid that telegram on me. Flee at once.

I began to walk slowly, telling myself that I'd had a bad reaction to the Novocaine, that the shock of the tooth-pulling had been more than I'd realized, that I had the flu coming on. I'm a bad liar.

When I went through the door into the lobby, Lucas was just stepping out of an elevator. Lucas Dymate—in another, later life called Lucas Dynamite—my oldest buddy. We started out together fifteen years ago as two young black reporters covering social notes on the South Side. Muggings, rapes and drug traffic, fires and murders.

'Brother, you look like shit,' he said to cheer me up.

'I've just come back from the dentist. Want to see a bloody hole where my molar was?'

He put his hand on my arm and looked serious. 'Listen, there's some heavy news.'

I said, 'Lucas, you got a bottle of bourbon in your desk, lower left-hand drawer if I put it back right last time, and you can either give me a drink or else bury me right here.'

He nodded abruptly, as if thinking about something else, and turned back toward the elevator.

In his office, I got a merciful ounce of Jack Daniel's inside me before he started talking. 'Listen. It came over the wire and it's on the radio now. The President has declared martial law in ten cities. Things look pretty mean.' He glanced down at a note pad. 'Cleveland, Philadelphia, Boston, Los Angeles, Atlanta, Detroit,

Baltimore, New Orleans, and Birmingham. And Washington itself.'

'Chicago?'

'Not on the list. Yet. Ten minutes ago, NBC had a bulletin about fires out of control in inner-city Detroit. Last night, Cleveland police headquarters were wiped out by an explosion. Near Rittenhouse Square in Philly, the cops fired on a black crowd. Blood on the streets, man, plenty of it. And more to spill.'

'Something told me,' I said, and took another stroke at the bourbon. 'Are they mobilizing? I mean the Black Republican Army.'

'What do you think? But its new name is BLAC, Black Liberation Army Corps—which signals that the hot war just started.'

He had inside lines because for about two years now he'd been covering that paramilitary organization along with the police and FBI attempts to destroy it. A lot he knew never got into his news stories.

Lucas Dynamite, old friend, you're dead now. And you're a hero, if there are such things, with a black brigade named after you and your portrait painted twenty feet high on the wall of a bombed-out building near the Merchandise Mart. I've never quite been able to visualize you leading your men in that shambles once called Evanston and no picture comes when I think of you dead in the street, but I can still see your intelligent, reasonable face as we sat in your office that rainy day and hoped to Christ that things were not so fucked up as they seemed. It's a kind of monastic face, with deep-lined brackets around the mouth, thought in the eyes and the scores of frowning etched on your forehead. In a better time, you would have died a scholar. Or a priest.

'I'm going to Canada,' I said suddenly. 'Come with me.'

He shook his head. 'For *you*—okay.'

What he meant, what he knew, was that I wasn't committed. I had no stake in the movement. I'd been divorced from Emily for nearly two years now. No kids. Earthly wealth: an apartment with some furniture I'd tastefully decorated with cigarette burns, a large case full of books, a stereo, three suits, a shambling idiot of an old Chevrolet.

'You're loose,' he said as he poured us drinks again. 'And anyway, we can't be absolutely certain that the country's coming apart.'

'Ifn he don, still gone be a bad-ass place fo niggers in de next few years. Remember Chile? Yugoslavia after Tito died? Spain when the Reds came in? Court-martial executions, concentration camps, mass graves.'

'I suppose,' he said slowly and thoughtfully. 'But we *could* win. . . .'

That new 'we' stunned me, coming in his calm voice. I'd heard it

11

often enough in the mouths of Movement speakers and had seen it everywhere in the literature. 'We-win' was code for the uprising they were working for. In usual conversation, 'we' meant the paper. Though the city was two-thirds black now—and the paper often covered whites as if they were a minority problem—the ownership was still in the Field family and white editors came in from Highland Park or Glencoe to keep the flag of racial harmony flying. (Nowadays, by the way, it's the *Black Sun*, great oxymoron that, and it's down to four pages of bad grammar. If the white man spoke with forked typewriter, at least he did it in passable English.)

'If *we* win,' I said, 'mass graves, concentration camps and court-martial executions.'

'No,' said Lucas abruptly. 'With the right kind of leadership . . . Force them to agree that they can have theirs and we'll take ours. Soul is really a remarkable man—not the dervish he sounds like. You're wrong about him.'

'Brother Lucas,' I said, 'think real. Another man once said all of those things and he had one third of the country behind him. All in one place. We have a scattered ten, maybe twelve, percent, if we could count on every black.'

'We've got most of the cities,' he said stubbornly.

I didn't realize it at the time, but you were the future brigade commander speaking then. 'Our Black Voroshilov,' as some writer later called you in the *Black Sun*. Nor did I know how far you had gotten into the BLAC movement by then. It was a week or so later, when the suits came off and you had the black diamond of a major on your collar, when I understood. You were wearing a bush jacket and a black beret, and in your hands was an assault rifle. Old friend, I never knew you.

We shook hands, I remember, in a long, silent clasp and we did not say goodbye.

The Kennedy Expressway was full of slow-moving traffic, nothing abnormal. I had the car radio on and the music was interrupted three or four times to give announcements about the state of national emergency. There had been violence in some cities, but the National Guard was being mobilized and order was being restored. We were asked to carry on as usual. The President would address the nation at seven o'clock tonight. At that, there was a sound of static and the broadcast—the only local one left—went silent for about five minutes.

Then a new voice came on the air. 'Not on this station, he ain't,' said the black voice.

I had the feeling of going over a cliff. I stared through the rain and the pendulum of the wiper blade and reflected that the only salvage from fifteen years of my life lay packed in two bags in the back seat. Sleeping pills and snapshots. Worn clothes and a few books. Bitter's the bread of exile and steep are the stranger's stairs.

But 'little did I know,' as people in terrible novels say. Still, little-know is the only grace God gives us.

The upper ramp at O'Hare was a logjam of cars and taxis and nothing was moving. Finally, after I'd inched as close as I could to the international terminal, where I could see an enormous crowd, I simply abandoned the car and took my bags and ran. It was a long, long way around the curve to Air Canada.

And the terminal was another mob scene, packed right to the doors with people and luggage. I had no ticket—only my passport and a thousand dollars I'd picked up at the bank. So catch as catch can, I began to work my way toward one of the counters. The loudspeakers were busy, first announcing a flight and then coming on to cancel it. As usual, there seemed to be about six airline clerks to deal with ten thousand passengers, who were getting more psychotic by the minute. I was finally halted, hedged in, next to a middle-aged man who was sitting on a scarred suitcase. He said he'd been waiting two hours.

'I want to get a flight to Canada, anyplace in Canada,' I said.

'You'n me'n the whole damn state,' he said. 'They talkin on that horn few minutes ago say the Canucks is askin fo a visa fo you kin fly. You got no visa, you fucked.'

'You heard anything about the other airlines?' I asked. 'North Central to someplace in upper Michigan, maybe?'

'Half the cities closed down. Nothin to Detroit, Kansas, L.A., La Guardia. The rest I forget.' His round black face was shining with sweat. 'I take anyplace. Fuckin Moscow, even.'

Just then, the loudspeaker came on with an announcement that all flights to Canada were full and that no more passengers would be accepted until further notice. There was a great groan and a woman's scream. Television screens farther down the terminal jittered with a change of posting. Domestic flights, one after the other, showed 'No Space' or 'Canceled.'

Luckily, nobody had stolen my car; it was still blocking traffic. I was home a little after five o'clock.

[*June 29*]

Backtracking more, I want to give some account of those early March-to-June days, that wild festival of death and hope when our revolution began. At first, I began to talk this journal into a tape recorder every night before bed. But one night I had a dream. Of the strangest kind.

I am in a clearing in the woods, or at least my eyes are. It's a long, long way from here. I see the trees with their leaves glinting in the sunshine. Along a path there comes a man dressed in some weird clothes that seem to be animal skins. He has long hair, tied at the back of his neck, but I can't see his face. He is leading a horse. I have been expecting him.

Now, so far this is not very odd, as my dreams go, but the chilling thing is that I am both looking at this man and I am in his mind at the same time. I am a part of his thoughts. He has come a long way and I feel how tired he is. But he will follow the trail on—because whatever the distance, he is coming after me. He will never give up until he catches me.

I woke up then, in the middle of the night, with the nightmare's chill still on me. And the afterimage of that savage man made me begin to wonder if there might not be a time when tape recorders were useless; there might be no more power to run them; even the idea of what they were might be forgotten.

Because in the dream, I was absolutely certain that I had been dead a long time.

That seemed so real and so shocking that I put the machine away in my desk and began to write in this account book, performing the act of Robert Scott in the antarctic waste before the expedition died, the act of Daniel Defoe in London in the plague year. Confreres.

There's another thought, though. All this might make an interesting story to show my grandchildren. Or it might be published someday as an eyewitness account of the trauma we passed through near the end of the twentieth century. I comfort myself with that observation by the poet Ralph Hodgson: 'The handwriting on the wall may be a forgery.'

I have a dark little cavern in the basement of the *Tribune* building for a private office and bed-sitter. Upstairs are the offices for the north and northwest sectors. Hanging on the wall is my steel helmet and beneath it my bush jacket with the green diamond of a captain. I am intelligence chief for the northern front.

In the street outside, an ambulance screams on its way to Passavant Hospital—I forget: on its way to Angela Davis Hospital. Michigan Avenue is ruinous now, but the rubble has been pushed into piles along the sidewalk so that military traffic can pass. At the street corners, there are sandbag shelters and barbed wire barricades where sentries examine your papers.

14

The Magnificent Mile of Michigan Avenue is now a little country road, two lanes, winding through the banks of rubble. And much of that rubble is glass—we never realized that half the city was made of glass! Now it lies in glistening banks of powder or cliffs of shattered plates. The Illinois Center buildings across the street from us are great, empty cages amid drifts of glass. Michigan Avenue is a long stretch of blackly vacant oblongs. The white rich lived in their great pueblo of highrises along the lake and this street was their bazaar. The looters picked it clean of oriental rugs, jewelry, paintings, furs, fine clothes. The only shreds left are the names on building fronts—Gucci, Saks, I. Magnin.

The water tower, those comic miniature castles that survived the fire of 1871, are still there. The marble slabs from the face of Water Tower Place almost choke the street. The John Hancock building is a gaunt monster; the Drake is a burned-out shell. The beaches are strung with barbed wire, and machine guns cover them from windows in the lower levels of abandoned lakefront apartment houses. Where yachts used to sail out of Belmont Harbor, a converted police boat—our navy—now creeps down the shore. The lion and the lizard keep those courts.

All revolutions must have the same standard footage and stock shots, I think. The vehicles and the clothes are different, but Paris in 1789, Moscow in 1917, Johannesburg in 1986 must have told the same stories to the eye. Trucks full of commandos racing through the streets to secure something or other—a bank, a television station, an airfield, a factory. Crowds of looters coming and going through the smashed windows of the stores eerily lighted by bonfires in the streets. A plane suddenly swooping off the lake to rocket the traffic on Michigan Avenue bridge, leaving smashed cars from which the blood runs as if the cars themselves were bleeding. Bodies of white refugees, their belongings scattered around them, lying in a vacant lot. Mountainous smoke rising from a besieged police station, where bullets still chip the wall next to you and sing away.

The mountains of smoke—that's one of my chief memories of the city in those days. Everywhere I looked along the rooflines, there was smoke. Here it was a black fountain, there it had settled into a vast, low-lying pillow. The city seemed to be pouring its black blood upward into the air. Day or night, the city was never quiet. Sirens and the screech of car tires, the snapping of rifles, remote detonations like summer thunder, voices in screams, voices in yells, whiskey laughter.

I can't account for myself in those psycho days. In plain and ordinary times, we keep our balance because we all have a secret room in the head where sometime we can lock out the world. Sort, revise, recollect. I am myself not because of what actions my body goes through but because of how I count and record those actions. And, in those frantic weeks, I was no longer accounting to myself. I lived outside my head.

I was—am?—a moderately balanced and reflective man. Of course, like all of us, I hated white-on-black injustice, but I suppose that my sense of the future was without anger. If people could adapt to the strangeness of deserts, mountains, ice lands and concrete cities, they could adapt to different skin colors in one another. All in one week—month?—I became a revolutionary and a soldier.

I was put in charge of the fourth commando, directly under Brother Soul, and our mission was to get some order in the city while the other commandos were being shaped into army brigades to stabilize the fronts. (Ironies—I can't help thinking of them. *Kommando* was a Boer militia unit in their war against the British.)

I had a collection of miscellaneous trucks and cars and about forty-five men, some veterans and some deserters from the USG army and navy. We had to stop the looting, pinpoint the pockets of white resistance in the northern sector of the city, send refugees to the centers being established, collect all weapons and explosives we could find, put guards on food stocks and vital matériel.

One night, in front of a blazing building on Lawrence, I put seven black men and four black women up against a wall and dropped my hand. The machine gun mounted in the back of a truck began to stutter.

A white security guard in a bank fired on us when we broke down the door. When our men brought him out, I told them to hang him from a fire escape.

I made everybody—black families—get out of a burning apartment house and then we dynamited it. The women were crying as all their possessions went up in dust and smoke.

Did I do such things to make order? I have recorded them almost without believing them. I was/was not there.

[*June 30*]

The dream again, with that savage in it. He has gone farther into his forest, closing the distance between us by a few miles. I can't remember much of this dream, except for that feeling of slow progression and, then, certain points when he suddenly comes into focus. He's fording a stream with his horses—there seem to be two of them

16

in this dream—and I can see very clearly the gray-green water swashing around his knees as he wades in. An overhanging branch with shiny green leaves comes in front of our eyes and he bends it back, breaks it off so that it won't brush the horses and frighten them. The surface of the water has a few ovals of bright green on it, floating downstream. There is a mossy boulder we have to make our way around.

He sits on the ground and unfolds a many-creased square of something, spreads it on the ground and stares. Two or three blueflies are buzzing in the air around his head. He pays no attention. I have the sense that he does not know that I exist, but that he is trying to meditate me into reality.

[*July 1*]

I was still in the dream—climbing a long hill and out of breath, it seemed—when the telephone rang at 0400. 'George Arrow,' said the voice in my ear. Arrow . . . Arrow? My mind fumbled, trying to make a connection with the savage hunter and arrows.

Then, slowly, I stagger into the waking world. Arrow, ex-con, now a BLAC colonel, north sector commander. His ghetto speech is so black and so quick that I often have trouble understanding him. He's asking for an update on our tactical situation, with some grid references. As if I stayed awake twenty-four hours a day, a human computer always ready to retrieve. I leaf through a pile of the last CB messages from our transmitters in the field.

Hampton Brigade still pushing forward on the Calumet front as of 2000—objective Hammond and a linkup with the BLAC force in Gary, expected within three or four days. (The Hamptons are a hard-assed bunch of paramils from Southlawn, one of the formations Soul trained secretly before the Declaration.) I tell him we had four tanks for sure today and two probables. The National Guard farm kids from downstate don't know what hit them. (I remember the voice on the radio saying, 'Fuckin cinders!')

Another scribble says we're holding the line along the Des Plaines River—just. Oak Park is one big bonfire. (The Luther King Brigade there—mostly middle-class kids who didn't grow up street-fighting.)

Fuck Des Plaines, he says. What are the motherfuckers doing on the Evanston front? Evanston—the Mousy Tongue Brig? (That was Lucas's, before he was killed.)

No, the USG is still in Northwestern University. And brought up

17

more stuff. Six new batteries reported and lots of shelling from 1800 to dark. The el (which we've been using for resupply) is knocked out. One Dempster Street position was overrun about 1830. Everybody dead, as far as we know. And more bad news—coast guard, or at least some kind of ship with guns on it, began shelling us from the lake at about 1730.

'We shittin blood,' he says, and hangs up. For a minute, those words seem to last in the air, like skywriting, before they bleed away in the wind.

And now, because I can't fall asleep, I'm at this journal again, my recollective therapy.

Why that persistent, progressive phantom of the ancient hunter in the forest? My mind must be trying to escape into the past of a primitive world. A simpler life and the silence of woods? I can't believe it.

A quotation I once copied comes back to me, more or less correct, here it is: Isaac Luria, the lion, demonstrated that the soul of a dead man can enter the lost spirit of another to maintain or instruct him.

2

Since the first gray stain of dawn on the forest floor, the man had been following the trail on foot, his riding horse and his packhorse pacing along behind. Tired as he was, he dreamed a dream of infinity—a green enigma of trees and bush, vaster than comprehension, stretching about him not miles but centuries. Through one narrow tunnel that widened, shrank, twisted, disappeared into scrub at times, a man and two horses walked. Often he had the illusion that the trail was not one made by other feet, but a wish traced by his own mind, and that it faltered just as his determination wearied. If he were to give up, lie down, that crooked string would disappear behind and in front. At the beginning, he had kept count; now he found it hard to remember how many days he had traveled. In his walking dream, the trail had become life itself, slippery and rough, crazy awhile and straight awhile, passing through thickets of despair, clearings of green hope.

For the past hour or so, he had been descending a long hillslope, the track plainer where runoffs of rain had eroded it to brown earth. From the sparse light drifting down through the green roof, he calculated that the sun must be nearly overhead and he looked for a place to halt. Then it appeared ahead, where the trail angled to a little clearing just at the bank of a stream. Beyond the stream was a thick growth of underbrush and there the path was lost again.

He unslung the saddlebags on each horse, loosened the cinches and let the two drink. After he had fixed their feedbags, he took off his leather shirt, arranged biscuits, dried meat and his canteen beside him on a kerchief and began to eat. When he had finished, he dozed awhile, in his sleep still pushing forward, footfall after footfall among the endless trunks.

He was a tall young man, tough and brown as one of his leather thongs. His black hair, with some kind of oil on it, was drawn into a short tail at the back of his neck and tied with a piece of yarn. He had a stubborn face, with a triangular nose and a mouth like a cleft, and he would have looked brutal if it had not been for the eyes. He opened them now and sat up. The eyes were gray and wide-set, with a hint of seeing things not present. He wore homespun breeches and rough leather boots that came to his knees.

He rose and went to his saddlebags and brought out a flat case made of leather. He knelt on the ground and withdrew a folded paper, yellow and brittle, which he handled with immense care. The topmost fold was almost covered with a stain, but some words could be seen. The man read them slowly: 'Esso Road Map: The North Central States.' Then he painstakingly unfolded the paper and began to examine it. The surface was covered with interconnecting, crooked lines, colored black or red. In many places where the lines came together, there were small circles, and in some cases, shaded patches with words printed alongside. He could read these words, but only a few of them had meaning for him. Clearfield, Fairview, Pine Grove Mills, were plain enough. But such as Pittsburgh, Akron and Erie were beyond guessing. The important thing, though, was his notion that these were all names of the ancient settlements.

He had drawn a line on the paper in walnut juice. It ran from a spot near the lower right-hand corner diagonally leftward and up. It crossed many of the printed lines, but it always skirted the settlement spots. On his travels, he had constantly compared map and ground to verify that the lines stood for the ancient roadways of the forefathers, and when he crossed one, that gave him his approximate place on the trail. At the end of each day, he had marked a little cross on the paper to show about how far he had come.

He wished that there were pictures of the enormous stretch of forest and the high hills, but there was the possibility that somehow the land had changed in the hundred, or even two hundred years since the old country of Esso had disappeared.

He had been traveling steadily northward for nine days along the trail. If his calculations were right, he was now not far from the greatest mystery. It was that broad, blue-colored place with black letters spread across it to spell 'Lake Erie.' He knew that the color meant water, but so much of it seemed impossible. There was a lake near his settlement, but a swimmer could cross it in a few minutes. This Erie lake and the other blue places to the left of it must be where all the water of the earth flowed.

He had hoped to find an inhabited settlement or, at least, some hunters along the trail, but the only living creatures he had seen were deer, once a bear at a distance, raccoons, birds, squirrels. Hunters had been through here, because he had come across the marks of their campfires and the bones of their kills. No doubt that was why the trail remained as clear as it was.

At last he arose, put on his shirt and made the horses ready. From a scabbard strapped to the packhorse he took a long, straight-edged bushcutter, forged for him by Harris-the-smith. After all these days of use, it had dulled a little. The man waded across the stream and began hacking at the bushes there to clear the trail once more. After about twenty minutes, he had cut a trail wide enough for the horses. Leading them across the stream and through the cutting, he picked up the trace once more on the other side. It led uphill and he began to follow the leafy tunnel again.

3

'The handwriting on the wall . . .' A lot of us thought we saw it in the 1980s. But in those days, we wishfully accepted the predicate: '. . . may be a forgery.' It's all there in my book (*Racial Polarization in the United States*, Times Books, 1986), the prescience and the self-deception both. It's true we were misled by that near-peace, that pause during the recession years of mid-decade. We didn't know what hatred—on both sides—had gone into hiding to grow in the dark. Or recognize the separate happenings as serial. The Supreme Court's much-debated reversal on Miranda. The increased apartheid as the cities grew 70, 80, 90 percent black and the white suburbs as much as hung out the sign 'No Niggers After Sundown.' The way the NAACP and the Urban League dwindled and disappeared, with the white money and the black participation gone. The slow increase of unemployment among blacks as general employment rose. The way moderate leaders such as Jesse Jackson lost following while ones like Brother Soul skyrocketed in front of our eyes.

And of course, there was the shock—deeper in the white heart than anybody suspected—of the overthrow in Rhodesia, the horrors of the South African revolution and the wars that came along next.

The smaller signs . . . The way whites began again, casually, to use the word 'nigger.' The new, subtle difficulties blacks encountered in white universities. But I'm beginning to paraphrase my chapter called 'The Dialogue Breaks Down.' I thought I'd exaggerated, just by way of warning. I didn't know what a sad understatement it was.

I'll always remember my interview with Brother Soul in September 1979. That ramshackle, fortified house in south Chicago, with a surly young bodyguard making me strip in the entrance hallway—and then dress again—before I could see the man.

He didn't converse; he spoke in ultimatums. Even so, he conveyed a remarkably detailed, statistical grasp of the extent of the white glacier that was moving on us. He struck me, I remember, as perfectly shrewd, perfectly ordered and perfectly mad.

Up here, I still have that hard-edged picture of Soul sitting at the bare table across from me in his war room, under a single, green-shaded bulb. On a peg in the wall behind him was an Armalite rifle, the only decoration (no revolutionary posters at the center of the revolution). He leaned on his elbows, his hands flat on the wood, and seemed to lance at my eyes. He had a bony, mahogany-brown, undistinctive face (now that he's grown fleshier, he seems to look more dictatorially striking). I recall that in my article—written for a left-wing black magazine—I indulged my historical weakness and made some references to Christophe, Toussaint L'Ouverture, Burning Spear, Nat Turner. Literary flourishes, bullshit. All I could see as I sat there was a copperhead. A powerful thinking weapon.

It may have been my questions or my nearly white accent, but something turned him off quickly. He began asking the questions, boring in. Where did I come from? Did I have any connection with the Movement?

The many times our scene has been repeated in ill-lit headquarters. One of the gentry trying to placate Robespierre. A bourgeois sweating to convince Lenin that his heart was with the workers. But I must get out of this bad habit.

How could I make any points for myself? My father had been a bank teller and then an official at First National. I grew up in a neat, clean house in Lake Meadow. I was a Boy Scout. I had a scholarship to Francis Parker School. I was the editor of the newspaper in a white university. Most of my life, I've worked for a white newspaper. So I gave him some fancy generalizations.

Finally, he said, 'Stop farting.'

He changed the subject then and went on with my interview. At the end, he rose from his chair and said bleakly, 'Brother, we gonna beat you black all over.'

[*July 3*]

This morning at 0700, I went to the radio-monitor room, where a dozen girls per shift copy the news from the air. We listen to all transmissions possible, though nowadays the U.S. radio is all government-controlled and there's little but music and carefully vague, carefully optimistic official bulletins. We glean from CB, ham operators, guerrilla radio, foreign broadcasts. CBC from Canada is the best source for hard news.

The Windsor station has a report on U.S. refugees. During the first weeks, the border was flooded with Americans, until about the middle of April, when they really put up the fence. Mounties, army, navy, RCAF, where only a bored customs inspector used to stare and wave you past. The prime minister has issued a statement outlining new, stricter regulation of Americans in Canada. Over 120,000 refugees in resettlement camps already . . . Essential to Canadian interests that the conflict be kept from spilling over the border . . . Et cetera, et cetera.

What I'm waiting for is the news from Brussels. At last, it begins to come in a flurry of pages written and torn off the pad. The UN, meeting there for the past week, has released some new resolutions. This isn't the old, debating-society UN. This is a new one, with Russian and Chinese teeth.

The big question is whether or not the Third World proposal for intervention—a peacekeeping international expeditionary force in the U.S.—will be ratified. The news all my hopes are pinned on.

Anita—a pretty girl, dressed in shapeless khaki shirt and pants, sexy on her—slides the pages over the desk to me with a little grimace. I read hastily, dying a little with each word. James Monroe, thou shouldst be living at this hour: here is your new Doctrine in reverse, spelled out in hasty shorthand. We are sold out.

In brief, the UN has agreed on a cordon sanitaire. There is, of course, a fairly long preamble to echo the Arab and African indignation. 'Vicious white racism in the United States has created a situation of civil war. . . . The nations drastically condemn the Washington government as a fascist and genocidal regime. . . . Recognition withdrawn by all but six countries. . . .' Then the cop-out. Moscow and Peking have shaken hands again.

In June, there were fragmentary reports of a Cuban-Nigerian volunteer force landed in Florida and on the Georgia coast. Then came some conflicting bulletins about battles in the streets of Miami and Savannah and a Havana announcement of the creation of an 'independent black southland' state. Then nothing. Our dream became our rumor became our official fact.

Now, in this UN report, I decipher that the expedition has been destroyed. Or perhaps it never was. I won't go into the labyrinth of official text, but in effect, the new Doctrine reads that the nations of the world have drawn a border around the United States and have left us to our desperation.

The Russians and the Chinese are thinking of all those ICMBs hidden in Dakota or Maine silos or under the ocean—still a danger in the hands of the USG. Of course, they will wait serenely as black and white gut each other over here.

The Europeans—France, Italy, Belgium, the rest—are filled with *Schadenfreude* to see their old, benevolent tyrant tearing apart. And they know that the wind now blows from the east. And so they vote correctly.

The statement goes on to endorse the Mexican and Canadian decision to seal off their borders and declares that all member nations have agreed to halt sea, land and air traffic and transport, including all movement of persons, to the United States until 'the tragic crisis is resolved.'

[*July 5*]

This morning I went to Frantz Fanon Hospital (formerly Cook County Hospital) to interrogate a young captain who was wounded yesterday in the Oak Park sector. It's not my area, but the G-2 man who usually covers it is missing.

The Eisenhower Expressway, now Uhuru Highway, looks more like Junk Alley. The roadside was littered with abandoned cars and trucks, here and there a huge semi. Our patrols had pushed them off to the side, though, and traffic was moving at a fair rate.

Planes were on my mind. I could see a few craters in the road and some of the trucks seem to have been burned out. Corlie, my driver, snaked through the meager traffic and I scanned the sky to the west.

The spring air raids have dropped off to nearly nothing and the sound of a siren is rare nowadays. We guessed that those were largely terror raids because few vital installations were hit—except for Midway and Meigs Field, where every plane was destroyed. The hopeful rumor is that the USAF has been grounded by sabotage; it has been halted because the Middle East cut off oil supplies; our guerrillas have destroyed most of it on the ground. Take your pick. I believe it's simply because the government wants the cities back more or less intact.

Occasionally, by day, a plane passes over—obviously a photorecon plane—and there are useless bursts of machinegun fire from the streets. The *Black Sun* has carried photos of the wreck of an old Convair with new-painted USAF markings, under the caption: 'Jet Bomber Downed by Our Troops Near Evanston.' Still, any aerial activity has intelligence-report priority A-1.

The hospital was surrounded by a waiting horde of people—the streets crowded and the little park filled. Farther on, I could see another crowd around the entrances to Presbyterian St. Luke's (March 15th Hospital). Corlie inched his way forward until we had to stop. I elbowed to the door on my own.

The armed guards had all they could do to keep a lane open for ambulances, but they checked my papers and admitted me to hell.

The lobby was packed. Bandaged people, weeping people, people in shock, noise and confusion of a kind I never saw before. I had to step over a stretcher where a boy of about seventeen was lying, his bandaged head and torso all crimson and his breathing a snore. His hands were folded simply on his stomach. Abandoned in the crowd, he was dying.

I yelled at two soldiers standing with their backs to him and told them to pick up the stretcher. They turned slowly to look at me. One of them had a black band across his eyes; the other had a right arm that ended at the elbow.

It seemed to take hours before I could fight my way into an elevator, and once inside, I closed my eyes and held my breath. I was almost surprised that it rose with its cargo of damned instead of descending into the earth.

The corridors were a little better than the lobby, but not much. The nurses and orderlies kept some kind of plan going, though the hallway was lined with mattreses on which lay civilians and soldiers alike. You could tell the soldiers because they had their armbands taped to the wall behind them.

At last, I found the room where Captain Gamal X lay. In peacetime days it probably held two beds, but now it held four. I edged to the far wall, directed by a nurse, and found a light-skinned young man, propped up on pillows, quietly smoking a thin black cigar. I'd seen that face before in a museum, cast in Benin three hundred years ago. A young, unknown prince.

'Captain Gamal X?' I asked, and introduced myself.

'I am he,' he said.

I lost my speech for a moment. For some reason, that oddity of correct grammar was a time shift and I was back in a university seminar room, years past, and a young black instructor was saying, 'I shouldn't make that postulation if I were you. . . .' The coolest of Oxford accents, from a black throat. Another seminar, and a young black woman said in a pure Parisian tone, *'Les lauriers sont coupés. . . .'*

I sat down on the window ledge and began to explain that I needed some details of the action in which he'd been wounded. I really wanted to ask: Who are you? What have you read? What do you think about? Tell me your life. Instead, I asked my questions.

'I had an infiltration squad of ten men,' he began, drawing on the cigar and looking straight ahead of him at the wall. He went on to explain that they worked forward by night, using all that obscure maze of channels in and under this decaying city—sewers, fire escapes, coal-delivery entries from the old days. By dawn, they would have niched themselves in some upper storey or rooftop that could command a street or crossoads. Then, as long as they could hold out, they'd disrupt the route with their fire. He stopped. 'We don't live long.' Then he added, 'While we do, we live on Benzedrine.'

'Some of my men collect ears,' he said later on. 'They have more than a hundred.' He turned his head and looked at me. 'But I've got used to that.'

He explained in a detailed way about the night before last, touching a place on my map to give the approximate location. They had tunneled through the cellar wall of an empty apartment house and, avoiding suspected booby traps, used ropes to climb up the elevator shaft. As he spoke, I saw them emerging onto the rooftop in the first, faint sunlight. I asked him to describe their position.

He shook his head. 'Somebody must have heard us or seen us going in.' Before they could even take up a position, there was a chopper beating in from the east, out of the pale sun, with its guns on them.

'Just one?' I asked. We had to know how many they were using for close support.

'We only had time to count to one.'

A man behind a parapet, firing to draw fire, had been cut in two. He'd been hit then. Two of the squad had dragged him to the hood of the stairway and, booby traps or no, carried him down it.

'They put on a tourniquet and found a rug to roll me in, to carry me. I looked like a blood sausage.' He smiled just slightly. 'A fresh blood sausage.'

I put my notebook away and we were silent while he finished the cigar. He was not very descriptive, but somehow I could see that tarred stretch of roof in the dawn with the men scrambling in the sudden 30-caliber storm and the rain of blood, could hear the cries and the whine of ricochets.

'When you're on your feet again, come to see me. Headquarters canteen has pretty good food and drink,' I said.

Then I saw him look at the flat place under the blanket where a leg should have been. 'Forgot,' I said. 'I'm sorry.'

'No,' he said. 'I can still drink.'

[*July 6*]

My dream of the skin-clad man in the forest came again last night and it seemed to me that he'd moved on to a new sequence. From a medium distance, I see him emerging from the trees into the sunlight, and just at that moment, I receive something from him that says frustration, unhappiness. Has he lost his path? Or come to a mountain he can't cross? Or are there dangerous wild animals facing him? I can't see past him clearly enough to get any landscape or to know what makes him pause. Since dreams have never impressed me much, I've always forgotten them in the morning. But this one is such a strong print that I even have afterimages in the daytime. It's not that great a dream, I tell myself, but the fact that I'm overwhelmingly sure that this ancient hunter is searching for *me* somewhere makes it eerie. And the fact that he transmits his feelings so powerfully to me, without ever speaking a word.

Looked again at the quote from Luria, the old Jewish cabalist, and tried to remember how I happened to recall that scrap of writing so completely. I remember: It just happened to strike me when I was in Palo Alto in 1980, doing a story on the precognition and paranormal research going on at the Stanford Research Institute. I arrived, I recall, thinking I'd do a very funny story about perfectly sober scientists in a great university fooling around with clairvoyance and telepathy like a bunch of old gypsy women. But I sobered up when I saw what they had done.

The work had been going on for about eight years, but the real breakthroughs had been pretty recent. I still recollect Dr. Robeson explaining about a faculty of the brain that seems to create a field of force different from the four known physical fields of force. I watched an experiment in telekinesis—a young woman, standing about three feet away from it, apparently bent an iron bar that was sealed in a glass tube; I saw it beginning to curve.

But the really wild ones were the temporal retrieval experiments. They found an old house that had been lived in continuously for about a hundred years but was abandoned now. It was in an isolated, semi-desert area of New Mexico, surrounded by open country. They sealed it off with a high fence and sensors and placed in the rooms long-playing recorders with a week's supply of tape. The house was locked and then guarded—both electronically and by watchmen—for a week.

I heard some of those tapes. There were voices on them, muffled conversations, even separate words that could be understood.

This was just after Ivor Dansk, the physicist, had produced his theory showing the possibility of 'time reversibility'—a theory I struggled to put into simple words in my article, though it was based on mathematics I couldn't begin to comprehend. Are certain events synchronistic—that is, relatively indifferent to the facts of time and space as we know them? The precognition experiments I saw at Stanford were strange evidence that it might be true.

I write this down because my dream has some of these tones; it troubles me just as those experiments troubled my sense of cause-and-effect. A primitive man from an unknown past is seeking me out, or so my unconscious seems to tell me. And yet I have the impression of seeking *him*. If there is a transmission here, which is the direction—from past to future or future to past?

No; I'm working too hard. I'm too full of anxiety. Every circuit is overloaded. I'll have to find some way to make peace with myself, get rid of my apparition. I confess, though, that I've begun to look forward to his recurrences. I've even found a name for him: Mortmain.

4

It was much later in the afternoon when the traveler on the trail caught the signal in the breeze. The track had crested some time ago and then had turned downward, becoming broader and more distinct. The forest had thinned out too, and he could see as far as twenty or thirty paces among the trunks on either side of him.

Something seemed to have happened to his perception, a blurring of overlays, during all his long journeying, and one passage of the trail had begun to seem very much like another, as if he were ascending the same hill and descending among the same trees time and again. Dazed by the long monotony of oak, elm and ash, his eyes no longer caught on details. But his nose and ears were still alert, like independent scouts. And now, in his nostrils, there was something new.

Amid the usual wood smells of leaf and decay there came a more acrid odor. It was a compound of smoke, cooking, excrement, animals, garbage—the stink of man on the wind, faint but sharp.

He went cautiously a hundred yards farther. It was keener still and, here, he began to notice V-cut stumps where trees had been felled by axes. In the near distance, the path became a bare track of earth.

He stopped to prepare. He fastened his deerskin shirt with the horn buttons, he took a fur cap from his saddlebag and put it on. Then he looked to his rifle in the long holster strapped behind the saddle of his riding horse, making sure that no mud or rust had clogged it and that the bolt worked easily. It was a good rifle, the best craft of Harris-the-smith. It had a polished walnut stock and a long, octagonal barrel that carried true. These days, most guns were poor, smooth-bore weapons, but Harris carried on the old skill handed down by his grandfather.

He noticed the tenseness in his muscles as he climbed into the saddle. He was wary and anxious. This north was unknown land. Occasionally, travelers came through his settlement from the south or east, but it had been years since someone had appeared out of the

30

north. There were tall stories about the north—such as the one the old men told about a land covered with ice and snow and called Canady. A savage brown people lived there, ruled by white men in red coats—but no one had ever seen such men.

Now, as he rode cautiously forward, he caught another scent on the breeze, apart from the habitation odor, a putrid smell of much decay. He shifted uneasily in his saddle.

At the brink of the hillside the cleared land began, and there he reined in to survey. He gave a whistle of relief. The valley spread out in a familiar contour, not much different from the valleys of home. There were the cornfields, surrounded by the jagged line of stump fences like great insects helplessly clawing the air, the settlement enclosure with its palisade of sharpened logs and its three block-houses, the little, rush-roofed houses of hewn logs clumped around a town square where the well and the flagpole stood, the watchtower of rough scaffolding where a lookout was already leaning as if to shout the news of a stranger's approach.

Thin rivers of smoke from the chimneys swayed upward in the clear, early-evening air. The picture was peaceful and reassuring.

Then, all at once, it was strange. The putrid smell came to him even more strongly, and looking beyond the village and its fields, he saw where another world began a mile away. It was a limitless swamp, a huge, desolate sponge of country stretching out to the very horizon. He saw areas of weed, channels of black water twisting among mud-banks where tangles of elder grew, wastelands of bare and ghostly pines, long carpets of green scum. He had a dizzy, somersaulted feeling. Earth's end? Did it finish here? Did he live on a little island surrounded by poisonous half sea?

Slowly, his gaze came back to the settlement and he began to notice odd things there. He saw a general air of neglect in the rows of stunted corn, the weed-choked fields, and in the palisade, where some of the logs had fallen, leaving gaps.

Now he saw doors opening and figures coming together in a little crowd around the gate. In front of it stood two guards, who must have been alerted by the lookout, because they were now holding rifles at waist level and staring in his direction. One was a short man dressed in dun leather and the other was tall, with some kind of blue cloth bound around his head.

He knew the first rule about an unfamiliar village and he made ready. He drew the packhorse alongside him and tightened his fist on the lead strap, taking the two down at a walk. 'E-a-a-s-y, e-a-a-s-y,' he crooned to them. 'S-t-e-a-d-y.' He knew he could count on the roan he was riding. He got set to dig his heels in.

31

They came out of the gate in a charge, yelping, snarling and making a great show of yellow teeth—at least ten lean mongrels. Beyond, he could see the guards slapping their thighs and yelling them on.

When the dogs were about twenty paces away, he put the horses to the trot, then into a gallop straight at the leading dog. Suddenly, his hand came up with the plaited rawhide whip and he cut the dog exactly across the eyes. It went down with a howl and the rest of the pack split and swerved. There were wild dogs in the country he wouldn't have risked this way, but he knew the settlement cowards. He came through handily, the pack at a distance but swearing in dog at him.

He reined to a halt about ten paces short of the gate and sat motionless as his horses wheezed and snorted.

The second rule of a strange village is to read faces. In the hills of his home country, each little stockade had its own notion of outsiders—fearful, hostile, or welcoming.

He thought now that the guards must be the fathers of their dogs, the snouts and bristles, the feral eyes and yellow teeth were so like. The shorter man had a grotesque harelip and the taller one had a purple birthmark that spread across one cheek and down his neck. Mastiffs.

He shifted his gaze to the crowd around the gateway and a gradual horror came over him. Every human proportion was wrong. There was a tiny woman in a homespun dress, bunched as if something had tried to roll her into a ball. A very tall girl like a thin weed, with a tiny pod of a head. Some of the children had blank, idiot eyes and heads that skewed on their necks. A man wearing a filthy blanket had teeth that thrust forward from his mouth like a pitchfork. A boy of about fifteen had a face from a nightmare and a withered arm. A pair of women, like hens, clucked with excitement and embraced each other. The traveler stared. The guard with the birthmark raised a three-fingered hand and spoke something.

Something, but was it words? The sound was guttural and menacing. He made more animal sounds. The harelipped man had brought his rifle to port and stealthily had begun to circle behind the horses. The stranger glanced closely at the man's rifle and noted that it was old and rusty, with a hole where the chamber should be. The tall guard's weapon was just as rusty and it lacked a trigger.

The crowd was silent. Their eyes shifted in unison to the harelipped man, who had now got behind him. He felt the packhorse shy a little as a hand was laid on its flank.

'Tell him to come back to the gate,' the stranger said slowly. 'I am going to count to five and then I will shoot him if he doesn't.' He showed what he meant by putting his left hand on the pistol grip of his rifle. But that was for distraction. His right hand had slipped down between the horses to grip the bushcutter's handle.

It struck him that he had thought of everything—everything but words. It had never occurred to him that he might come to a place where the people had no language, and this idea chilled him. He waited tensely, slipping his feet out of the stirrups and calculating how he would turn and spring.

Suddenly, the tall guard snarled with a sound that seemed something like, 'Hkimer-Som! Hkimer!' Then there was a shuffle of feet and the harelipped man returned, the crowd watching every step with fascinated eyes.

So the traveler tried the next test. He reached into his shirt pocket and drew out a piece of paper and held it up to view. There was a murmur from the crowd at this. The tall guard stretched forth his hand and said a word, or a nearword: 'Guvme.'

The traveler was relieved and he smiled. In the more isolated settlements, English had fallen away into local speech that was hard to understand, but he had never heard anything so warped as this.

He said in a loud voice, 'No! This is a paper. It has words. Do you have a man who can read words? Can your sheriff read words?'

The tall guard had been mouthing, trying to keep up with the speech and, at the end, he grinned and said, 'Ya, sherf!' delighted with himself. The crowd picked it up and began imitating. 'Sherf! Sherf! Sherf!'

5

I am exhausted with reality tonight. I've just spent an hour by myself, sitting on the lakeshore and looking at the night sky, feeling as if my ghost were rising into the dark. Overwork, exhaustion, Benzedrine, dreams—the wheel of night and day is spinning so fast that I no sooner wake up to the fantasy of the city than I seem to plunge again into the fantasy of sleep.

Last night, my savage Doppelgänger was lying in a forest clearing, looking up at the stars.

And that thought slid into an older dream I remembered again as I sat by the lake. It comes from the astronomer's theory, scientific nightmare itself, first conceived in the eighteenth century, of the 'black holes' in the universe. I recall my fascination when the news was published in the early 1980s that new observations by the Russians, the British and the Americans had confirmed the nightmare: a tragedy conceived by some cosmological Sophocles.

In the beginning, there is an enormous star, possibly greater than our sun. At some point in its course through endless time, its nuclear fires begin to die. The star compresses. It gives birth to a mighty helium flash that drives its temperature as high as one hundred million degrees and it becomes a supernova, the most brilliant fire in the sky. Then, for thirty million years, more or less, it crescendos in size, an imperial monster, until it has grown four hundred times as great. Yellow at first, it changes to orange and then glows as a red giant, swallowing the planets that orbit it. This is natural drama on a scale so big that our small spasm in time and space seems annihilated. I cannot conceive it, but I can dream it.

In time, this giant stops growing, and now, its core loaded with carbon, it begins to collapse inward from its own gravity.

Now there are two possibilities. If the star was no bigger than our sun, it will become a shrunken corpse the astronomers call a 'white dwarf.'

If it was more than half again the size of the sun, its tremendous compression will continue—until even electrons and protons are crushed into abstraction. Crushed at last into an infinite mass of nothingness, an empty place of sheer gravity, so powerful that no light can escape from it and even time itelf has vanished. Some scientists think it might be an aperture through to another universe, where all dimensions are different.

I wish all this had remained astronomers' fiction; when reality catches up with fiction, life is altered. I remember the feverish sense with which I read every report in the early eighties as observation began to confirm the existence (how can pure Nothing exist?) of a black hole. The white supergiant Cygnus X-1 was proved to be wandering through space in the tug of an unseeable, almost inconceivable force.

A death so complete that it only persists as the Idea of death. Yet still so powerful that a giant star is helpless in its embrace.

In my dream, I have seen all this through a different telescope and it has become earthly. Black hole, white dwarf.

After I wrote this, I felt a great urge to look at the sky again and so I went out of the building and into the street. Two sleepy sentries in the courtyard nodded to me. A messenger climbed into a Volkswagen and drove off down Michigan Avenue with a diminishing engine growl. After that, everything was silent.

I looked up and saw the old stars. There was the Ethiopian king and his daughter, the princess. There was his wife's rocking chair. Once, she'd dared to say that a black girl was the most beautiful woman on earth—and so had angered the white sea god. Does anyone else alive remember that the son of Zeus rescued, loved and married a black princess?

[*July 14*]

There was a food riot this morning in Grant Park. A company of the reserve was hastily brought in from the west central front and they used tear gas. Rumors of scores of wounded. Does anybody remember other times, other police using tear gas on black people?

Soul hasn't had a staff meeting or been seen in public for more than a week. Once he was omnipresent in the flesh, on posters, on the radio.

Soul is shut up in his bunker. He and his girl smoke hash all day long. He is drawing up the constitution for the Republic of Africa in

America. He has had a nervous breakdown and when a doctor was called secretly, he found him crying uncontrollably.

He has a new, secret plan for ending the war in just a few weeks and something wonderful is going to happen, just wait.

Soul was assassinated by one of his bodyguards three days ago and they are keeping the body hidden until the new chief takes over.

Soul has had a private peace offer from the USG. If he sells out, he will get a personal island in the Caribbean and live in luxury the rest of his life. And he is ready to sell out.

Two nights ago, a submarine from one of the Arab countries picked Soul up from Navy Pier and carried him off to Canada.

An old woman in one of the resettlement buildings, said to have gifts of prophecy, had a vision in which a black Christ appeared to her with bleeding hands. He told her that the way of salvation was to dynamite the river and let Lake Michigan drain south into the Mississippi. Then His people could walk to freedom over the lakebed, with dry feet.

Some patients died of typhus last week in Angela Davis Hospital. Their bodies were taken away in secret and burned.

A man listening to a CB radio heard air-to-air transmissions in Russian between two bomber pilots. The Russians are sending planes over the North Pole to help us. (No explanation of how the man knew they were speaking Russian or how he found our they were bomber pilots.)

Soul is getting ready to purge a lot of officers who've been negotiating with the enemy and have planned a coup.

Somewhere on the northwest front, a white officer was leading his patrol down the street when one of our machine guns caught him and shot his head off. He just kept on walking, headless, until he stumbled into our barricade. When our men examined him, they found out that he was an electronic robot, radio-controlled.

I was drinking beer in the canteen this afternoon with some of the others from headquarters. This is what they said; this is the gossip of our city.

What nobody talked about, or cared about, is a fragment I took from the radio-monitor reports this morning. Two or three half sentences from a Tokyo bulletin to the effect that Russian nuclear missiles last night struck Chinese installations in Sinkiang province and . . .

So no more America, no more balance of power, no more entente; what we've dreaded this half century is finally happening? I've been trying frantically all day to get some further information, but nothing seems to be coming through from Europe or the Far East. I seem to be the only one here who cares.

6

'Sherf! Sherf! Sherf!' the whole crowd was chanting; piebald faces, open, snag-toothed mouths. The traveler's horse shied and began to back up. He could almost feel its nerves beneath the skin. He took a tight grip on the reins, preparing to wheel.

'The sheriff will be glad to see you.' In the gateway, suddenly, there stood a man in neat clothes, clean-shaven, with a human face. His dark hair was clipped close to his long head; he wore a clean gray shirt with a leather vest over it, homespun breeches and good half boots. 'Sorry I was slow getting here. Don't trouble yourself about these ones. They just haven't seen a stranger in a long time and they're always ready for a show.'

'Well, I provided,' the traveler said. 'And I guess they liked it, except for one of the dogs.'

The dark man stepped forward, extended his hand, and they shook. 'My name is Greenberg-storeman and this place you are in is named Erie Place.' He spoke precisely, but with a pronunciation that seemed slightly strange to the traveler.

'My name is Kinkaid. I come from far south on the trail.'

Greenberg smiled. 'Well met, then, Kinkaid. Follow me to the sheriff's house.' He turned to the tall guard and said, 'Gut, Els. Okay-nu.' He waved the crowd back from the gate and Kinkaid followed him through, his horses a little more placid now.

'They meant no harm—and they even understood a bit of what you said. Their own talk, though, is what we call 'Nonglish'. For instance, the one called Els—I'd guess that long ago, the name was Ellis. And the little sentry, Gdr—that was Gardener, likely. Their words are mostly like that.'

At closer range, the settlement was even more dilapidated than it had looked from the hill. The houses that faced the road on either side were crisscross—corner log cabins with clay daubing and a heavy mat of rushes that formed a pitched roof. Some of them were no bigger than corncribs and most were ill-built and crooked. The chimneys were made of heavy sticks and fire-hardened clay. Windows were few and the people, crooked as their cabins, stood in the doorways to stare at the stranger and his horses.

They soon came to the village square with its well, the watchtower and an old iron bell mounted on an oak. Greenberg led on toward the one large and solid building facing the square. It was about fifteen paces long, two-storeyed and made of square, deeply notched logs, so smoothly cut that they needed no chinking. Expect for a heavy oak door on iron hinges and a line of loopholes, the first storey was blank. In the second storey, there were four long windows with real glass in them, a leaded patchwork of small panes behind vertical bars. The steep roof was covered with shakes. At either gable end were chimneys built massively of fieldstone.

'We'll tie your horses here for now,' Greenberg said, taking the reins and looping them over two hitching posts that stood by a horse trough. Then he went to the door, knocked three times and pushed it open, waiting for Kinkaid to enter.

Once inside, Kinkaid felt astonished. They had walked into a big keeping room, fine things abounding. The puncheon floor was a smooth expanse; the walls were covered with planed boards; the fireplace, with its cooking spits and great iron kettle on the hob, was large enough to enter upright. In the middle of the room stood a great trestle table at least seven paces long. There were ladder-back chairs with woven rush seats, benches and stools along the wall, a high settle by the fireplace, a spinning wheel in the far corner near a big cupboard with paneled doors. Kinkaid noted a gun rack to the right of the fireplace, with rifles that looked oiled and in good repair. He stood, turning his head at all these riches.

'Well come, sir'—a musical sound out of nowhere. He looked around quickly and saw an armchair in the shadow, a man sitting in it—the voice. 'I am the sheriff of this settlement, James Cochrane. I'm sorry not to rise.'

Kinkaid saw a small man in a white shirt, swollen legs outstretched on a low bench in front of him. A weed patch of longish gray hair falling across a white bank of forehead; an overhang of black eyebrows; a pointed nose and a downdrawn mouth. Except for the eyes, a sick man's face. He held out his hands.

'My legs are cranky today.' When they'd shaken hands, he said, 'Greenberg friend, there's a jug of wine and cups in the cupboard. Pour, then sit.' With a try at a smile, he turned his head. 'And where do you come from, sir?'

'I'm Kinkaid from River Cross Place in Pennsylvan-land. I've been walking nine days on the trail and never a settlement until this one.'

'So you weren't bound here?'

'No; to a place farther westward. It has the name Michigan-land.'

The sheriff shook his head. 'It's not known among us.'

Greenberg looked very seriously down at his sunburned hands, clasped on the table in front of him, and said, 'I think there's nothing to the westward—no settlements and no people. No one ever came from there, but I've gone a little way. Without a trail, how would you go?'

Kinkaid was silent for a few minutes. For such a long time he'd spoken nothing but a word or two to his horses that now his tongue found the going hard. And, too, the answers had nothing to do with anything he had ever seen, had only felt, dreamed, suspected. It hurt his pride to sound foolish.

Slowly, he said, 'There's great water in the north. I hoped men there would have a boat big enough to float me and my horses, going west.'

'Have you seen such a boat?'

'Never.'

Cochrane, head tipped back, stared at Kinkaid from under his furze of eyebrows. 'What is your work? What do you do in your settlement?'

'I'm a healer, what we call a doc. I go out from River Cross Place and the settlements round and treat folk—fevers, broken bones, wounds, childbirth.'

'And then you left and decided to trail westward?' Kinkaid knew the thought in his mind.

'I'm no outlaw man. I have a paper written by our sheriff. It tells my name and asks friendliness from settlements on my trail.'

'And what's the name of this big water?' Cochrane asked quickly. 'Is there a name?'

'I don't rightly know the sound. I've seen it just in letters, ee-ar-eye-ee. Part of the water is named that.'

Greenberg and the sheriff looked at each other, careful not to show expression, though it was as if a word had been passed.

'Erie,' Greenberg said softly. And then, leaning forward on his elbows, his brow wrinkled, he said in a coaxing voice, 'And it was written on a piece of paper that this is the word for a big water?'

'No,' Kinkaid said. 'A picture paper where blue stands for water. Esso-road-map-the-north-central-states—though I'm not sure if I have the right sound of all the words. That's the name of the paper.'

Greenberg's voice was even more gentle and patient. 'Road map?' He shook his head slightly. 'And how did you find this paper? Where does it come from?'

Kinkaid, irritated, pushed back his chair and put his hand to the inner pocket of his shirt. Then he dropped it and decided to answer fairly. 'Eight winters ago, when I was still a boy, we found a dying stranger in the snow, in the forest. They carried him to our house and my mother tried to heal him.'

The firelight on the sweat-glazed face and the matted yellow hair came back again. When no one was near for a moment, the boy had edged close and whispered, 'Who are you?'

'He couldn't speak. In the night, he died. My father spread the things he carried out on the floor the next day. There was a short bow with a stock on it and one arrow left. Some other things. And the paper.

'My grandfather was an old, old man and he wandered in his head and they'd got used to not hearing him. Except me; I liked to listen. Once he took the paper in his hands—his hands trembled—and he told me it was a small picture of the land. Not exactly a picture, but a plan the forefathers used, to show them how to go from one place to another. I believed him and I kept the paper.'

Kinkaid reached into his pocket and brought out the leather case. Slowly, he unfolded the map until it lay open on the table, discolored, heavily creased and much mended. He put his finger on the blue patch and said, 'Lake Erie.'

Cochrane and Greenberg bent over it, staring, touching it with tentative fingers. Greenberg read a few of the names from it aloud.

Then they sat back and Greenberg poured three more cupfuls of the wine, making a small ceremony of handing the first one to Kinkaid. The sheriff sat, breathing heavily, his face pale and his hand, like a blue-veined leaf, against his heart.

After a moment, he said to Greenberg, 'No, it's all right,' and made a feeble attempt to sit straighter.

Then he looked at Kinkaid. 'You've come to it, your lake.' He raised his hand to stop Kinkaid from breaking in. 'Now let me tell this to you. There are a few old stories nobody really believes—but they're still told. And then, once in a while, somebody brings in some strange object found in the mud. Greenberg and I, being the guessing kind of men, listened to the stories and looked at the findings and made up a notion about it all.

'A big sea in ancient times, blue water as far as you could look. Men going out in boats and pulling fish out of the water. That was our notion.' He stopped and nodded at the map as if it were a fourth person. 'But the swamp has always been there, they said. In my father's time, my grandfather's time, in his father's time.'

Kinkaid felt stunned. 'But beyond the swamp?'

'Only more swamp. We've gone out until we couldn't go farther.'

Cochrane and Kinkaid sat quiet for a few minutes. Greenberg was running his finger over the paper and saying, as if to himself, 'Clev-e-land. Toly-do. Det-ro-it.'

'I'll find a trail,' Kinkaid said. 'I'll make my way to one of the old forefather roads and follow it west.'

'Why?' Cochrane asked.

Kinkaid leaned over and put his finger on a spot on the map where there was an X mark. It was a place far to the left of center, on the border between another blue space and a gray one. Then he traced along a faint line that had been drawn on the map. It followed a wavering path downward and then to the right. 'The stranger came from up here and along this way. The line stops in Pennsylvan-land, close to River Cross Place.'

'And so?' Greenberg asked.

'I think he came to find us.'

'That may be,' Cochrane said in an uninterested tone.

Kinkaid was on his feet. 'I'd be obliged for a little food and some feed for my horses. And a place in your stable to sleep. I'll leave at first light tomorrow.' He began to fold the map again.

Greenberg looked up. 'Because you found a dead man once, you're going on a long journey to a place that may not even be?' He shook his head and looked upward to the rafter beams

Kinkaid did not mean to speak any more, but he was irked and, without intending, he said strongly, 'The sheriff said you are guessing men. I don't believe him. Haven't you ever guessed about strange things of the forefather times we come across everywhere? Stone paths not made of stones, ruins of great settlements, all odds of things we haven't even names for? Why did the forefathers leave them and go away? Or do you believe the ghost-and-shadow stories old folks tell by the fire?'

7

Kinkaid waited for an answer to his question, but Greenberg and Cochrane sat stock-still, staring at each other. Were they alarmed at the talk of forefathers and the strange relics they'd left behind them?

Then Kinkaid realized that just a moment ago there had been a shrill whistle from outside and that the two were silently deciding something. Cochrane nodded. Greenberg sprang to his feet and ran to the rifle rack. He took two rifles from the pegs and, thrusting one of them to Kinkaid, butted the door open with his shoulder. He took a cautious step outside and Kinkaid followed.

A bear—not a bear, but a short, burly man like a bear—was at Kinkaid's riding horse. As the animal stamped and shied, the man was half lying across the saddle, trying to keep his balance and tugging at the butt of the rifle in its sheath.

On the trail, when there was no sudden need, Kinkaid left the holster strap buckled to keep the gun dry and secure. He'd fastened it automatically before tying up the horses. This man didn't understand a buckle.

'Kuk, stopt! Hkimer!' Greenberg said in a barking voice.

The man took his hand from the sheath and dropped to a crouch this side of the horse. Four teeth, like rusty nails, showed in a gap in his beard. Then he launched himself at Greenberg. Greenberg slid aside easily as if he had danced this kind of dance before. He swung his rifle butt no more than a foot and caught the man exactly alongside the head, and the man doubled and went down on the doorstep stone. Greenberg stepped back and then swung his boot in a heavy kick. The man groaned. A little dust flew up from the furry black shirt, which was all he wore.

'Give him one more!' Kinkaid looked up and saw the lookout, whistle still in his hand, leaning from the tower platform. He was a boy of about nineteen, with close-cut hair and good homespun breeches, much like Greenberg's. 'You got his attention now; give him one more!'

Greenberg shook his head. 'G'hum-nu, Kuk,' he said. The hairy man got to his knees, avoiding Greenberg's look, and went off down the street at a shamble-trot.

'That's Kuk. Cook, I suppose. I should have remembered to bring your rifle inside. They're not allowed to touch any weapons. And never load one in front of them—that's settlement rules.'

Kinkaid walked over to soothe his horse, stroking the roan's neck and making his 'E-a-a-s-y' noise. Suddenly, he turned to Greenberg with a frown. 'My bushcutter's gone.'

Greenberg came over and looked at the empty scabbard. Then he turned and made a quick, beckoning motion for the lookout to climb down.

'Did you see Kuk take a bushcutter from that horse?' he asked when the sentry had arrived.

The boy rubbed his freckled forehead. 'There was a mixup out by the gate. Some man was beating a woman and a crowd came around. For a minute or two, I wasn't watching the horses, I guess.'

Greenberg's eyes were closed and a muscle in his neck twitched. Finally, he said, 'Call Jeffs-son and tell him to lock the horses in the stable. You go back to lookout.'

When they went inside again, Kinkaid was carrying his rifle and the pouch of ammunition from his saddlebag.

Cochrane was lying flat on the floor near the table and a white-haired woman in a homespun Mother Hubbard was bending over him. She looked up and her face was distraught. 'Oh, Greenberg, it's come again.'

Kinkaid dropped the ammunition pouch and the rifles with a clatter and bent down beside them. He could feel that the sheriff was breathing, even stirring. Then, in a small voice, Cochrane said, 'All right. Right. Just help me to the chair.'

After a minute or two in the chair, with his legs propped again and a blanket around him, he seemed to recover. He kept his fingers laced and his hands flat on his chest. 'Now, tell me,' he said.

'Something new,' Greenberg said. 'One of them has begun to think.'

'No,' Cochrane said, and smiled—a lip-parting with no humor. 'I've hanged six men in my time for thinking. I always knew there would be a seventh. Find him.'

Kinkaid slept that night in a room in the sheriff's house. Almost as he dropped to the narrow, feather-stuffed bed, his dream mind sprang free, just as it had so many times in his solitary going.

Again, he was following the trail into green infinity before him, but his feet were not heavy and they scarcely brushed the leafy ground. In the dream before, there had always been something waiting for him at the far end of the journey that never seemed to end, beyond the trees, remote as a star. But now, as he went lightly, he was visioning the other place, as if one eye saw this scene and the other a different one. He was eager to arrive. In the dream, he was running.

There are very tall lines of cliffs with deep valleys running among them and much fallen rock and rubble. In the distance, there is a pall of smoke against the sky, and somewhere near the cliffs, there is broad, blue water. He moves in the valley and in the distance he sees the figures of men, but they are going away from him.

Without transition, he is standing in an entry, looking into a cave, but it is not a cave. It's a room with smooth walls and ceiling, and before a tablelike thing is sitting a man who has been waiting a long time for him.

The man appears to be asleep. He is dressed in strange clothes, with loops on the shoulders and a figure on his collar. But the strangest thing about the man is that he's the color of shadow. Kinkaid cannot understand how any human can be so burnt. There is something he has heard long ago about this, but in the dream, he can remember nothing. The man breathes quietly in his sleep and the dark hands are motionless in front of him in the lamplight. They are resting on a book and, not knowing how, Kinkaid knows that he has been writing words in that book. He is about to awake and open his eyes on Kinkaid. Kinkaid is to awake at the same moment.

Kinkaid wakes. He is in the forest again. 'Why didn't you tell me what it was you had to say?' is in his mind, but the forest is empty and he keeps walking forward on the thin trail through the enveloping green.

In the early morning, Kinkaid was following Greenberg-storeman up a series of four ladders. It was a longer climb than it had looked from the ground—thirty or forty feet—and Greenberg, moving with an easy swing from rung to rung, got well ahead. They were in shadow, but the new sun caught the lookout platform in a pure light. It was a square, open box of timbers and roughly sawn planks with a pitched roof for shelter. In winter, Kinkaid thought, it would be like death.

Greenberg caught the edge of the platform and a hand came out to help him through the open place in the siding. Kinkaid tried not to pant as the hand reached down to him.

'Jeffs-son. Kinkaid,' Greenberg said. The watcher was young and tall, with a blond haze of beard and hair. He smiled and shook hands. He was dressed in a mottled, capelike thing of pony skin.

'Now that the sun is up,' he said, and pulled it over his head to hang on a peg.

'We'll do the watch for a while, friend,' Greenberg said. 'Eat some breakfast and I'll call you when we go down.' Jeffs-son nodded, swung onto the ladder and was gone.

As they now leaned on the rail, Kinkaid made a slow circumvolution of the settlement with his eyes, catching a few bits and twists he hadn't noticed before.

After a time of silence, Greenberg spoke. 'What do you see?'

'In my mind, a great blue water out there.'

'You can see the dark side of the moon, then.' Greenberg waited. 'But it may be you can. When I first saw your eyes, I had a notion that you could see beyond.' Kinkaid said nothing. 'But around us here what do you see?'

Kinkaid tapped the railing. 'Everything looking inward. This is meant to watch the streets. Your palisade out there is falling down.'

'Yes,' Greenberg said. 'You saw the dogs when you came. They're as much outside guard as we have. The worst we've had to fear is a curious bear or two. Go on.'

'I see two guards at the gate with useless rifles.'

'We tell them they're guarding. They enjoy it.'

'The watchtower is your eye. You—I mean, it's plain that there are two peoples here: your kind and then the crooked ones—your kind is afraid.'

'Afraid!' Greenberg said abruptly. Then, 'Oh, yes. Afraid if we left them to themselves they'd burn the settlement down and go into the woods to starve. We teach them to work—they don't work very well.' He paused, but he had no reply from Kinkaid. 'Am I right, though? You do have a sight of inner things?'

Kinkaid stared at the great ranges of cumulus above the swamp in the morning sun. 'In my settlement, they always said that one of the old women at the bedside when I was born was a witch. Foolish—but that's how they explain things. Yes, I have sights and thoughts I can't reckon account for, sometimes unnatural.' He was reluctant to go on. Then he added, 'I can dowse for water better than anyone I've ever seen. Sometimes, I seem to know the kind and course of an ailment almost in a flash. A little magic helps in my trade.'

Greenberg picked a splinter from the rail and dropped it down, a bright, momentary needle until it disappeared into the shadow. Some ragged children were playing a game in the square below. Three or four women were talking and filling wooden buckets at the well.

45

Beyond the palisade, there were figures of men at work in the fields, slow and listless-seeming even at this remove.

A call from a long distance sounded through the air and Kinkaid saw three men and two scrawny oxen coming out of the woods where the trail ended. The team was dragging a tree trunk by ropes and two of the men were helping to pull. The other one, standing a few steps off, carried a whip.

'And do you see ends too?' Greenberg asked in a low voice, glancing at Kinkaid. 'I mean, what isn't yet but will come?' He tried to make the question sound light, as if they were merely passing the early morning awhile and taking the fresh air, but Greenberg had no real lightness. His tone had a current in it.

'Cochrane, the sheriff, is going to die soon. But nothing's unnatural about knowing that.'

Greenberg turned his head away to stare at the treetops in the distance. 'And so you saw what was in my mind to ask you. Now, do you catch the next question? And the answer?'

Kinkaid smiled. 'Yes. It's a question you've asked yourself a good many times. And find only one answer for. I don't have a better.'

Three birds in flight swerved past the lookout post, their white wings ricochets of light. A report that sounded like a shot—then its duller echo—came from the forest a long way off. Two men came, dragging a creaking cart down the village street in the direction of the gate. The playing children broke into a noisy argument.

Greenberg straightened up and shook his head as if to clear it. 'Come,' he said. 'I'll show you my storehouse.'

When they'd descended the ladder, Greenberg called for the watchman again. Then they crossed the settlement square toward the street of poor cabins that led to the northern palisade. Near the end of this street, close to the blockhouse, Kindkaid noticed several better-built houses with roofs of split shingles, glass-paned windows and even a few flower beds.

Greenberg was pointing out buildings. 'Our smithy over there—we barter for all our iron, what we can get. Or try to dig it up. The butcher's yard is behind that fence.' A cow lowed, confirming it. 'The tanning shed next to it. And over there is the midwife's house. She can dress wounds, treat boils and burns, put on splints and make herbal drinks. We have no doc here. Could you teach her some art? Ah, and here's my storehouse.'

It was a long, low building of square-dressed logs, with a heavy door on iron hinges. It was, like the sheriff's house, windowless below, with a row of loopholes in the front wall. Two dormers in the roof let in the light. To Kinkaid's surprise, Greenberg brought out a

46

big iron key and fitted it into a lock. At home, the inside latch with a latchstring that could be hung out through a hole was the common fastening. But he had seen a lock once or twice before.

'A smith in Stony Hill can make these,' Greenberg said, turning the key and bringing the door open. 'It cost me a sow, but I had to stop the night stealing.'

They entered a room that had little except a long table with a crude set of scales atop it and passed through a gap in the curtain that separated off the storehouse room. Greenberg crossed to a little table and sat himself down there, extending his hand in the direction of a stool. But Kinkaid did not sit immediately. He paced the length of the room, staring at the shelves of goods and supplies.

'It's the common store,' Greenberg said. 'What we make or raise is brought here and then shared out. But some of these are things I trade for in the other settlements.' He watched to see what Kinkaid was noting.

'We are the poorest settlement. All the crafted things—mill boards, powder and shot, barrels and so on—are made in other places.' He spoke as if he had little interest in what he was saying, as if his mind were carrying on another conversation—a troublesome one—in another room.

It was a sparse enough store of goods, though stacked and arranged neatly. Homespun stuff, piles of pelts in a corner, tallow candles, a big box of salt, some kegs that seemed to hold meal, three or four hanging fitches of bacon, a coil of rope on a peg, bags of dried peas. Kinkaid wondered if there was a more private store somewhere else. Walking back to the stool, he felt his boot heel strike an iron ring let flush into the floor and he thought of a trap door.

The sun came into the room in a shaft from a kind of dormer above the roof beams. The pattern it cast on the floor neatly divided in squares and Kinkaid looked up to see an iron grating that guarded the window. All forethought, all skill, he reflected, were spent to make this settlement secure. And so it must live meagerly.

'Have your folk lived here always?' Kinkaid asked.

Greenberg gave his thin and serious smile. 'Oh, the old tales are something to hear. If you believe it, our people lived on an island in towers taller than mountains in the times before the troubles. Shining engines, shaped like rooms, carried them over the land and water and even into the air. There was so much good food that they would throw it away. Engines of other kinds kept them warm or cool, cleaned for them, raised buildings, cooked and made pictures appear on the wall. Old folk by the fire can whistle up any kind of foolery.'

'And what was the name of the place? Why did they come away?'

'Its old name was N'york Place. Well, you've heard of the troubles and the starving time. The folk who were first here—the crooked people—lived in rush huts. In the cold time of the year, they killed each other for food. My folk found them and settled here. In time, they built what you see.'

'But why did your kind leave N'york Place and come to the swamp shore?'

Greenberg seemed to be listening for something else. At last, he said, 'Driven out, I think. They came with a few oxen, a couple of wagons, carts they pushed along. There are one or two old songs about that. When they found this place, they wintered here. And because they had guns, they saved themselves and the crooked people from starving. Cochrane knows more about all of us—'

There was a soft tapping sound from beneath the floor.

Greenberg got up, went over to the iron ring and hauled open a trap door. One young man, then another, climbed through the opening as Kinkaid watched. The first was Carlsson, the lookout he'd seen yesterday. The other was a red-haired boy of about twenty with muscular arms and shoulders.

Greenberg stood with his hands on his hips. 'From your looks, I don't think you found them.'

They glanced at Kinkaid, then back to Greenberg. 'He's a friend; I want him to hear,' Greenberg said. 'Tell me.'

'We dug up the hearthstone in Kuk's house,' Carls-son said in his nasal voice. 'Just as you thought, there was a hollow place under it. But no bushcutter, no guns. Just this.' He held out a small round thing and Kinkaid saw that it was the kind of plug generally used to stop up the muzzle of a rifle when it was carried in the rain or through streams.

'Kuk and Kuk-wife, what did they say?'

'Lies—that they didn't know the hole was there. We locked Kuk in the jail cabin. He's yelling through the bars at everybody who goes by, saying he's been thrown in just for looking at the stranger's horse.'

Greenberg hooked his thumbs into the armholes of his vest and, with bent head, paced up and down the storeroom. 'So somebody stole the bushcutter and sent Kuk back for the rifle. At the same time, got the man to beat the woman and get your attention. Next, the one with the bushcutter thought that we'd probably search in Kuk's cabin. I think he took some guns away from it last night.' Greenberg made a nervous 'mmh-mmh' sound in his throat.

'I'll wallop Kuk and make him tell,' the red-haired man said in a confident way.

48

Greenberg stopped walking and put his right foot on a stool. 'Good. But I don't think he has much to tell. Likely he doesn't know more than who it was passed the order to him.' He picked a piece of chalk from his table and juggled it from hand to hand. 'Four steps,' he said quietly. 'One, he steals. Two, he hides it. Three, he takes it away, guessing where we'd look. Four? We've never had to deal with one who could think more than two steps away, steal-and-hide.'

'Robs-son!' asked the sentry. 'Your guess?'

The red-haired man was squatting on his haunches and looking up at the rafters. 'Wod stole a sickle once and hid it in his roof. Keler is shrewd enough to always win the threestick game they play. But they're cowards.'

'Well,' Greenberg said, 'if there are guns still in the village, we'll make them move. Search some of the cabins—random ones, any will do. Tonight have men and dogs—quietly, remember—outside the stockade. We'll see if he tries to take what he has into the woods tonight.'

A fly spiraled in the sunlight from one of the dormers; Robs-son straightened up and caught it with a quick swipe. 'They can't load or aim a rifle,' he said.

'I calculate one of them has found out,' Greenberg said. 'And I don't want to be shot in the back to prove you're wrong. Talk to everybody who was near the square yesterday after Kinkaid rode in. Write down any names you hear.'

He turned abruptly and walked over to a set of shelves piled up with bags that might have contained wool, or feathers. He reached behind an upright and seemed to pull on a string. Then the whole shelf section swung out on unseen hinges, as a door opens. On the wall behind it was a gun rack with seven rifles. They were of different sizes and shapes and they looked well oiled and useful. There were ramrods, cleaning patches and pouches of ammunition on a shelf below.

Greenberg took down the shortest two rifles and handed them over, then passed two pouches of ammunition. 'Take five men for the watch and a boy to run with messages. I'll be at the sheriff's tonight.'

The two men smiled at each other. They were enjoying this game. Greenberg waited a minute or two after they had gone and then closed the trap door carefully. He sat down at his table again, after he'd put the shelf back in place.

'We were talking about the second sight when we were on the lookout tower,' he said. 'Yours, Kinkaid. Now you've heard these things, does any picture come into your head?'

Kinkaid smiled. 'If I had such powers, I'd have taken the rifle and bushcutter inside with me. No; whatever I see that way comes at strange times—and it may be something I can't make out at the time.'

'But you have some thought about all of this?'

'Maybe.' He stared at the shaft of sunlight from the dormer. 'Maybe I'd walk and look and think. Maybe I'd notice something that one of the people did that was different from all the rest. A planned thing that took time working out—whatever plan it might be. One, two, three steps, as you said.'

Greenberg sighed. 'I would have noted that. But no. It seems that there are things I haven't noted.' One of the sacks had fallen off the shelf and Greenberg, seeing it now, went over and kicked it against the wall. A cloud of dust rose up in the shaft of sun and, for a moment, it seemed to Kinkaid that Greenberg was enveloped in smoke.

8

[*July 18*]

Arrow's staff meeting had a kind of manic desperation. On the southwest front, the Stone Brigade has lost two out of every three officers and the advance to Gary is still stalemated. There are no reinforcements available. 'It's fuckin high noon and we gotta bust sompcn soon,' Arrow said, and karate-chopped his desk. 'Les hear yo shit,' he said to me.

'My plan of attack, sir,' I said, 'is this.' I picked up my notes and began to go over the idea we'd talked about.

It wasn't going to be one of the great maneuvers in military history, but it did have the merit of being slightly insane. There's the insanity of Alma and the insanity of Balaklava—and I hoped mine was the first one.

I got the idea when I'd gone into the motor pool garage on Hubbard.

It's hard to keep cars running nowadays. The supply of gas—bad enough in the whole country when the revolution started—is now desperate. Parts are harder to find because the motor pool garage guys have cannibalized just about every available car to keep military vehicles in operation. I was talking to Sam, the oldest and the best mechanic, when I noticed an odd shape in the shadows at the far end of the garage and asked him what it was.

'Piece a shit. One them Brink's arm-cars we use las May.'

And that was when I'd had my idea. 'You think the ordnance dudes could mount some MGs and recoilless on them? Could you keep 'em running for about three hours?'

He spat. 'Reckon.'

'And are there still a few of them around?'

'Brink's, Purolator, Wells Fargo. Mos laid up in garages.'

'How long would it take you to get 'em in running order? We

want to take a little ride.'

He cocked his good eye upward as if looking for the God of Internal Combustion to shake his head. 'A week,' he said, 'but I hopes you ain't got nothin foolish in mine.'

That was a week ago.

[*1500, July 19*]

Yesterday, just at twilight, we brought the cars up to the Stone Brigade front, one by one—that was to avoid the spotter planes that hover incessantly in the eastern sky. Now they are dispersed in wrecked buildings or camouflaged near the jump-off points. The crews are ready in the bunkers.

Booner, the brigade commander, shakes his head at one of the gray-painted cars and says, 'Them old shoeboxes.'

'You didn't get very far with the building-to-building, small-arms stuff,' I say. 'Wait till they see our wheels. *Les taxis de la Marne.*'

'Lay tahksees what?' he asks. 'Don't think I don't dig your plan. Them honkies see the cars and they drop their guns and run out—think somebody comin' to deliver their payroll checks.'

[*1850, July 19*]

I'm scribbling this by candlelight in a cellar. Outside, the light is just beginning to shade off a little, and when the sun is at our back and in their eyes, we'll start. The crews have all been awakened and a few of the officers have come to shake my hand. I'm writing this because I'd hoped to think of some deep and moving sentence to express what might be my last words. But I disappoint myself. All I can think of is that ancient phrase *Morituri te salutamus.*

[*0200, July 20*]

Did it. We done busted their ass.

And they broke our heart. Now I know that it's all over.

I wish I'd been killed instead of coming home to find what I found.

I'm sitting here in my room again, dirty, worn out, a leaking bandage around a hole in my shoulder, hopeless. I'm supposed to be writing a report for Soul himself, but this is all the report there's going to be.

I'll never forget those cars, like big, oblong elephants lumbering

52

down the ruined roads, through every open space, into the enemy front. Some of the lead ones turning into fireworks in front of my eyes—but more of them than I expected getting through.

As I'd guessed, the enemy hadn't looked for anything like this and they had nothing in the way of antitank around. White soldiers spilling out of their OPs and running in a sleet of tracers.

A haze of smoke and dust in front of my eyes. I don't remember much in any detailed way. I must have been standing up in the jeep when that motherfucker came out of a wrecked gas station with a laser-aimed submachine gun and cut Corlie in two and hit me in the shoulder.

Then I was lying on the ground and everybody, everything seemed to have gone off in the distance, just disappeared, leaving me with the burning cars and the ruined buildings around me and no sound—no noise at all. I raised my head a little and he came walking toward me, walking from out of nowhere. The savage man in my dream.

For the first time, I saw his face—a white man's but very sunburned, a square face with a thick nose and thin lips. He seemed to be wearing some kind of an animal skin on his head. He looked directly into my eyes, but I couldn't speak. At first, I thought he was coming to kill me. Then I knew that he was coming to take something and I knew it was this book. I must have blacked out then.

Booner has described the complete success of the breakthrough—our men fanning out through their defenses and the point column, with Booner in the lead, barreling down the highway into Gary, everybody screaming and cheering.

To find Gary nothing but a burned-out graveyard, a lot of the buildings smashed, the streets eerie and empty. His men found a few whites in a rear-echelon depot and killed them, that was all.

One of Booner's captains found the mass graves, a couple of them still open and in the process of being filled with quicklime before our attack.

Gary had been a city of about 180,000 people, most of them black. Most of them are lying in those endless rows of huge pits.

Booner had headed for the BLAC radio station, where the Gary revolution bulletins had been coming from for months. He found it in pretty good repair and he went inside, went into the deserted offices, began to examine the papers there and found—

Found that it had all been a paper game. Scripts of broadcasts about the Gary brigade gallantly holding the front, orders to the people, bulletins from the BLAC provisional government inside the city—all fiction. The USG must have taken the town and the radio station back in June.

Riding back in the staff car with Booner, I didn't have the heart to talk. But we both knew, now, what the scam had been. Knew why there'd been no gunships in the sky to turn back our attack, why their artillery had been silent, why their defense melted. They *wanted* us to break through that white paper front. And they wanted us to have a good look at those enormous graves. Those graves, all over the country, would be filling now. *They* are our new Africa, our promised land. And we are to possess this land by being laid in it.

In a few minutes, I'll lock this journal in its steel box and hide it again in the hollow I've made in the wall. The block fits so well that even the most careful searcher would have to be lucky to find it. But I think that someday, far from now, it will be found by one who dreams it's there.

I turn back to the first page and see that phrase 'one fingerprint of my own left on earth.'

There is a knock at my door.

9

Never before in his life had Kinkaid seen such a dazzle of candle flares, heard such crosswinds of rising and falling voices, seen such a swarm of people in good clothes. There must have been more than thirty of them in the sheriff's big keeping room and more were coming to the door. He was dizzy with names and smiles, hands shaken and names forgotten. Sometimes in River Cross Place, there were roasts around an outdoor fire, with some old songs sung and some dances danced to the tunes of three whistle pipes and a drum, but never a company like this.

There was a smell of new-baked bread from the oven built into the fireplace, and at the fireplace itself, women were coming and going, busy with iron kettles that hung from the bar inside. There a young boy stood, slowly turning the crank handle of a spit and the juices of the meat fell into a pan, sizzling. Two large tables were laid out with wooden trenchers and knives, a folded cloth alongside each. There were pottery jugs and some bowls with fruit.

As the crowd grew, Kinkaid edged to one side of the room, where a smaller table was laid out with cups and jugs of what seemed to be wine. A young woman standing there smiled at him.

'Will you have a cock tail?' she asked.

Kinkaid stared. She was wearing a neat gray dress with a white collar and her hair was long and light and loose. The women at home simply tied it at the nape, or made it into a braid.

'A what?'

She repeated.

He looked inside the cup and asked, 'But where's the tail?'

She laughed. 'I don't know. That's just an old word for a drink. Wine or turned cider—anything like that. In the old days, they may have put a feather in the cup.'

'But stopped when too many drinkers choked to death,' Kinkaid said, taking the cup she offered.

She laughed again and Kinkaid suddenly felt successful.

'My name is Mary and I know yours. Jeffs-son is my brother.' Kinkaid wondered why women before this hadn't thought of loose and curly hair. In the candlelight, it was a marvel. And her old-kind of name was music. He didn't know how to say any of this, though, and so he just drank from his cup. To his surprise, he tasted the tang of grapes, not berries. They began to talk and he forgot the rest of the room.

Then women were bringing platters and bowls of food to the tables and people were beginning to sit down. He couldn't think of quite the right words to ask Mary to sit with him.

'May I sit with you?' she asked, taking his arm.

Fine talk with a woman—he could scarcely believe it. He had slept with some, had treated some, had attended a lot of them in childbirth, but as he recalled, no girl had ever talked with him in this easy and equal way.

And as they took places at a bench beside one of the long tables, women's voices mingled with the men's, even cutting in, to make a strange tune in his ear. At home, women served the food silently. The tones of River Cross Place were the rumble of male voices, men's heavy laughter, terse orders to a woman or child.

Now another woman was speaking to him, a gray-haired woman with high color in her cheeks, who was sitting across the table. 'Where do you come from, Mr Kinkaid? Is your settlement much like ours?' He noticed that she and all the others had taken the big pieces of cloth from the table and tied them around their necks. Wondering why, he did the same.

Mis-ter. He had heard that word once or twice before when some old-fashioned man was pleading his case to the sheriff. Mister Sheriff.

He tried to describe River Cross Place with its meadows and cattle, the water mill, forge and market—so busy a village that they were already building cabins outside the stockade. 'I am the doc there,' he said, and spoke of his rounds in the little hill-farm settlements, some of them no bigger than a dozen families.

She led him on with questions, others put in, and almost before he noticed, the women were clearing the dishes from the table. He could hear their voices in the kitchen as they put the food away and began the washing.

'Tell us,' Cochrane said from his seat at the head of the table. 'Tell us about the country round you. Don't you have travelers from far settlements, east or west?'

'Yes,' Kinkaid answered. 'Now and then a family with a horse and cart come to settle in our place. Traders with packhorses and goods to

56

barter. Then there are the scavengers, who even go far east, over-the-mountains, for months at a time. Against the law, of course, but these days even the sheriff turns his head.'

There were whispers at this. But looking around the room, Kinkaid could see iron things and copper that were never forged at home. He'd noticed a few books and an ornamental object with a face where the numbers one to twelve were arranged in a circle.

A man called M'Vay-smith—he remembered this name—a lean man with a horseshoe of gray around his pink scalp, said in a nasal voice, 'Over-the-mountains is fearful places, hear tell.'

Kinkaid suddenly found Mary's hand in his, resting on his thigh under the table. Then she gently brought both their hands to her own thigh. He shivered, not only in surprise.

'It's hard to sort out the lies and bragging in the stories,' Cochrane said. 'Some of the scavenger men tell tales about forefather ruins so wide you can't see the other side. Or walk across them in two days. Full of wild dogs, they say, and rats as big as the dogs.'

Mary tickled the palm of Kinkaid's hand with her fingertips. He didn't dare look at her.

'And terrible sickness,' said a woman at the far end of the table.

'I don't take stock in that,' Cochrane said, lolling back in his padded wing chair. 'The forefathers had a great sickness in their times, that seems to be true. But it must be gone after all these years.' He seemed to be sitting easily, without the spasms that had come over him yesterday. This afternoon, Kinkaid had mixed a herbal draught for him and it seemed to have had effect.

'There's one vasty settlement over-the-mountains,' Kinkaid said, 'with the most contrary tales about it. It's far to the east and it stands by a big river—some of it is under the water now. On the hills that overlook the river, salvagers tell, there are more tall, wide houses than you can count. Much has fallen down, but much is left. And many of these are something else than houses—what, they don't know. Long flights of stone steps leading up to them, big rows of stone tree trunks across the fronts. They talk of one that had a high roof shaped like half an egg—but the roof's fallen in now.'

Mary was rubbing his hand along her thigh with exciting slowness. He wondered if any of them guessed at this under-the-table game. It made his face feel hot.

'I got that from a salvager named Kodi, a mean old man who's not afraid of rats or ghosts or anything else. He said inside the building with the egg dome he saw people made of stone, some of them lying on the floor smashed and broken. It gave him a wind at first, but then he went into a big chamber with nothing but rotting benches in it.

57

'Farther away, by the river, he said he saw another great hall and when he climbed up the steps and went inside, he saw a stone giant sitting on a chair. But the face had been smashed. Everywhere in this settlement were stone people and stone animals. Ghosts turned to stone, he said.'

The hands were resting now where he dared not think. He felt the touch of her breast against his arm. He was thankful for the long neck cloths and he took a glance at Mary.

'Please go on,' she said sedately.

What had he been talking about? 'Ruined and plundered,' he said. 'Kodi saw places that must have been burned out by fires long ago.'

'And are these lies, d'you think?' the sheriff asked.

'He lies when he's bartering. But no, I think he told me the truth about what he'd seen. There was another look on his face.'

'Well, what did you make of it? What was that settlement built for if the forefathers didn't live there?'

There was a stroking motion and Kinkaid wondered if he was getting red in the face. He had to keep the talk going because he couldn't stand up now.

'No; Kodi saw houses too. But the main thing, I think, is this.' He paused for a long minute. The caressing hand was having an almost trancing effect and the mystery picture that had come time and again after Kodi's words was before him—the great, empty rooms in the midst of overgrown meadows, sightless stone eyes, the sky-reaching stone pillar, the wide, crumbled roadways. 'It comes to me as a village of the dead.' His voice floated away from him. 'The forefathers could make their dead into stone and this great settlement was the place of the unforgotten. Across the river, there, is a great burying ground for the dead who once guarded the dead.' Kinkaid had lost all sense of the room and the watching faces.

Suddenly, the gray-haired woman across from him was speaking in her sharp voice. She was agitated and her fingers kept turning over the crumbs on the table in front of her. '. . . and things we should be feared to pry into,' he heard her say.

Angrily, she went on: 'All of you know the Doom Story, handed down. I heard it from my grandmother, who never told a lie in her life, and she heard it from her grandmother. How just after this world began, the tall forefathers, white as the snow, knew a magic to build all kind of great things. And how the shadow people came from another place. So black that nobody ever saw their faces. Then the fearsome fighting when the shadows tried to keep the sun from rising and make it always night.

'You know the story as well as I do—how all the forefather great things were ruined even though the shadows died. Then the long sickness and starving time when just a few of the forefather children lived in the woods. That's the old story. It tells us not to turn over the forefather places or to raise the dead. It tells us not to pry into terrible things better left alone.' As she finished, her face was unnaturally red and her fingers were shaking among the crumbs.

'Weel. Humph!' M'Vay-smith said. 'I guess it's true if it's always been said, Marthie. Still, you can't blame me for pondering if there's much salvages in them settlements. Just pondering, see?'

But, Kinkaid noticed, the woman's outburst had seemed to subdue the talk. People were already beginning to rise from the benches and go to the sheriff to say their goodbyes. The front door was opened and the cool night air came into the room.

As a boy, Kinkaid had heard almost the same white-spirit-and-black-shadow story about the war at the beginning of time and it still held a dread, though he no longer believed in it—or at least, believed in it as it was told.

He was standing with Greenberg, saying good night, when Robs-son came running through the door and into the room, the rifle cradled under one arm.

He said to Greenberg in a low voice, 'There's something. Will you come?'

Greenberg nodded, patted Kinkaid on the shoulder and said, 'Tomorrow, then,' before he went off with Robs-son.

The last of the crowd was beginning to leave. Kinkaid turned and saw Mary waiting for him. He said to her, 'I want to talk with you.'

'You can,' she said. 'But not here. Outside.'

The square was moonlit and they took a turn around it, Kinkaid fuming but not knowing how to begin. She slipped her arm in his and this made him feel even more uncertain.

At last, she pulled him into the shadow where a little lane alongside the sheriff's house entered the square. 'Well?'

'Why did you do that to me?' he whispered. 'To make me look foolish?'

'I'm sorry,' she said. 'I was being foolish.' They were very close. He could smell some kind of herb scent in her hair. Silence for a minute—then it seemed to Kinkaid that they met in midair, arms and bodies and lips, for a long time.

They were walking again down the lane; twenty paces and she paused and pushed open a gate in a sapling fence that stood a little higher than their heads. She took him by the hand silently and drew him after her, into a little yard, then through a door. They were in a room with a wooden floor, black except for one bar of moonlight through a window high in the gable.

She put her hands on his face and they kissed again, longer. Then she drew away and there was a rustling. 'Mary?' he whispered.

'Yes?' She was back in his arms, Kinkaid startled by her sudden nakedness. He ran his hand down the smooth curve of her back.

The bed was a feather bed, all billows, and they seemed to sink in clouds as she guided him gently inside her.

Kinkaid's experiences had all been quick and fierce. At home, a man spoke a word to a girl and they found a loft or a shed. There was no caress, no kiss. She drew up her dress and he plunged to his shudder. A transaction between man and hole.

Now he scarcely believed the things that could happen—slow, warm, murmurous, lost out of time. At last, she gave several quick gasps and cries. Then she astonished him again.

With an agile movement, she rolled on top of him and sat up, straddling him, thrusting with her body. Kinkaid had never imagined it, a world upside down.

The beam of moonlight cut her in half, falling across her left side and breast, leaving the rest of her body in darkness. The nipple eye seemed to stare at him and he was spellbound. Until their spasm came.

He woke later to find that she'd left his arms, and he heard a soft scraping sound from the other side of the bed—strange, then familiar. He reached over and took the flint, steel and tinderbox from her and made a spark catch. She took a candle, lighted it and put it on a stool next to the bed.

'Kinkaid?' she said, and hesitated a long moment. Her face was amber in the candle glow, framed in the disordered hair. 'Stay with me.'

'The sheriff's household will wonder.'

She laughed. 'Oh, not just tonight. I mean stay on. Don't go traveling on the trail again.' She was silent.

Kinkaid saw before him the long trail receding into the twilight of the thousand-tree forest. He saw himself squatting as he made a fire in a clearing, taking food from his saddlebag for a brief, soundless meal. Asleep, he felt himself waking as the wind began to gust and the rain dripped from the leaves onto his face.

'No,' he said. 'I can't.'

She put her arms around him. 'I'd make you happy.'

'I know you would,' he said.

As he dressed, he looked at her once more. 'I'll think on it,' he said.

Kinkaid ate his breakfast in the company of Cochrane's wife and the two young daughters of the house. 'Will you go to him afterward?' she asked. 'He wants to see you.'

Kinkaid got his bag of medicines and walked along the gallery to a room at the end of the second-floor half storey. Cochrane was sitting up among pillows, floury-faced and coughing.

'Good morning. Kinkaid. Not good, but better than last night. I couldn't sleep.'

Kinkaid drew the bedclothes back and looked at the sheriff's legs; they were swollen like white sausages. 'The pains in your chest?'

'Come and go—a little less this morning. Give me some more of your herbal stuff, Kinkaid. It makes me drowsy, but it keeps the pains off.' He motioned toward an old, much-scratched bottle that stood on a table.

'I'll leave you a good supply, but remember, there's a strong drug in it. Take it only when you have real need.' Kinkaid poured a little into a cup and the sheriff drank and sank back.

After a few moments, he said, 'Sit down and we'll talk.'

Kinkaid pulled a joint stool up alongside the bed. 'Yes, it's time for me to thank you for your welcome. I go away with good memories.'

Cochrane smiled his naïve, child's smile. 'Accepted and returned.' He made a gesture toward the bottle. 'But I'd hoped you'd stay to help me get well again.' He glanced down at his legs beneath the covers. 'I should be walking before summer's out.'

'I'm good for wounds, colic and broken bones, not much more. You'll improve by nature.'

Cochrane sighed. 'But you see we need a doc here. I've seen many people die when a little knowledge could have saved them. What do you want, Kinkaid?'

'It may happen that I'll be back this way.'

'Look, Kinkaid, you're a lettered man. There are forefather books on that wall.' Kinkaid got up and drew back a little curtain that hung in front of a shelf. The books were very worn and stained.

'A man who has the interest can learn a lot in them. There's even a book about healing. With secrets even you don't know.'

Kinkaid slowly read the words on the backs of the scarred and faded bindings. *Home Radio Repair. Lawrence Welk: The Man and His Music. Ben-Hur. Practical Accounting. Learn to Invest Wisely. Shorthand Made Easy: The Gregg System. Caring For Your Parakeet. The Songs of Stephen Foster.*

'Where is the book about healing?'

'The red one on the end. I can't make it out, but you will.'

Kinkaid took the book in his hands and read, *Better Health Through Zen.* What is Zen?'

Cochrane looked up at the ceiling, nodded wisely. 'Oh, he was a great doc among the forefathers. All of his teaching is there.' He waited for Kinkaid to sit down again and, after some hesitation, said, 'There's a house vacant since Corelli butcher died. Well chinked and warm. I'd give it to a doc, if we had one here.'

Kinkaid nodded and said nothing.

'A doc, say, could have all his food and clothes and firewood, double share. And a gun for hunting.' He paused and smiled. 'In the fall, the ducks come down from the north and the swamp is full of them. My wife roasts them to something better than you've ever tasted.'

'I'm sure,' Kinkaid said.

'The smith's youngest girl's strong and willing. Sixteen or thereabouts. She could do the washing and cleaning.'

'You must get some rest now,' Kinkaid said, rising. 'Thanks—and I'll think on it.'

In the afternoon, Greenberg asked Kinkaid to walk with him outside the settlement. 'You can tell me if our woods have any herbs useful for medicine,' he said.

At the gate, Kinkaid noticed a change in the sentries—there was just one man now, tall, straight, dressed in homespun and carrying a good rifle. 'I'll be somewhere near the south trail, Zabriskie, if you want me,' Greenberg said to him.

Kinkaid and Greenberg walked slowly along the track into the woods whence Kinkaid had come. He pointed out a few medicinal herbs, but Greenberg seemed preoccupied and took little notice.

In time, he said, 'We caught him last night.'

'Ah, you recovered the bushcutter and the rifles, then?'

'Bad luck, no. He'd say nothing. But he was coming back from the swamp very late and our dogs sniffed him out. Fishing, he said. He did have some fish.'

'Who is he?'

'One you don't know. I'd rather not say just now.'

'And to make him tell?'

'We put him in a cellar. All of them have a mighty fear of the dark. In their cabins, they keep the fires going all night, even in summer.'

Kinkaid broke a twig off a sapling and began to chew on the end of it meditatively. 'Friend, be prudent about this. Are you sure this one is the man you want?'

Greenberg halted on the path, a stubborn look on his long face. He hooked his thumbs in the armholes of his vest—his move, Kinkaid had noted, when he was set on something. 'We found out some things. He can count higher than ten. He can understand our talk and even imitate it. When we searched his cabin, we found a bow and some arrows he'd made. Maybe for hunting, maybe not. He had a canoe hidden by the shore—hollowed out from a log—and he fished from it. Under his lean-to is a log-lined cave where he keeps winter food for his family. This man can think ahead.' He paused. 'There's a fallen tree over there; let's sit.'

When they were seated, Kinkaid said, 'I see your train, Greenberg, but you've come at it from the wrong way. The man you have is not the one you want.'

'D'you have a vision of that?' His tone was sarcastic.

'No. But try to match the two ends—the end this man has in his mind and the end you're fearful of. They don't match.'

'Well, I'll be cautious, then,' Greenberg said. 'But I came here to talk about something else.' He was silent for a minute, breaking one twig after another in his fingers. Finally, he said, 'The settlement is poor because we are poor in people. D'you know, Kinkaid? There are fifty or so of us and maybe three hundred of them.' He stared up into the branches of a maple tree, where a squirrel stared back at him.

'It could be different. I ask you not to tell this, Kinkaid. I'm a salvager, as you've guessed by now. This spring, I was southwest of here, poking in a forefather ruin, and I found a buried place that had never been robbed. A storehouse of some kind for metals. Copper, lead, I don't know what all. More than I could tally in a month.' He threw a pebble and the squirrel scurried to a higher branch.

'I'm a doc, not a smith, but I can see the worth of that.'

'The worth is that hoard turned into other things. I see it turned into a water mill, into a smithy three times bigger than the one we have, a marketplace, new buildings. But first it has to be turned into numbers—new settlers.

'They'll come where there is land and trade.'

'Kinkaid, nothing grows without a strong hand to direct it. Cochrane is dying—you saw that. I will be the new sheriff. But I am a salvager, trader, builder. Somebody else has to hold the other rein.'

'One of your people?'

'No; men like M'Vay-smith are too narrow. The boys are too young and thoughtless. A stranger would do better—if he was a prudent man and a strong one.' He hesitated and smiled. 'Why should a man waste his life on the trail trying to find an unknown settlement, lost farther than beyond in the wilderness?'

Kinkaid chewed the twig until it was shredded, then he spat it out. 'Since I was a boy, half high, I've wanted to know. All about what the forefathers built, all about them. And why they came to grief. D'you understand, Greenberg? It's hard to tell. But we have to learn those meanings if we want to know where we're going. I have a sense I can find out some of that if I go over beyond. Just a sense, but it stays with me.'

'What do you believe to find out there?' Greenberg asked. 'This X mark on the paper?'

'Well, you said that I can see the dark side of the moon. Think of it that way. The place of the X has words beside it that spell Grand Haven. Sometimes it comes to me that I can see through the thickness of the moon—that is, through the thickness of the forest westward.

'Greenberg, you're a man with a hard, good head and you'll shake it when I tell you that I'm saying something from a dream and yet once was or once will be. It waits outside our time. There—you see, you're shaking your head.

'Shut your eyes. This is a cliffland where the forepeople lived, in cliffs made by their powers. They are high enough to shut out the sun. In the valley roads there are more people coming and going than we have ever seen and strange big shapes moving too. Then the people are all gone and I hear the wind blowing among the empty cliffs. This is how I dream the Grand Haven place.'

Greenberg raised his head and looked narrowly at Kinkaid. With stress on every word, he said, 'Listen to me, my friend Kinkaid. Here's a dream of something likely true. One winter night, you are lying dead in the snow under the trees and wild dogs are coming out of the bush to eat your body. Now think if my offer isn't better than that.'

'I'll think on it,' Kinkaid said.

10

On the seventh day—two nights ago—they were overdue. On the ninth day, their food and the boiled water in their canteens would have run out. Tomorrow they would have to drink swamp water and eat what fish they could catch. She dug her nails into her forearms so hard that the pain made her eyes water.

Glyn Havensdotter smiled a rigid smile and tried to narrow her mind to the children, the lesson, the questions and answers. But her eyes kept swerving off across the sandy clearing toward the small dock over there. The shoreline wilderness of reeds was split in one place—and at that place stood the plank landing dock and an open channel of graygreen water about twenty feet wide where she'd waved to them as they poled the canoe away.

'What is the name of our settlement?'

'Ha-ven Place is its name.' The children's voices sang it. They loved the naming of things, this who-we-are, where-we-are part that always began the lesson.

'And all the big land around us, what—'

Snap: The phantomscape in her head came on again. She seemed to see the reedtops about thirty yards out from shore bending as something glided through them. Another agitation where the channel made a turn; two birds shot violently into the air. Then a shadow on the water, followed by the familiar prows pushing slowly into sight, then the whole length of the double canoe sliding alongside the landing dock. Piet-mechanic rising to catch the post. She saw his sunburned torso and his buff-yellow head. He laid down the paddle and stepped carefully onto the planking and, for the first time, he looked at her. He looked at her despondently and slowly shook his head. Alone; he was home from the marsh alone.

'I didn't hear. The big land around us, what is that?'

Cheerfully and obediently, they sang out, 'Mich-i-gan-land.' Their faces were intent on hers to see if she was pleased. It was painful to see how little they knew and how eager they were. They had been working in the cornfields or vegetable gardens since sunup, and after this little luxury of a class in the shade, they'd go back to the same toil.

'Now the big, big land that takes in even Michigan-land?'

They knew the answer, but they never said it unless she said it first. Not because they'd forgotten the word but because it didn't fit any idea. No one had ever been farther than a few miles from the settlement—no one who'd ever come back again, except for her father.

'Berk Weavers-son?' He was the biggest boy in the class, of seventeen summers or so. He was a muscular boy, a wrestler, swimmer, runner, climber of trees. His friends made jokes about his sitting to learn letters with the little kids. But he stayed, red-faced and half resentful most of the time.

'Called Usa, I guess it is,' he finally said.

'Good, Berk. Usa.'

'And now, what were our forefathers called?' She chalked it on her piece of plank in big letters. But nobody wanted to try the hard word. 'A-mer-i-cans,' she pronounced. 'Say it.'

They tried. It came out something like 'Amurrytins.' Everybody knew that the only people there were had the name Haveners—except for the few scattered settlements along the nearby shore.

Snap: The double canoe, its small sail limp, lost in reeds and seaweed-choked water. Behind them, the channel had disappeared. They were trying to work eastward, in the direction of the sun, but the weeds fouled their paddles at every stroke and they made little or no headway. The sun was like fire. Clouds of torturing mosquitoes surrounded them. Then the canoe slowed to a stop in the green mass. Her father, kneeling at the bow, dropped his paddle wearily. He turned around and she could clearly see his sane, strong hunter-searcher face with the blue eyes under the rough gray outcrop of hair. He looked at her slowly and shook his head.

What? What? 'I go hunt deer with Dader,' Bills-son was saying. He'd hardly been able to talk when he first came to the class; now he exploded a sentence or two at a time. 'I saw a stone path. Big, long.' He stopped for a moment, trying to get off his last shot. 'Ani't gotno end!'

'Yes,' said Glyn. 'That was a path—called a road—the forefathers used to come and go on. And on the water, they had great canoes that were pushed along by the wind.' They nodded, but she wondered if any picture came. She wished that she could explain better, but all her store of learning came from the five broken-backed books—with many pages missing—her father had given her. In his workroom there were more, as many as twenty, but those were his study books and she was not permitted to touch them. And he did not abide impractical

66

questions very gladly.

'And now it's time for letters—I brought our new book again today.' The smaller children laughed and clapped. After two days of patient word-by-word deciphering, they'd mastered the first two pages fairly well. Then they'd seen that it began to make a story about people like them, but different. She unfolded the cloth wrappings and brought the fragile thing out. It must have passed through fire and water down through the years before it came to her hands, because the pages were stained, colors of the drawn pictures faded and leaves charred at the edges.

'Mara reads first,' she said. 'Hold the book carefully, Mara. The rest of you look over her shoulder and see each word as she speaks it.'

'Once—upon—a—time—there—lived—in—Sher-wood—For-est—a—band—of—out-laws. . . .'

Snap: The two men had landed on a strange shore. There were forefather ruins all around, high ones. It was bright moonlight and there were no colors. She saw looming shadows, chasms, thickets, masses of boulders. The men were moving along a straight pathway, coming in and out of shadow toward her. About fifty paces away, they passed into a bigger shadow. She heard something. Though she waited, they didn't reappear.

'. . . while—Kink—Rish—ard . . . Richard?—was—in—the—Holly—Land—on—his—Crus . . . Crus . . .?'

She came to herself. 'While King Richard was in the Holy Land on his Crusade.'

They began to ask all at once, 'What's Holy Land? What's Kink? Where is Crusade?' Now that they had found out that the words fitted together to make a story, they hated to let any small meaning slip.

Holy? She wished that she knew what that word stood for. Nothing in the books had ever told her. In her teaching, there were many guesses.

'King—not "kink"—Richard was a leader of the forefathers. Like a sheriff, but greater. In those days, there were many people and the sheriffs of all the settlements did what a king said to do. We'll read about a sheriff later in this book.

'And "Crusade." Well, the king went on a big hunt with some of his men'—she paused to invent—'to a woods called Holy Land. But let's go on. Babra Mortsdotter, it's your turn to read now.' The little girl took the book tenderly and began to read. She was already going faster and with fewer mistakes than the older ones.

Just at the end of the fourth page, the noon bell sounded. Glyn rewrapped the book in the cloth. 'Say the words of the story over to yourselves while you work and try to remember how the words look on the page.'

'We will! We will!' they said before they ran off, shoving and shouting to try to be first in the food line.

Glyn stood up and brushed the seat of her short breeches. She was an ant who had just carried one grain of a sand dune away. And tomorrow she would make it one grain less until, in ten thousand years, it disappeared.

This was all part of her father's plan for Haven Place. The children must learn to read and write and calculate. He ordered it, he threatened, he made a speech whenever it crossed his mind. Most of the people shook their heads and let Haven have his way. A few of them stubbornly kept their children in the fields. Knowing the little black bugs on a piece of paper didn't make a farmer better. Maybe worse. Muller-cowman said it soured the brains, like milk.

She walked quickly, her stride like a man's, across the clearing toward her father's house. She was in no mood for cornmeal mush flavored with watery maple syrup—or for talk about village quarrels and village pregnancies. She had saved some bread and cheese in the cupboard and she would eat and worry by herself.

She knew that her father was right about the reading, as he was right about almost everything else. Just looking at the row of clapboard, slant-roofed buildings under the dapple of sun and shade reminded her. In Old Haven's time—her grandfather's—the people had lived in the swampy place a few miles north with nothing but bent-sapling huts for shelter. In winters, they had starved and frozen; in summer, they had died of fevers. They'd lived, all the stories told, in terrible fear of the dangers in forefather ruins, fear of bears, wild dogs, snakes, fear of death, which came often and quickly. One day, her grandfather, a man from nowhere, had walked out of the woods. And then life had begun to change.

She passed by the corn mill with its two huge grinding stones and the horse patiently dozing in the sun. That was her father's doing, but it had been Grandfather who found Haven Place. Searching along the shore, he'd found this forefather place, different from the others, a little row of half-fallen houses that had somehow escaped the fires and destruction that had consumed the other places, and the invading forest. Weeds and vines had been cleared away, old walls shored up, sunken roofs rebuilt, the big stone chimneys cleaned.

It was her father who had caught the first two wild horses and tamed them for the plow, had made them clear the cornfield of stumps, had built the forge out of which came his ideas—ax heads, plow points, candle molds, knives, hoes, fishhooks and other things from the iron he'd salvaged. Over beyond the mill was the apple orchard he'd made from trees transplanted with care from other places.

When the old man had died, Glyn was still a child. Her father had become the new Van Haven, sheriff of Haven Place, without anybody questioning it.

Now she went into the big, littered main room of his house and so intensely was he there that she heard the quick, questioning rumble of his voice and felt his stare in her eyes as he swerved from his stance at the table. But he was not there.

He had the knack of making her—anyone—say things wiser than she knew. He had a look that said, 'Yes, speak!' and another that said, 'Quiet, now!' and very few mistook them. What she cherished, a lot of the others hated.

A map lay unfolded on his big table—one of his treasured maps, which he called 'our land'—and there were piles of his books and papers, the lantern he read by, quill pens and ink, three big bottles of strange-colored liquids. She could not imagine his never coming back to his things.

To get to the cold cupboard for her bread and cheese, she had to open the back door, and for a minute she stood looking at his high-fenced salvage yard with its pole-supported pitched roof. Here lay the piles of strange salvage, mostly machine things of iron, he'd brought back from his sailings across the swamp. The toothed wheels, he told her, would go into the big scaffold he called the iron mill, when it was finished. It would have great sails on arms turned by the wind. How that would happen she couldn't picture, but the things had been built and were ready to hoist into place when he came back.

All the things he was building or had built—that made her think again of the double canoe. Everyone had whispered that it was a foolishness that showed Haven had gone off his head—two wooden canoes side by side, with a strong frame across them and a platform atop that. And a thing he called a sail, a homespun square stuck up on a pole with a crossbeam, with ropes at the corners and other ropes to pull it up. Haven and Piet had made it, but what would they do with it? people asked. Too clumsy to work very well in the narrow waters of the swamp. And the sail thing for the wind? The wind would catch it and just run the whole double canoe into a mudbank.

There's blue water out there, Haven had told them. Half a mile out, the swamp is gone. No shallows or seaweed or sandbanks; just blue water as far as the eye can see. Nobody had believed him except Piet. And Glyn—half.

She took her bread and cheese and went to sit in front of the house, where she could keep an eye on the landing.

She had just finished it when she saw Berk walking across the clearing toward her, Berk-bear, as the children called him, with his muscular, pigeon-toed walk. They pretended to talk bear to him and he, enjoying it, answered in bear. He was a strong boy and his chore was herding the cows; he came carrying a coil of rope over his shoulder, the kind he used to tether them.

'Faithful dog waiting for master,' he said.

'I guess I look like that,' she said. 'Sit down and talk.'

He dropped the rope and squatted on the ground, a smile on his sunburned face. She noticed the first thin signs of a yellow beard along his jaws. 'What've they been doing all those days in the swamp—salvaging again?'

'He went back to the big ruins he found, far away. He doesn't tell me, much, what he's looking for.'

'Must be queer things out there under water. I reckon that it was all dry land you could walk on in forefather times.'

'No; a lake, Haven says—you've heard him. The canoe boats with sails could let the wind blow them far to north and south. He says that's what the old map shows.'

Berk shook his head and ran a brown hand through his thick hair, which had been whitened to corn-tassel color by the sun. 'I've seen roads and ruins offshore in the swamp. I swim down to dig for bits of salvage.'

'I don't know,' she said uncertainly. 'The water may have come higher since forefather times. Haven says that the swamp wasn't there long ago.'

Berk smiled again. 'Well, I won't say no against Haven,' he said, but what he meant was that everybody knew that the swamp had always been there. 'Come along with me and I'll show you what I mean. I'm going up River Place way to catch a heifer got loose this morning.' He jumped to his feet and took her hand.

'But—Haven might come back.'

'You'll sit here moody all afternoon, waiting. Come on; we'll be home again long before sunfall.' He took her other hand and helped her to her feet.

'A little way, I guess,' she said. 'But not as far as River Place.' That was a small, woeful collection of huts where about ten families lived. Around the river mouth nearby there were many ruins half covered by sand and shore growth.

They started walking. 'Is it true your father told the river people to come settle here with us?'

'Offered, not told. Three of their babies died of cold or sickness last winter. But they're shy folk—they didn't say.'

'They never say. Gwauk, gwibble. They hardly know ten words you can understand. And wild and dirty!'

'Don't be so judging,' Glyn said. 'They aren't that bad—and we could teach them. Haven's asked the settlers from Shore Place and Ho-land to move here too.'

'So they can steal our pigs better? That's what they love to do.'

'Haven has plans. He always talks about making our settlement as great as the forefathers' and he says we need more people to do that.'

Berk laughed. 'Them?' He bent into a crook-backed walk with his hands before his face, peering through his fingers. 'The river people? Why, the forefathers were tall as trees and fine to look at and they knew magic.' He dropped Glyn's hand, jumped straddlewise over a stump and ran a few paces ahead. 'Glyn,' he called back, 'did you know that the forefathers could talk to each other over far distances, too far to yell? How could they do that?'

They were now beyond the northern edge of the settlement and they were passing through a sparse stand of pines among the willow and cottonwood, but many of the pines were dead. Ahead of them, the sun shone on a tawny slope of dune.

'I can see her tracks!' Berk yelled. 'Straight on. I just hope the river ones haven't caught her and butchered her by this time.' She ran a little and caught up with him.

After a few more paces, he said, 'Look. Over there is where a stone forefather road runs under the water—points right out into the swamp. D'you see where that big stump of stones is? Wait, I'll show you.' He ran across the dune and made a skid-and-jump descent toward the margin of the swamp.

Glyn followed more slowly. First, there was a broad strip where the dune grass and spiny bushes grew, changing to a lush band of reeds and cattails as the sand gave way to black muck. At the water's edge, there was a thicker growth of cattails and a mass of bulrushes. Farther out, she could see patches of water almost carpeted with pond lily pads. Great dragonflies cruised amidst the vegetation and gnats appeared in sudden swirls.

Berk was standing near a stretch of water surprisingly free of weeds. As she came up, he pointed and said, 'That flat place down there—see? I've dived here lots of times and followed it out as far as I could go.' Beneath the floating patches of algae, Glyn could make out a grayish stone surface crisscrossed by wide cracks and half covered with mossy weeds, but still clearly something built, not natural.

Berk said, 'Why would they build a road under water? Now tell me they could live on land and under water too. They were giant turtles.'

She laughed. 'I don't know. But it's getting late and you haven't caught that heifer yet. Listen. I'll go just as far as River Place with you, and if we don't find her then, I'm going back.'

He looked disappointed that she showed so little interest in his discovery. He sighed and said, 'All right, but someday come swimming with me here.' They turned back toward the path that began on the other side of the dune and led inland in the direction of River Place.

This was a kind of corrugated land now, with the dunes rising a few feet, then sloping off. The path, when it could be seen, snaked among tracts of sumac and coarse grass, disappeared in windblown sand, then reappeared alongside a line of driftwood stakes. This was a strange part of the shore. Sometimes, after a winter of heavy winds and snow, the spring would reveal the skeleton walls of an ancient building jutting out of its sandy grave. On the surface, it was a lonely, bird-inhabited, wind-haunted place. But buried beneath, she felt, were the bones of things and the bones of people.

She had fallen behind and Berk was some distance up a rise, heading toward a weatherworn post that marked where the path surmounted the dune and began to descend toward the settlement. She thought that it wasn't quite so much the heifer as a wish Berk had to waste some time in the settlement.

He liked to barter for odd bits or curios that one of them had found in the sand or the swamp. She couldn't wait for that. She thought that she'd turn back now. 'Berk!' she called out. He had almost reached the marker post.

Suddenly, he fell to the ground, twisted to face her and made a gesture with his hand to stay low. He was playing some game, she thought, and she was in no mood for it. He could be very childish at times. She was already a grown woman of twenty summers and too old for make-believe. Perhaps he'd sighted the heifer and was going to make a great show of pouncing on it. She walked deliberately up to where he was lying.

'Get down,' he said in a low voice. 'There's something uncommon.' She dropped beside him and tried to peer through the clumps of coarse grass to see whatever it might be. The heifer wasn't there. She saw nothing but the low huts along the river—

which was actually an ancient channel—and a few clothes drying on bushes in the sun.

Then she saw them. They were moving about among the huts and the scrub, men she'd never seen before. They were not dressed in homespun or buckskin, but in dark brown clothes of some kind, and they wore broad hats. They carried rifles. Just then, two of them came out the door of a hut dragging a woman between them. She was struggling and Glyn could see her mouth opening and shutting in terror.

Berk tapped her on the shoulder and pointed off to the right; she looked and gasped. In the middle of the settlement's scanty vegetable garden, the strangers had rounded up and roped four scrawny horses—and had done the same with most of the people. They were standing there, hands tied behind them and a long rope linking them neck to neck—bewildered women, wailing children, men in long, ragged shirts, with blood on their faces.

'Berk, who—' She began to ask the useless question but stopped herself. She could hear both of them breathing hard. For a few moments, nothing changed except that gnats swarmed on the dune in front of them and a hawk circled in the calm blue. A woman with long gray hair was trying to bend down to a naked child. One of the strangers was roping two bags on either side of a horse. A tied man, on his knees, vomited into the sand.

Then she felt Berk's fingers digging into her shoulder. 'Slide back slow,' he whispered. 'Keep on your belly and follow me.' With elbows digging like paddles into the sand, he began to scuttle back into the gully behind them.

For another paralyzed moment, she stared at the scene. Four or five of the horsemen came at walking pace into the open and halted. One of them, a little to the fore, was a long-legged man with a small black beard like a prow. He wore boots to his knees, stained buckskin breeches and a gray shirt with no sleeves to it. On his head was a broad-brimmed hat with a round crown. He seemed to be looking straight toward her. He raised his arm and pointed and seemed to say something. The horses began to move in her direction.

At that, she quickly dug knees and elbows into the sand and followed Berk as fast as she could. When she got to the bottom of the sandy dip, she said, 'Men on horseback are coming!'

'Horses are slow in this sand. Keep down, follow me. When we get to the next hollow, we'll run. Stay on the path and meet me at the forefather-road-under-the-water. I know a place in the swamp they'll never find.' His blue eyes under the blond forelock were very close to hers and they had a confident look.

73

He ducked his head and started working his way up the rise, into a shallow depression among the sumac. Glyn followed, so close to the soles of his feet that he kicked a little sand against her cheeks. All the while, she was listening, but her own panting was all she heard.

She told herself that they couldn't possibly have seen her—they were busy with their strange work in the settlement. Then she heard a thin whistle, far off. Her knees and elbows were getting chafed from the sand and beginning to sting.

As soon as they'd crossed the next hollow, Berk came to a crouch. 'Now!' he said, and, head kept low, he broke into that easy, long-paced run of his. He was over the slope almost before she had started and he was ten paces ahead by the time she had got on the path and had begun to gather a little speed.

'Don't look back,' she told herself—and looked back. In the near distance, where they had just lain staring, the head and shoulders of a man rose up next to the marker post. But the westering sun struck him in the eyes for a moment and he raised his hand for shade. 'He missed me.' In that instant, she had lunged down the next slope, panting now.

Fifty paces farther, she began to get a little new courage. She glimpsed nothing behind her among the sumac and now she was on a long, easy descent to the foot of the last large dune before the swampline and Berk was waiting, gesturing her on, crouched in a little saddle where they could cross.

It was hard to run in the soft sand and her legs had begun to tire. But it was not far now and they had got away. Just then, behind her, she heard a long-drawn 'Ey-e-e-e-e!' on the wind—a hunter's sound.

She was a pair of laboring legs and lungs, no sight, no thought, just pain. Berk and the duneside drifted slowly, very slowly nearer when she opened her sweat-clouded eyes. She began to stumble helplessly and suddenly she felt his hand on her arm.

'Now quick, while he's still out of sight!' With an arm around her waist, he almost carried her across the saddle and down through the knee-high grass to the marsh's edge. He guided her into the reedy water. It felt cold on her sand-burned feet and her breathing was so hoarse that it was almost a bark; she tried to quiet it. When they were up to their hips, she felt the flat, gritty surface of the ancient road under her soles and Berk drew her down until their chins were under water.

'Over there,' he whispered, and nodded. She saw a thicket of cattails and other weedy growth that stood up above the surface two or three feet. 'There's stone underneath that, part of some ruin. That's where we hide.' He propelled her along, one hand at her waist and the other on her shoulder.

The green slime clung to her face and something spiny caught in her hair for a moment, but with Berk clearing the way, they worked into the thicket and, at last, found a resting niche among the roots. Below, she felt mud ooze halfway up her calves, but there was something solid beneath it and they could stand without sinking. Berk raised a handful of dripping mud and plastered it across her face and on top of her head and then he did the same to himself. They waited, as deep in the water as they could crouch.

A white cloud drifted slowly across the sun, making the swamp shadowy. A bird chirruped in the marsh behind them. The reeds bowed to the wind in a long swath. Beyond the boggy margin, the sun shone again on the dune's tawny flank.

Such a long time seemed to pass that she began to feel the swamp growing around her, into her body. She was very tired now and she wished that she could lie on the sand and sleep. 'A few more minutes,' Berk whispered. Sunshine again and the buzz of a bluefly in the silence.

The dunetop suddenly grew a horseman, as if he had emerged from the sand. They could see his face—he was a young man, bareheaded and fierce-looking, with a band around his head and long, reddish hair flaring in the breeze. He wore clothes of butternut brown and in his hand he clutched a whip some six feet long. He reined in his horse and stared at the marsh's verge. Glyn's fingers dug into Berk's arm.

Then the man turned his head to the left and voiced the shrill 'Ey-e-e-e-e!' again. His glance seemed to have caught some sign in the mud. He walked his panting horse slowly down the dune and stopped to lean from his saddle at the place where Berk and Glyn had entered the water.

In a minute, four more of them appeared, these wearing the broad hats and carrying rifles in holsters slung behind their right legs. In his hand each one carried a whip.

The first rider came slowly into the squelching mud, testing the ground for his horse's footing, and the others circled around and spread out a little of left and right. They said nothing, as if each knew his own work. The only sound was the sucking noise as the hoofs rose and sank again into the mud.

Apparently finding the ground firm enough, the lead rider urged his horse through the reeds and into the water. The others, fanned out in an uneven line with about six paces between riders, began to move forward. Squinting through the reeds, Glyn calculated that one horse would pass about four feet to the left of their thicket and another some twelve feet to its right. Now that the riders were closer, she could see no more than two of them through the screen of weeds. She held her breath.

They waded their horses in, though the animals, skittish and unused to swamps, it seemed, snorted and shook their heads. Glyn had a partial view of the man on their left, a narrow face with the look of brown, porous rock. From a string across his forehead hung a black leather patch that covered his right eye. Now he was raising his whip.

From all about them came the sound of whips slashing into the reeds and water. They were beating every hiding place. 'Just as he gets here, sink and stay under. When I pinch you, take a breath and then follow me,' Berk whispered into her ear.

The whip struck the reeds about ten feet in front of them; she saw it plunge, then emerge like a dripping snake, into the air. Berk's hand was pushing down on her shoulder and, her eyes still open, she sank into the black water.

This time, the whip cut across the reeds less than a pace in front of them. Though she heard nothing and saw only a burst of whitish bubbles, she felt the water tremble violently. They waited, lungs straining. There was an agitation from the water on either side and then a slow subsiding. They came to the surface, noses just touching the air, and drew breath again.

After a minute or two, Berk slowly raised up a few inches to look and she followed suit. He pinched her arm and then began a slow struggle through the roots toward open water on the side they'd entered. She followed him, fighting the weed growth under the water with her hands. She was caught for a moment, then pulled free.

They had come clear. He pinched her arm and she could hear him inhaling deeply and then he sank beneath the surface again. She saw his feet flash once in the green dimness as he began to swim. This was the forefather road he'd explored so many times and she knew that he was following it for a reason, that there was some chance here.

But she'd had no time to tell him: she couldn't swim. With a shiver of green-white under the surface, he was gone.

And now all she could think of was to get ashore and run. The men were some distance away in the swamp and she had at least a few minutes before they would turn to come back. She rose. She noticed something different about the shadows on the water. She looked up.

Horse and rider stood silently in the shallows about thirty feet away, waiting. It was the young man with the band around his head and the reddish-brown hair, who must have guessed that they would surface after the hunt had passed by.

For a minute, they stared at each other, predator and prey. But she saw no cruel satisfaction on his face, just a sober scrutiny. At last, he raised his whip and gestured toward the shore, saying one word: 'Git!'

She made her way there, dripping and exhausted, while he peered out into the swamp, apparently expecting to see Berk surface. She could have tried to make another break, but when she took a step, she found that she was too weak to run. He made a gesture to her to go on and slowly turned his horse and came to shore.

She walked on the path back toward River Place and he followed, holding the horse to her slow and stumbling pace. The walk seemed to take hours. Mud had dried and caked in her hair, on her face, over her clothes, but she had no energy to brush it off. She knew that she should be frightened, but she was only stunned and angry.

The settlement was empty when they came to it. The doors of huts swung on their leather-strap hinges and a few broken possessions—a corncob doll, a bucket, a sandal, a piece of cloth—lay scattered in the roadway. She looked back at him and he motioned her on to where the trail entered the woods. From their tracks, she could see that the others had gone this way.

She had no idea of how far they went on the trail, but sometime before dark, they approached a clearing and could see fires. There the River Place people, untied now, were sitting on the ground. They had been given a ration of corn cakes and water and they were eating in bewildered silence. The strangers were making camp—unrolling blankets and cooking their food over a fire. All around was the busy stir of men coming and going, the neigh of horses, the sound of hatchets splitting wood. She was too weary to eat and she lay down under a tree.

She awoke at some commotion later on, about twilight. Two of the horsemen were bringing Berk in, his hands tied behind him. She recognized his stumbling figure on the road. One of the men raised his boot and sent Berk sprawling on the grass.

She ran to him and untied the rope. 'Oh, Berk, what did they do to you?' There were two red welts across his face, but otherwise he seemed uninjured. He was too humiliated to talk with her. He turned his face away and lay silently.

Glyn sat for a long time, thinking in anger. Sooner or later, she'd find out who these men were and what reason they had for all this. Then she would make them regret it. She had to think how Haven, if he were here, would make them regret it.

11

In the night, in sleep, Kinkaid trailed westward, the thought of the settlement vanishing and the green, illimitable thought of the forest closing around him, dream rivers to cross and dream thickets to cut through, until he came to a place where the trees grew greater in width than ten men in a row and the spaces were so narrow that he could barely slide between the trunks. All silent and soundless until now, the air suddenly cracked as one of the giants fell across the trail. Kinkaid woke.

The grainy half light showed the sparse details of the bedroom in no color, in blacks, whites and grays. He listened for a wind in the shingles, but none blew. He swung his legs over the bedside and pulled his breeches on, then opened his door. The sheriff's house was quiet. He stood on the cool boards of the gallery and looked down into the empty keeping room below. A few embers from last night's fire smoked in the fire-place and the air smelled of wood ashes. Noiselessly, he moved around the gallery to where the front windows looked onto the square. And peering out, he saw the tree.

It was the lone oak that stood beyond the lookout tower, almost in the center of the open space. It was drawn in black. From one of the lower limbs was a black downward stroke and at the end of the stroke was a dead man.

His head hung forward in a broken-necked way, his black beard flat on his chest. He was naked, and except for the black detail of his genitals, the body seemed to bleach white in the rising light. He turned slowly from east to west, west to east, as if in some ritual movement.

Then Kinkaid noticed some figures, of women they seemed, in the shadow on the far side of the square. In the lookout tower there was a silhouette with a rifle.

A man learns to understand the talk of his rulers. A man shapes out a bow and some arrows to hunt game. Secretly, for a long time, he

78

labors to hollow out a log for a canoe. He fishes in the swamp. Then he builds a store cranny for the fish he's dried and the meat he's smoked and the vegetables he's saved—to feed his family in the winter. Then they hang him on the end of a rope.

Kinkaid shivered once for the man. Then he padded noiselessly back to his room and finished dressing. He packed his things in his saddlebags, slung them and his rifle across his shoulders, and with boots in one hand, went down the stairway into the keeping room. He passed through the empty kitchen and out the door that led to the stable.

In the hay-smelling dimness, he put on his boots and saddled his horses. He led them out and down the lane, keeping close to the outbuildings and lean-tos, avoiding the lookout's sight.

The horses were restlessly glad to be out of the stable at last and they trotted quickly after him. Just at the end of the lane, he stopped them and mounted. Past the corner of the last cabin, he could see no guard in view at the stockade gate, nor was there any movement by the blockhouse. The early summer morning was dewy and still; the new day yellowed the rough log walls and the beaten ground. Kinkaid took a deep breath. 'No,' he whispered unhappily. 'I have thought on it and the answer is no.'

He put the horses to a trot, then a gallop, and as they passed through the open gate, the dogs came again on the run, their barks breaking the silence.

This time, Kinkaid used the whip even more ruthlessly. Ten feet out, he cut the legs from under one big mongrel, swung to the other side and caught a second across the back. A third leaped at his right leg and, just in time, he plunged the whipstock down to strike it between the eyes. Snarl changed to howl as the momentum carried the dog among the hoofs, and Kinkaid was nearly thrown as his horse trod the body. The losing game was over and the dogs dropped back.

Still at a gallop, Kinkaid headed directly down the path between cornfields that led toward the edge of the marsh. The other day, from the watchtower, he had noted what seemed to be the start of a forefather road going westward along the marshside. After a few minutes, he slowed the horses to a walk.

It was, in fact, a forefather road, but not one of the broad kind. Masked by bushes and broken by frosts and erosion, it was worse than the forest trail. He led the horses down this twisting way, trying to skirt the worst fissures and heaps of loose debris. Greenberg was right to say that no one had passed here for years. It was midmorning when his real troubles began.

The old trace finally became too cracked, tilted, bush-grown to follow and he backtracked to a vestige of another path that led inland. In time, this brought him to a thick growth of scrub, through which he couldn't pass without his cutter.

He found a little pool of water for his horses, sat down, chewed a piece of dried meat and consulted the map. It showed him the thin line of the road running along the edge of the blue Lake Erie and then a broader one, roughly parallel but farther inland. He rested awhile and then began to double back.

It seemed to take an unaccountably long time to follow his own tracks back to the ruinous road. The sun was high. The horses sweated and seemed stupid with the heat, balking at the slightest obstacle.

The sun was far westward when he found what he was looking for—another, more promising trail tending southward. He stopped to rest and saw, over the brush, no more than a few miles away, the upward trails of smoke from Erie Place.

It was close to twilight when his new path—bad enough, but better than the other—came to the inland forefather trail. He stopped and stared. The surface was cracked and buckled by roots in places, but it was a broad and easy passage. He looked to the eastward and it seemed to curve back in the direction of Erie Place, not far from where he had started out this morning, and he knew that Greenberg must know that too.

He tied the horses and fed them. Then, on the surface of the road, just at the south edge, he built a fire and lay down to eat his meager supper. He wished he'd brought vegetables with him from the settlement. In his pack he carried a small iron pot; he could almost smell a fat rabbit stewing with vegetables in that pot slung over the fire. Kinkaid smiled. Two days of good table had spoiled him for lean living.

After that, lying there, he dozed, half pictures moving through his mind—moonlight on long hair, rooftops seen from a dizzy height, meat sizzling on the fireplace spit.

One of the horses whinnied and he started up. He listened. There was nothing in the silence except the drone of tree toads, but he sensed some change. Slowly, he looked around the clearing, as much of it as he could see by his fire-light, and saw nothing.

Then he looked upward. On the trees at the westward side of the clearing, on the highest leaves, he caught an unnatural flicker, as if they'd got a momentary light from a long distance. He watched for it and saw it again.

Somewhere to the east of him, there must be a forest fire. A slight breeze sighed in the woods, more from the north than the east, he thought, but there was no sense taking chances. This forest was dry and he'd seen fires helped by the wind that leaped ahead faster than a running man. He would have to get the direction of the fire and then move upwind on its flank. The play of light on the high branches dimmed, then brightened again.

He caught a burning faggot from his fire, for precaution took his rifle and ammunition pouch, and began to trot eastward on the stone surface of the forefather road.

As he went, he caught new glints on the higher leaves, but he smelled no smoke. Nor was there any sign of what he expected, a distant cloudy uproar and ragged flame among the undergrowth ahead.

In puzzlement, he began to slow. An illusion? Maybe it was the reflection of summer lightning somewhere far off in the sky. Then the breeze must have shifted a little, because he suddenly had a whiff of burnt wood. He stuck his torch in the ground and went upwind of it a few paces. The smell was there. He picked up the torch again and increased his pace.

As he had guessed, the road bent back in the direction of the swampline and a stark thought struck him. He began to run.

After a long time, he saw the trees begin to thin and then he reached their edge and stopped, panting.

There, on its flatland, was Erie Place, edged in flame along its rooflines and palisade, smoke blurring the outline and ascending in a yellow-lit cloud to blot out the stars. Then he heard several sharp cracks together, what might be the snapping of dry timbers. Or rifle shots. The gate of the stockade was wide open, but he could see no people coming out. He doused his torch in the ground, dropped it and began to run again.

With his second wind, he reached the gate easily and halted in the shadow, staring into the settlement in the fitful red glare.

The lookout tower in the square was brightly lit, like a giant insect wading in smoke, its legs fringed with small flames, but the platform seemed to be empty. There was a heavier cloud from the direction of the sheriff's house, but this side of it, the rush-covered roof of a cabin had become a wild torch and it was hard to see beyond.

Above the busy crackling of the fire he heard several more sharp reports and now he was sure what they were. He leaned inside the gate and looked at the blockhouse. Its door was open and a body was sprawled in the doorway, cut in half by shadow. He unslung his rifle and made sure that it was ready.

Kinkaid edged inside, then made a dash to the corner around which he'd brought his horses this morning and was in the lane quickly.

It was darker here. The fire seemed to be burning the northern and western parts of the settlement; the outbuildings along the lane were still dark shapes in the smoky haze. Keeping as much to shadow as he could, he ran lightly along the edge of the pathway until he came to the broad bulk of the sheriff's house. There was no sign of life. He tried the back door and found it stoutly barred from inside. On the front side of the roof's pitch, the dry shakes must have caught fire; he could hear their crackle and could see the red sparks they spat into the air. He turned at the cross lane and ran southward until he came to a sapling fence.

Its gate was open; the yard and the little house were dark. He looked back down the lane and saw a few burning sticks on the ground. As he caught one of them up, he heard scared horses whinny from inside the sheriff's stable.

Holding his rifle cradled in his right arm, finger on the trigger, and the torch well away from his eyes to the left, he came back to the gate and entered the yard. He stopped before the open door.

'Mary!' he called softly; there was no answer. He stepped forward.

She had died hard. The body of one of the crooked men was lying doubled over just inside the door. His stomach had oozed a puddle of blood on the boards. Kinkaid saw her hand first—it was clutching a knife. She lay on her back across the bed, her dress strangely neat, almost as if she had smoothed it out at the last moment, but her white collar was shiny red.

Her gray eyes were open, death's most horrible detail, and Kinkaid closed them with trembling fingers. He remembered them in the candlelight, an age ago, and he remembered the sound of her whisper. 'Stay with me.'

Sick and nerveless, Kinkaid stood in the dark yard for some minutes. Until another series of cracks from far off awoke him. He saw a reflection, saw that it came from a rain barrel and bent to soak himself as best he could. 'One, two, three, four. Steps,' he said to himself as he straightened up.

He walked to the gate and peered out into the lane. Cochrane's big house was outlined in red now and all the village on the north side of the square was ablaze, the smoke no longer drifting, but pouring into the sky.

He saw no figures. Kinkaid ran to the crossing of the lanes and turned right. Here a few outbuildings were beginning to catch fire and he no longer tried to conceal himself. He knew that a rifleman would have to be a steady shot to bring him down in this flickering light—and he calculated there was only one such man.

It was little more than fifty paces to the rear of the storehouse.

Kinkaid stopped under the eaves of a lean-to, his back against the wall, and looked carefully around him. There was still no sign of men. Set back ten paces from the storehouse stood a low shed built of heavy logs and closed off from the lane by a pole fence. The shed door must be on the other side.

Kinkaid drew breath, then rushed the fence and was over it in one vault to land lightly on the other side. He found the thick plank door of the shed closed securely on the inside. There was no outer lock or fastening that he could feel. With his hands, he began to search carefully around the edges of the door until at last, near the bottom of the right-hand corner, one of the logs gave a little to his pressure. He knelt and pushed harder; a section of the log swung inward on a hinge and he could reach inside. As he had hoped, there was an iron latch.

When the door was free, he opened it just enough to edge through and shut it quickly after him. He was in a woodshed so low that he had to stoop a little, but faint light from a barred window showed him piles of split firewood against either wall. He tried the slabs on the north wall, but they were loose and he could feel nothing beneath them. He leaned his rifle against the wall and began to clear away the cordwood on the north side. After a minute or two, his hands met a solid mass of logs and he found that this could be pushed aside on some kind of rollers. He groped and found a rectangular hole and a laddertop, as he had expected.

The tunnel was narrow and damp, just wide enough for one man and probably about fifteen paces long. Kinkaid moved cautiously through the absolute dark until he stumbled against the foot of another ladder. He mounted it until his raised hand touched against boards. He took his rifle and rapped three times above him with the muzzle and said, 'Greenberg! Kinkaid here.' There was no answer.

With his bent neck and shoulers, he heaved upward; the trap door rose and smoke descended. Kinkaid, choking, swung himself quickly into the room. High in the roof, the dormers showed dirty red, and the whole storeroom was a dull crimson cloud. The heat was so great that he had a feeling the entire building might ignite in an instant.

He kept to the floor, crawling and constantly turning his head to see what he could. After a minute, he bumped against some shelves— the shelves that moved out from the wall—and fanning away the smoke, he could see that the rifle rack was empty.

Working with knees and elbows, his rifle cradled across his arms, he reached the little desk where Greenberg had sat during their conversation and found the chair overturned. He was coughing now and the smoke was a heavy weight in his lungs. His eyes watered and he tried to clear them. 'Greenberg!' he called again. No answer.

So he turned in what he thought must be the direction of the anteroom and crawled blindly until he touched the dividing curtain. His lungs were dying. It was as if he were breathing burnt porridge.

He didn't stop until, choking and sweating, he nudged up against the front wall. Kinkaid was dying. The only hope was to find the front door, unbar it and step out into the blazing street. He got to one knee and found that the other knee dragged slowly. He felt a faintness, dizziness, as if he were baked unconscious. With feeble fingers, he began to search along the wall for the crack at the bottom of the door. His hand touched a blunt tip of leather, a boot toe. Greenberg was lying under one of the loopholes, his rifle beside him; Kinkaid had to lean very close to his face to make him out. He slapped the face. Greenberg's head turned limply to one side.

Holding his breath, using his final strength, Kinkaid managed to unbar the door.

In the cool dark of the forest, he tried, but he couldn't remember any of the rest of it. He must have opened the door, dragged Greenberg out of that furnace into the street. Unbelievably, he had even brought Greenberg's rifle along—because there it was on the ground. He must have crawled, dragging body and rifle, somehow around the corner of the storehouse without being seen. A child could have killed him with a stick.

And somehow, he had got down that burning lane to the sheriff's stable. One detail came back. He remembered the strange slipperiness of his hands as he put a saddle on a horse. Now they were covered with dried blood. He did not remember going through the gate or riding free of the settlement. But he was here, alive and awake, lying on the forest loam with the red haze dull in the distance beyond the trees.

He looked up and saw that Greenberg's body was slung across the horse.

There was a groan. Then, very faintly, he heard Greenberg whisper, 'Hold on, Sarah. I'm coming.'

12

When the first, misty forelight began to pale the woods, Glyn opened her eyes onto a wrong world. She lay still and silent, thinking the daze would adjust itself. Her feather bed had grown hard and rocky under her back. Tree trunks had appeared around her bedroom. Her warm blanket had changed to a scanty layer of leaves. In the farther room, men were moving around a fire and frying meat.

The smoky sizzle of fat in the pan was what had awakened her and its pungency in her nostrils was the thing that was real, the thing that made her know this was not a dream. Slowly, yesterday, like a shooting pain, came to her mind.

She could see them moving in half light by the fire, lean young men who walked with a wildcat spring in the step, the race of one-eyed horsemen. In the misty-smoky clearing, she could see their faces, shadowed under the brims of the wide hats they wore, one with a stump of black beard, some with boys' faces just beginning to harden and thin, but nearly all wearing the black shield over one eye.

She raised up on one elbow and watched. She knew she should be anxious and frightened, but strangely, the scene was so common now that no fright came. Without their black whips and horses, these men looked like settlement hunters making their breakfast in the woods. She listened.

'Huryon with theter hawg belly. Cunel sayta move out fas tiday.'

'Gime theter skillet, Price. . . .'

'Sho gotus a passel a sorry-looken . . .'

'Colden ma bones; wisht ah had a drank a corn. . . .'

' . . . outa theser woods an you git a whole jug.'

'Sheit.'

'Yawl smell like a poke a dead fishes.'

'Ah ben taken a bath in the swamp.'

'Sheit.'

The tune of the voices was a kind she had never heard before and

85

the words, most of them, were meaningless.

Now she looked around her and saw that the River Place folk were waking up and, with dazed, animal looks, staring at the horsemen. Their hair was long and matted; nearly all of them were barefooted; their ragged clothes left them half naked.

A few of them clutched some home thing or other, caught up at the last moment and clung to automatically—a wooden spoon, a ball of yarn, a clay bowl. The women held the small children close in their arms. The men looked suspiciously toward the fire and then back at the roadway down which they had come.

When the horsemen had eaten, four of them came around with a blanket piled with pieces of the fried meat and corn cakes, offering them with hand-to-mouth gestures and cries of 'Takem, takem. Eat.' The River Place people took timidly, not very much, and tested, their eyes looking up at the horsemen.

A short, solid man in butternut brown with a mask of curly brown hair across his lower face and a triangular daub of white on one sleeve came over and threw two small leather buckets on the ground.

'Theys a branch ova yonda. Yawl gitchasef some wata,' is what he seemed to say. They listened in awe at these sounds. Nobody moved. They waited for what he would do next.

He laughed a kind of snort and then pointed to a little run a dozen yards off in the woods. With the toe of his boot, he nudged two of the crouching boys. 'Yawl git,' he said.

Glyn looked behind her and saw that Berk had awakened and was trying to shake the sleep out of his head. He sat up, clasped his knees, looked around at the scene and slowly turned to Glyn.

'What is this? Who are they?'

'I don't know,' Glyn said. 'They caught me first and brought me here. I thought you'd got away.'

'Why didn't you follow me?' he asked sourly.

'I forgot to tell you—I can't swim.'

Berk groaned. 'Next time I'll know. I almost lost them. If I hadn't snagged on a branch under the water. Where do you think they're taking us?'

Glyn, eating, simply shook her head. 'Let's never find out. When it's dark or when they aren't watching, we can get into the woods. Look out for some rough ground with a good thicket, where the horses can't follow.'

He nodded quietly and crossed his two forefingers.

In a few minutes, the riders had begun to pack their blankets and cooking things into saddlebags and had saddled the horses. Some of them kicked dirt onto the fires and others began to herd the people into a line again. One older man would not move but sat still, staring at the ground between his knees. One of the riders came up to him, seized him by his gray beard and jerked him to his feet.

This morning, they did not use the ropes. Two horsemen, clucking to their animals, got into position at the rear of the line and started it moving, almost treading on the heels of the walkers ahead of them but, it seemed, measuring the pace to make it bearable.

Glyn walked beside Berk near the center of the column. She was trying to judge just how far they had come, a few miles inland from the swamp and then, turning, south to follow this forefather road. It was one of the narrower of those ancient trails. It rolled slightly, up a shallow rise and downhill on an easy slope, was buckled in places, was root-broken to rubble in others and often was thinned to a narrow corridor by the twigs and branches that crowded in on either side. Off the roadway, the ground was wet and spongy; they would come to a place where a run flowed and the stone trail would be lost for ten paces or more under a sheet of water. Occasionally, they would pass the overgrown ruins of some kind of forefather structure and again, where the forest broke and grew ragged, whole clumps of ruins where a settlement must have stood.

At first, she tried to talk, but Berk was morose. He seemed to blame her for being caught and he walked with his eyes stubbornly toward the ground.

In time, moving through this slash in the green world as if it were unreal, Glyn began to have a strange, detached feeling. She forgot to look for likely escape places and her eyes were entranced by the forest itself. Except for the scuffle of feet, there was a great stillness here and she felt held in it. The newly green leaves of the oaks, last of the trees to unfold in the spring, were like a roof of silence. Then, suddenly, the breeze would stir them and their thousand tongues whispered. Now and then, huddled in the shadows, she saw a clump of paper birches, like a ghost family, and, again, they came on stretches of broad sugar maples. When the breeze left off, the stillness closed in again, with none of the familiar frog sounds, bird calls and insect noises of the swamp.

Occasionally, when they came to an oak opening, the horsemen would let them rest by the roadside for a few minutes. Here the forest sometimes thinned away to what must have been stretches of meadow and cultivated fields a long time ago. Even in the shoulder-high grass, Glyn could see traces of ancient boundaries and, beyond, they would sometimes pass an old, overgrown orchard where the trunks of apple trees ranged in straight lines.

It was hard for her to imagine what this land must have looked like once when, it was said, there were settlements everywhere and more farms than forest. A ditchline; the slant of sagging walls seen through the tall grass; a vine-grown, topless round tower sticking up; scattered signs of corn or wheat growing among the wilderness of scrub, were parts she could not put together.

At noon, the riders stopped the column and let them rest for a longer time. Two boys brought water from a pond in the leather buckets, but there was no food. The River Place people lay or squatted in little groups, hardly talking, now and then giving Berk and Glyn a distrustful look. This morning, she had noticed how easily they were herded, how fearfully they looked at the whips and the horses. But except for a few of the smaller children, they seemed to endure the march well enough and it struck her that marching all day, for them, was no harder and not much different from ordinary life. They were in their fields or garden patches at first light or setting their primitive traps in the woods, and in the evening they lay down on beds of rushes as comfortless as the forest floor. As far as she knew, they were a people without games or rituals or celebrations or dance or music or ornament—and nearly without words. She shivered.

'They must have missed us at Haven Place by now,' Berk said. 'What will they do?'

'They'll think we were lost in the forest.'

Berk shook his head. He seemed to have got over his sullen mood. 'No; this is what I have been thinking. Haven has come back. He will take the hunters and look for us and they'll read the story in the footprints.' She noticed that his right hand was working in the grass. 'Don't look at it, but I am making a letter H,' he said. He picked up a twig and began to scrape. 'The next place we stop, you make another one on the ground.'

Glyn sighed. 'I wish I believed Haven came back.'

'Believe it!' Berk whispered fiercely, a man's scowl on his boy's face. 'And now he's on the trail with the hunters. You're too . . . Glyn, I've watched you and I see you dream off on your own ways. Keep your mind narrow and just look for the place where we can get away. It's ahead of us somewhere.'

'Last night they had guards in the woods. I heard them moving.'

'I've hunted animals and cornered them—then lost them. You know why? I was thinking about three or four things and they were thinking about only one.'

'I'll try,' she said, but in her mind she saw the horsemen moving through the swamp, working together with scarcely a word, hunting their game as if they had done that all their lives. 'I wonder where they come from.'

Berk shrugged his shoulders. 'From far. Their talk is queer. I think they live beyond the forest somewhere, because they have so many horses.'

'And why do they want to steal the River Place people? No one would want the River Place people for anything.'

Berk put his hands over his eyes and lay back of the grass. 'Forget them. In a day or two, we'll be gone.'

But she could not; their faces, their small gestures of hopelessness or protection, drew her eyes. Now, not very far away on the grass, two women were bending over a prone child. One of them, with long, graying hair, dressed in a leather shirt so torn that it left bare one pouchy breast, seemed to be the mother. At least, the anxious look on her raw, ugly face seemed to say it. Glyn got to her knees, but she could not see the child very well.

She walked over. The thin little girl lay with her forearm across her eyes and her cheeks very flushed. She breathed as if she had just stopped running. She gave a whimper as Glyn's shadow fell across her.

The mother looked up and spoke the first words any of them had addressed to Glyn. 'Bab-by sick.'

Glyn reached up and tore off the short left sleeve of her shirt. She turned to a boy who was lying nearby on the ground. 'Bucket,' she said, pointing. 'Water.' She pointed toward the pond.

When she put the wet cloth on the child's face, the little girl stiffened and gasped with fright. Glyn smoothed her hair and caressed one shoulder. She relaxed. 'Keep the cloth there. But make it wet again every few minutes.' She had no idea, from their looks, whether or not they understood.

Glyn walked over to the place where the horsemen were and found the man with the mark on his sleeve. They were preparing to take up the march again and the sleeve-marked man had his back to her as he tightened a cinch on his horse.

Slowly and distinctly, she said, 'There is a child sick. She can't walk and so we'll need a blanket and some rope to make a stretcher, please.'

The man slowly turned his upper body and looked at Glyn over his shoulder. It was a look neither forbidding nor angry nor wary, but slightly perplexed, the eyes searching and the brow creased a little, as if he had suddenly heard his horse speak to him and was about to deny that it had. And a truth that she had not realized before came to Glyn: These men stole animals. Faces, voices like those of humans—but the horsemen looked and saw only beasts. This man, quietly cinching up his horse, might as well have been nudged by a calf or a she-goat.

'Listen to me!' she cried. 'I'm talking to you! Over there is a mother with a sick child. It may be dying. It must be carried on a stretcher. It needs medicine.'

He stared for a moment and then the broad face slowly relaxed and the interest went out of his eyes like snuffed candles. He turned back to test the cinch.

Glyn looked on the ground around her. Then she saw, just beyond the horse's forefeet, the man's blanket lying on the ground. It was rolled up and ready to be tied across the saddle back. She was so angry that she moved without a moment of thought. She took four steps and scooped up the blanket.

A meaty hand came down hard on her wrist and began to tighten. She twisted around and, just a foot away, stared into the man's eyes. He did not speak, but his tightening grip said: Drop it now. *I will not.* I will break you. *Break me, then.* Before her eyes there was a mist like blood.

'I am going to make you speak to me. I'm going to make you scream like a wounded animal,' Glyn whispered. She was almost fainting with pain, but she knew she had enough strength left for one sharp plunge of her right thumb before he could loose her and bring his arm up. His left eye was very close.

'Sarjint!' said a harsh voice behind them suddenly. 'Leter go, Sarjint Hurt!'

Slowly, the hand unfroze from her wrist. Glyn caught her breath and the mist began to fade. She turned and the tall man with the black prow beard was standing there, looking at her from under the broad brim. He looked at her long, as if he were about to speak.

She said, without knowing what made her say it, 'I have seen you before. In a dream, maybe.'

In a low, very distinct voice, he said, 'But dreams never come back by daylight.'

Then quickly, behaving as if he had not spoken to her at all, he turned to the sarjint and said, 'Givem blanket an sticks and calomel for the chile.' He strode to his horse and mounted.

All the long afternoon, through leaf shadow and lattices of sunlight, over broken roadway and through knee-deep floods, Glyn carried one end of the stretcher. She talked to the child and told her a story, but there was only a murmur now and then. Glyn kept the cloth as wet and cool as possible, but she did not ask the sarjint Hurt for any more calomel. Gradually, she and the child's mother, at the other end of the stretcher, dropped back until they were at the rear of the column, then ten paces back, then twenty. A slight turn in the road ahead, and they were suddenly alone.

Glyn saw herself gently putting the child down by the roadside. On the right side of the road, about twenty paces into the woods, there was a bushy, thorny, abrupt ravine that angled off to the west. She saw herself running, dropping prone at its edge. She saw a tunnel into the underbrush, made by foxes or wild pigs, no doubt. She could feel herself squirming into it and losing herself completely. The child moaned then and Glyn did none of those things. She kept on walking and carrying.

A minute later, she heard the clop of a hoof on stone and, looking back, saw a man pacing his horse slowly there, keeping a distance from the marching column.

Late in the day, they skirted a place where some sizable ancient settlement lay. The late sun picked out details of window and gable, weathered façade and ruined wall, painting them all with the same yellow. They arrived at a crossing with a much broader stone roadway going west and they could see the junctions of other roads, but the black beard led forward on their same narrow trail until at last, in the hazy amber of the day's end, they stopped and sat down by the shore of a little lake.

After food, she and Berk lay in a grassy place, wrapped in each other's arms, and slept.

In the night, the sick child died. She died silently. Toward dawn, the mother, waking to tend her, found her body still and stiff and let out a low wail. Glyn, dreaming, was at home in her bed on a winter night and somewhere out in the frozen swamp a voice she knew was calling to her, Come! Come! Come! but she could not raise so much as one hand.

In the pale, gray light, Glyn watched to see what the River Place people would do. A few of the women stood singly, a little distance from the body, gazing at it. The mother sat apart, her head bowed, hands over her face. The men and boys behaved as if nothing had happened, but they all moved to the other side of the roadway.

Glyn thought: Too poor, too dull, too simple even to make a ceremony for meeting death. That made her sadder than the death itself.

Then, slowly and silently, the women began to move. With bowed heads, they converged on the body, pulling up tufts of grass to strew on it. Then one woman bent and put a little knot of wildflowers on its chest.

On the fourth day, in the afternoon, the thunderheads built up in the west, cloudy cliff on cliff, until at last all the air was tinged by their blue-black. Some of the riders, made nervous, brought their horses at a fast trot along the length of the column, shouting, 'Huryon!

91

Huryon, yawl!' and cracking their whips now and then. The wind swooped and the column was lost in a dust cloud. Lightning creased the black western sky; thunder boomed; the first rain came like shot.

They had arrived at a sparse grove of trees with the outlines of a few dilapidated walls. The riders drove their horses for the most substantial ones, where a sagging shelf of roof still remained. The marchers scattered to find trees, banks, burrows, anything.

Berk caught Glyn's hand and ran through the grove to a bush-shrouded wall; in the flash of light, he'd had a glimpse of a ruined chimney with a fireplace just large enough to hold them. They clawed the rubble out and snaked inside.

'Listen!' Berk said. 'Here's the chance. They can't see much in this light and they're busy with their horses.' Through the rain, they could see dim shapes of horses shying and rearing at the thunder and lightning and the men trying to quiet them. 'I'm going around this corner and into that bushy field beyond. After I'm gone, count ten and run after me. I'll wait.'

He was on his knees. He sprang out, swerved around the chimney and was gone. Glyn counted to ten, but she could not move. She kept counting, oddly, to fifteen, twenty. She got to her knees, but still she could not run.

There was the sound of hoofs and, in the half dark, a rider galloped past in the direction Berk had gone.

In a few minutes, they were back. The rider gave a downward cut with his whip and a kick from the stirrup. Berk, arms outstretched, came tumbling back into the shelter and Glyn caught him in her arms.

'You didn't follow me! You didn't follow!' he said, almost crying.

'No,' she said. 'I couldn't. Something stopped me.'

Berk put his face against her neck and she could feel his panting against her breast.

The wind was whipping the trees and the rain slanted through the grove. Someone had tried to build a fire under a half shelter some distance off, but its smoke died in gusty rags. Glyn did not know why she felt so passive, so powerless to run. She put her arms around Berk and stroked his back. She drifted.

And so she had no strength to resist when, later in the night, she felt his hand under the homespun on her breast and the other stroking between her legs. In her waking sleep, she dreamed that she was lying in warm water and something, somebody, was pressing her gently down. Then he bucked against her suddenly and, with a boy's wild haste, spent himself inside her.

In the morning, she remembered that for just a moment, but it came back to her as a night-born fancy of her own, a happening just on the edge between might have and done, and she decided to say nothing to Berk. She had a sense that nothing was continuous any longer, nothing repeated, no incident of the day led on to something else. Everything was made up of dislocated minutes.

After the rain, the morning was fresh and cool and the road cut down through a long meadow that looked like silvery-green fur in the sunlight. The weeds and grasses hung inward over the sides of the old stone trail, giving it the look of a sunken path that led to some abandoned place. As they walked, Glyn began to notice something odd. Most of the River Place people seemed to have adapted to this new way of their lives, this long walk. When a rest halt was over, they arose and moved back to the roadway before the horsemen had sig-naled. They walked patiently, tirelessly, almost without complaint; they even seemed to grow stronger.

But there were others among them, here and there along the line, whose limping and stumbling began to grow worse day by day. A few—not many—were children and others were the older men and women, but most of those who lagged seemed to be young enough and healthy enough.

Glyn noticed, too, that the River Place people seemed curiously powerless to help each other. Except for mothers who tended to their children and sometimes carried the smaller ones for stretches, the rest were indifferent. If a walker staggered, the rest drew away and passed him by; if he fell, they stepped over him.

Suddenly, a young woman with long black hair, just in front of Glyn, began to wobble as if all her muscles had gone slack in an instant. Arms swinging loosely, she veered sideways and fell into the shallow roadside ditch. The others walked stolidly on.

Glyn ran to her, knelt, wet her face from a puddle, tried to make her speak. She would not open her eyes or say anything. The starved face was motionless, the shoulders limp under Glyn's arm. She breathed, but the spirit had given up.

There was a clack of hoofs on the paving and the black beard came riding up from the rear of the column, leaning a little from his saddle and looking curiously at Glyn.

Glyn looked up, straight into his eyes, as he halted.

'She is alive, but she can't walk on,' Glyn said. 'Are you a killer?' He did not answer; his face had no expression.

Then Glyn said something she had had no thought of saying. 'I'm going to stay with her, whatever you do.'

He stared an instant longer, then wheeled his horse and trotted away. The walkers had stopped to listen and now they slowly took up the march again, indifferent again.

Then she heard voices and looked back to see several of the riders leading their horses forward toward the place where she lay. A thin young man, with the usual eye patch, stepped into the ditch, knelt down and gave the woman a drink of water from his canteen. He picked the woman up easily and swung her onto his horse, mounted behind her, supporting her limp body with his left arm around her waist.

The other riders were doing the same with others along the line who seemed to be near collapse. She saw a young boy with staring eyes, his head rolling, lifted into the saddle, and saw him fall forward on the horse's neck. The march began again.

After a while, Berk whispered to her, 'So they do care whether or not we die. Not much. But a little bit.'

Since the second day, Glyn had been trying to protect her sandals. She would walk barefooted half the day, both to harden her feet and to preserve one of the few things left to her. Now one of the straps had broken and she tied the sandals to her belt with the thought that they and her clothes made up the four things she had left in the world.

They came to no settlement that day or the next. The land they passed through was gradually changing, and though there were still areas of old forest and stands of young trees, at times she could look over long distances, miles of grassland. As the wind moved across, it shuddered and rippled like green water. Again and again she noticed the signs of ancient farmlands—in half-obscured fencelines, bramble-covered ditches, the remnants of crops among the grass, in the very outlines of squared fields—and she thought of a race of giants consuming all the grain and corn these fields once bore.

And it was hard to get used to enormous space. Unbroken and unlimited by branches, the sky seemed desolate. Without its protecting trunks, its thickets, its margin of swamp, the land seemed to lack all edges, limits, shelter.

The days grew hotter; the early freshness in the air was burned away by the morning sun. By noon, each step on the roadway seemed to sear the foot. Now there was seldom water in the ditches and, with throats dry, she and Berk gave up talking. She had sweated, then dried, in the hot breeze so often that she felt covered with a crust. She looked down at her dirty arm. It was a crust. She walked doggedly, head bent.

'Look!' Berk said suddenly in the midst of empty time.

She raised her eyes and squinted against the glare and the heat waves. A line wavered a long way off.

It was a winding snake of treeline, probably along a river. The road, diminishing to a thread, struck straight to it and through it to the other side.

'I can see the points of a stockade wall,' Berk said. 'And I think, a gate and a big, square house beside it. The settlement, Glyn. Look. At last!'

At the head of the column, two horsemen set out at a trot and dwindled in the distance. The walkers kept on—there was no rest halt this noon. In a daze of heat and fatigue, they brought the wavering treeline nearer step by painful step. As long as she could bear it, Glyn looked down at the road, then she raised her eyes for a moment to see the line of far-off wall just a little more clearly cut against the sky. Then, for twenty paces, she would look down again.

The bridge surprised her. She must have lost track of time. But there it was suddenly; the whole road, borne in dips and rises straight across the water. She found herself looking over an eroded side wall at the black water flowing directly underneath them—a wonder. Haven Place had log bridges, none more than ten paces long, but here was a roadway itself supported high over a stream.

As they reached the end, a dozen of the horsemen rode past them with a hollow clatter of hoofs. At the stockade gate, men raised their arms in greeting and swung the heavy gates inward. In a billow of dust, the riders passed through.

Overshadowing the gate was a thing Glyn had never seen before—a building that looked like one cabin with a wider one set on top of it. There were loopholes in the lower part and a few narrow window openings in the upper, and on top was a railed platform where two watchmen stood looking down at them.

The line passed slowly through the gateway and came to a halt inside. Glyn looked around, perplexed. Instead of the settlement cabins and roads she had imagined, there was a large open field, uneven ground, grassy in patches and worn brown in others. Except for a row of log buildings against the palisade at the far end, the only structures were roofs about ten feet above the ground, supported by bare poles. There was no order to them; they were scattered over the field as if they had grown at random.

Here there were more people than Glyn had ever seen in her life. Some were walking around, others lay in the shade under the roofs, a crowd of women was gathered around a well. Still others were busy cooking, it seemed, around fires that burned smokily here and there in the enclosure. Clothes were spread out to dry on the slopes and the shelter roofs.

Many of those people stopped to stare at the newly arrived for a minute before turning away again. No one approached, no one spoke.

A horseman rode up to the column, motioning with his arm, and said something that sounded to Glyn like 'Yawl follerme,' then started off at a walk toward a shallow dip in the ground not far from the south wall, where there was an unoccupied shelter. When they had arrived, he glanced once over his shoulder at them and was off at a trot.

Under the shelter they found a few open bags of cornmeal, a wooden tub full of water, an iron cooking pot and a pile of firewood. The River Place people sank slowly to the ground in the nearest shade, crouching or sitting as if they expected to be roused again in the next moment. They looked like creatures of dust, with only their fearful eyes moving in the gray-brown masks. It was Glyn and Berk who started the fire and put the pot to boil with water and cornmeal for porridge.

13

Oak leaves overhead stirred in the wind and a flicker of sunlight touched Kinkaid's eyes. He raised himself quickly to one elbow and looked around the green hollow. Dangerous to lie asleep with the sun up.

He thought he heard feet moving in the dry leaves behind his left shoulder and he reached for his rifle and rose to one knee. But it was only the breeze again.

Keeping close to the ground, he went up the slope and looked to where the horses should be. They were tied just where he had left them the night before, peacefully nosing at the grass at the end of their tethers, like three elders contemplating something on the ground.

Kinkaid circled the hollow and found no sign of any disturbance. He went down the slope again to where Greenberg was lying, still asleep, his forearm across his eyes, last night's horror still plain in his burnt and smoke-blackened clothes. When Greenberg moved his arm, Kinkaid saw that his hair had been badly singed and his eyebrows burned off. The face Kinkaid had always seen as fresh and clean-shaven was a crust of sweat and charcoal. Greenberg's hand sought his right thigh and he groaned in his sleep.

Then Kinkaid saw that the whole thigh, from hip to knee, had been badly seared, the scorched cloth and the burnt flesh almost indistinguishable. Kinkaid ran to his saddlebag to find his kit with the ointment and bandages.

Greenberg took the offered canteen but held it in his hand without drinking. A stunned man, he looked around the little glen and stared at Kinkaid as if he had never seen him before. Then he took a drink and shook his head.

'You went away,' he said. 'I saw them setting the fires. I have to get . . .' He started to rise and then saw the knife in Kinkaid's hand.

'Friend,' Kinkaid said, 'your leg is badly burned. Now, I'm going to cut the cloth away, wash the place, put on some ointment and bandages. You'll have pain, but I'd best do it now.'

Before the cutting and bandaging were completed, Greenberg had crushed a stick between his teeth, but he groaned only twice, at the worst part. When it was over, he lay back with new runnels of sweat on his smoky face and neck. Kinkaid got some water from a rivulet in the woods and gave him a wet kerchief to clean himself.

'It was simple luck I found you in the storehouse,' Kinkaid said. 'I don't remember much of the rest. At least, we didn't get our throats cut in the night.'

The absence of eyebrows gave Greenberg an astonished look; he was still shocked, in fact, and he spoke meaningless sentences, as if to himself. 'A little to the left, that's better. Throw the lard out before . . .'

Kinkaid built a fire and fried some of his salt pork and cornbread in an iron skillet. Then they ate in silence.

Finally, Greenberg struggled to speak. 'Wist,' he said, 'or West, the name must have been once, a tall man, it took three to hold him down and get the ropes on him.' He stared around the grassy glade.

'Kept telling me no, he wasn't. No rifles anywhere. And I said, "You liar." ' Greenberg put his hand to his throat and said nothing more for a minute. Then, 'Where is my horse? I have to cut the body down.' He was lying propped against a fallen tree, where Kinkaid put him, a folded blanket behind his back.

'Stay still,' Kinkaid said. 'It's taken care of. What else do you remember?'

'I heard the rifles later on.'

'Yes,' Kinkaid said, 'but Wist was dead by then. Somebody else had them. You were in a mighty hurry to hang that man.'

'Hurry,' Greenberg said.

'Yes; you couldn't wait.'

'Wife and children squalling,' Greenberg said. 'The ones who came kept saying he didn't. Wasn't. "He goodmin, goodmin." I said, "If you love him so, find them." '

Greenberg stared, as if charmed, at a spot on the ground in front of him. He tried to break a stick in his hands.

'I've found out if you start off with a mistake, you just keep making more. Your luck and your head go bad.'

'Kinkaid?' Greenberg said. 'You rode out.'

'Yes, friend. I tried to speak some sense to you yesterday. When I saw the hanged man, I saddled my horse.'

Greenberg put the stick down and ran the fingers of one hand over his bandaged thigh. 'What they hated me most for . . .' he said, 'in

98

their eyes . . . when I made them put out the hearth fires to search the chimneys. Fires. Curfew. Only the dogs moved in the streets. Cochrane talked to you, asked for some more medicine to help the pain. Can't get out of bed.'

'What happened then?'

Greenberg turned his head to gaze at Kinkaid, seeming again surprised to see him there. His eyes were wide and staring, as if they still reflected some other sight. 'One of the smith's sons—he was crying. "Robs-son," he said. On lookout and a rifle killed him. My eyes and ears. I missed it, sometime long ago, missed it. A little thing I should have noticed. Cochrane, who did we hang?'

'The wrong man. But go on.'

Greenberg said nothing for a long time, his blackened hands scratching lines in the grass. 'Close,' he murmured finally. 'In the logs six inches away from my head. He can shoot. They were setting the roofs afire. To bring us outside, d'you understand? Get to the blockhouses, all of you.'

'And so you ran to your storehouse? I take it all your people knew the strong points they had to defend?'

'Bodies over there,' Greenberg said. 'Two of them.'

'Were you alone in the storehouse?'

He seemed not to hear. 'Four,' he said. 'One, two, three. Surprised by four.'

The wind bothered the forest leaves gently over their heads. A gleam of sun played across Greenberg's eyes and he suddenly clapped his hands to his face and bent his neck. The backs of his hands were raw, patches of black and red. Kinkaid looked at him anxiously and started up.

Greenberg seemed to choke; then he said in a clearer voice, 'Sarah and Rochel. Sarah.'

'Your wife and child?'

Greenberg didn't speak, but he seemed to be trying to say yes. Kinkaid thought of him standing at the loophole, smoke curls coming down from the roof and the sound of shots in the distance, trying to decide between guarding the food and stores of the whole settlement or protecting his own. Kinkaid shivered at the man's choice.

'I'll go back to look for them,' he said quietly. 'You can't move with those burns and I don't want you to try. Stay here and rest. But tell me where your house is. One of those near the north blockhouse?'

Greenberg was finally able to speak. 'Shutters,' he said.

Kinkaid rubbed a patch of wool over Greenberg's blackened rifle, worked the bolt and decided that it was still in order. He left it within Greenberg's reach and stood up to go.

'Horse,' Greenberg said.

'Ah, yes. Better take the horse so they won't have to walk.' Kinkaid had thought to go on foot for better concealment. He realized that he'd assumed he would be coming back alone. 'I'll take my roan.'

But he led the horse, scouting carefully ahead as he reached the forefather road. Far in the distance he saw a deer crossing it, but there was no other movement as he waited. The sunlight through the leaves made a moving stipple on the gray stone and the birds were loud in the trees. A woodpecker flashed into the open and was gone. He began the road to Erie Place for the second time.

As he walked, he thought about the reasons that had made for his stubborn fury. Cochrane, was it, or Greenberg who'd told the girl what she had to do with him? And all the time she obeyed, was she hating him? He remembered her eyes by candlelight. No, he thought, she wasn't. I don't think she was. He remembered his trembling fingers closing the lids.

Where the trees began to thin, he left the horse behind and, crouching, moved up to the edge of the treeline. Erie Place lay charred and ended under the bright morning sun.

The whole southern half of the palisade was down, a jumble of blackened sticks on the ground, and most of the cabins at that end had disappeared. The ground was a field of ash, still giving up feeble smoke in places, and the southern blockhouse was a charred stump. The watchtower had vanished. On the northern side, sections of the stockade still stood and the blockhouses were roofless but standing. Cochrane's house, roofless too, looked like a great empty tub of some black stone, its cindery walls glistening in the sunlight.

Among the piles of ash, the roadways were no longer evident, but the solid houses of the new-comes, a few at least, remained in their cluster near the north wall, a cough of smoke rising from one of the shells now and then.

When Kinkaid had looked enough and had seen no sign of life, he mounted and rode down the rutted track between the hopeless cornfields. A light breeze blew from the northwest, lessening the acrid wood smoke in his nostrils but bringing in the odor of putrefaction from the swamp. Two smells of death.

When he'd first come here, the fetor of habitation had nearly turned his stomach. Then there was the aroma of roasting meat and the bayberry candles in the sheriff's keeping room. Then the herb scent from a girl's hair. Now all turned to the smell of ash.

There was no sound except the muffled thump of the roan's feet as he drew near the gateway. No dogs came snarling from the shadows. But something moved. Just as Kinkaid got to the gate, there was

100

a sudden clank-clank and he raised his rifle and stared around him.

It was only the links of a chain, once used to secure the gate, which dangled from a burnt post in the breeze.

He reined in the horse and sat looking. What he'd last seen through billows of orange-colored smoke now lay drifted like a gray snowfield. The remains of cabins looked like charcoal cages; black logs projected at odd angles from sooty banks. In places, there were still-glowing pools of embers and the wind played with the smoke and ash, making ghosts in the sunny air. These spirits rose from the dead, stretched and curled for a moment, then vanished.

Kinkaid wanted to move, but he stayed on for minutes, kept there. The roan bobbed its head impatiently and shuddered its skin. Ruins, Kinkaid thought. He seemed to see high, broken walls of stone and steel. He was another man standing at the edge of other devastation, trying to understand. He had a sense of enormous complication in this feeling, as if something greater than habitations, vaster to conceive, had passed away. He felt doom in the heart as that man turned away toward the forest. Kinkaid felt one click of time away from seeing into the mystery.

The horse shied at something and Kinkaid came back to his own moment. He looked at the smoldering drifts and decided not to try to walk his horse through them. Instead, he turned and rode northward along the outside line of the stockade, stopping now and then to look through a gap in the wall to spy for any evidence of life.

When he came to the north blockhouse, he dismounted and tied his horse to a fallen timber. Then, moving cautiously, he stepped into the blockhouse doorway.

Sunlight came through the opening where the roof had been and fell on a shoulder-high pile of ashes and cindered beams. The place was a shell. Nothing moved. Then, slowly, he lifted his gaze upward and saw the thing that had been waiting for him.

Where the second floor of the blockhouse had been there was still a shelf of blackened beam ends jutting unevenly from the wall. Crouching next to a loophole was the motionless figure of a man. In horror, Kinkaid saw what it really was.

The raven-black body was burned flat against the wall like some huge gingerbread man in an oven. Kinkaid stared at the crumbled face where no features remained, saw the outline of one hand, fingers spread and strangely distinct against the wood, traced the fire-drawn shape of the rifle that was no longer there, looked again at the crisp ash of the crouching torso and legs.

Dazed, struck still in all his muscles, Kinkaid could only stare in a dream. It was the black man, his heart told him, he'd seen so many times on the horizon of his dreams, the one who always bore trouble, an unexpressed message of great trouble and sorrow, toward a meeting with Kinkaid that the dream never seemed to permit. Unable to move, he waited for the other to move, to materialize out of the black ash and speak to him. Every moment seemed just the moment before a sound of a word would come. All surroundings were erased from Kinkaid's sight and the black man appeared to loom in a dark sky above him, heavy with a meaning untold. And yet, Kinkaid began to feel, the words were in being, like thunder in the mountains that hadn't yet time to sound in the plain.

Then it did seem as if the burnt man spoke to him, but voicelessly; in no formed words but in pictures of fire and smoke. In which I have died, he seemed to mean; in which you could die.

Kinkaid woke, sick and dazed, in the sunlight. Somehow, he had stumbled outside the blockhouse shell and away from the horror. He was leaning against a charred beam, his whole body drenched with sweat, his heart travailing. He wiped his face with his sleeve and pulled himself up and tried to remember. He tried to rid himself of the pressure on his mind. Greenberg.

He looked around. Across the roadway was a solid, squarebuilt house, marked by the fire but still standing. Shutters dangled at odd angles from the sides of the front windows. Shutters: the word came back. He moved unwillingly toward the doorless threshold.

The keeping room was unnatural but not destroyed. A layer of ash covered the floor and the table. There were ladder-back chairs tilted or fallen in their places. The iron cooking pot still hung on its hob in the fireplace. Nearby stood a charred cradle. The spinning wheel had collapsed on the floor and the still-standing cupboard displayed a few smoky plates. But the loft ladder mounted into emptiness and a waft of gray came from the farther room.

The name came to him. 'Sarah!' he called. He was surprised to hear his own desolate word in the silence.

There was a creak. He waited, motionless. A burnt pole from the remains of the room fell to the floor, raising a soft puff of ashes. He listened to the wind breathe through the walls. Then he stepped across to the doorway of the farther room and saw a churn, a bedstead with the covers and mattress burned away, an empty frame on the wall.

He left the skeleton of Erie Place at a canter, with no wish to look back.

'Gone,' was all he could manage to say to Greenberg when he walked into the clearing again. They looked at each other without speaking. At last, Kinkaid began to go about small tasks—gathering firewood, making a lean-to of sapling sticks and leaves, getting water. As he worked, he spoke without looking at Greenberg. 'Erie Place is mostly cinders. No trace, one way or tother, to say if your people got away. But I'm afraid . . .'

When he finally looked, Greenberg was lying flat on the ground, his hands covering his face.

14

First light, with knife edge of morning just barely seen at the rim of the world, rising slightly above the blue-black mass of forest on the land to the east; nearer—about a mile away—the broad march of swampland still shaded in night. Around the boat, alone out here, the new light touching the water and turning it a fish-scale gray; and the water, slowly swelling and subsiding beneath the hulls, itself like a great round fish belly. This is what Haven saw when he opened his eyes.

He lay near the stern end of the plank deck built across the two big canoe hulls, his back against the low storage hutch and the lashed tiller just overhead. There were the shapes of blanket-wrapped, rope-bound bales of salvage placed evenly around the deck; the low mast, with its cross spar, divided earth and sky into four sections in front of his eyes. Beneath him he felt the gentle ride of the water, but the boat was held more or less steady here by the two great buckets on ropes beneath the surface. He glanced toward the bow and saw that Piet was still asleep, wound in his black blanket.

Haven gave himself a little more time in the cool quiet, to lie still and to wait for the sun and, if they were lucky, an eastward breeze. In a while, he would get up and begin to search the swampline for the ragged red blanket hung on two poles on a sand flat, which marked where the entry channel was. It might take a little working along the shore to find it, but he felt sure his course across the lake yesterday had brought him close.

It was good to feel so certain; he remembered the time when every move was a hazard and he was like a blind man walking among snakes. Now it was two years past when he finally put his trust in the map and believed in the huge loop of blue water it showed, launched the canoe with Piet and set out to cut a passage through the marsh that had always walled off Haven Place from the western distance. No one else in the settlement had believed that there was open water beyond the swamp. Now the story of that first water-going was one of the hearth tales in every house.

He remembered the day-long, mosquito-plagued poling and cutting through the tangles, the moment when sunblazed blue water struck his eyes like a blow, the days of cautious paddling southward, just off the shoreline. Then, finally, the morning when the mist cleared over the water and beyond the low marshland they saw thrust into the sky those unbelievable ruined towers, high as bird's flight. The map had shown him a settlement at the far curve of the water, but it bore no idea of this.

He and Piet had been back there many times now, first in the canoe and then in the double canoe they'd built and rigged with the square sail. Had gone there through sheets of rain sometimes, had come back in wild wind and bucking waves enough to smash their little leaf on the waters. But they had brought back queer wonders—the metal pieces and machines that he and Piet calculated how to put to use.

Haven stood up abruptly and stretched his arms over his head. Recollection of those trials and actions always made him impatient to be moving on. There was a world to be accomplished and in his mind there was a rage to go on with it. 'We've put two sticks together,' he had often said to Piet. 'Just two sticks.'

He stretched to his full height and began to search along the swampline for the marker, but the sun was just at the verge of rising and the marsh was still a long-lying blackness. He began to scan beyond it toward the distant forest, where the yellow-gray now had tinged the highest treetops, and suddenly he stopped. Just at the paling horizon two miles or more to the north, there was a whitish line of smoke against the dark green—the first cooking fire of the morning in Haven Place. And just at the same time, there was a freshening air against the back of his neck. 'Piet!' he called. 'Get up! Home's over there and we've got one step to go.'

The blanket twitched, dropped away as Piet sat up. His head shone bright as a yellowbird's breast in the fresh sun—he had turned toward the shoreline, searching. His arm came up and all the exaggerated musculature of his strong torso showed in light and shade; he was pointing at one spot in the long smear of dark that edged the water.

Haven put his hand to his forehead and saw, far off, a speck of no color, not much different from swamp, but he knew, because Piet had caught it, that the speck was their red blanket marker. He had come to realize that Piet had a strange adeptness for seeing shapes and forms, where they fitted each other and where they repelled.

Piet got up and went to the sail and began to loose the lashings. 'One step!' he said. The words were separate beats, like the heavy beats of the big drum that called the Haveners to assembly. To speak anything was his worst trial and hardship; sometimes Haven saw the sweat begin on his forehead before the slow sentence came. Haven always elaborated these brevities: What Piet meant was that they had hours of poling through reeds and shallows, swamp stench and mosquito clouds, to make that one step. Time ahead always reeled through Haven's mind so fast that the day he was living in became long-past history. Piet inched toward the moment just ahead.

And true enough, the whole morning went in Piet's time, not Haven's. With their sail canted to north-south, they took the breeze and ran upshore; then, as the day brightened the swamp into all its separate details of knitted green growth, mazy black waters and spiky branches, they coasted down toward the oblong spot which slowly grew to be a dirty red. And past it, they slid into their channel mouth and furled the sail.

Then they had the long, laborious passage. The swamp had swallowed some of their markers, had grown new mudbanks to ground them, had put up brushy walls.

All morning, Haven poled and sweated patiently and in his impatient head traveled far away. He came into his settlement, stared at its familiar lines, saw all the empty places of things yet to be. He went back in time to the beginning.

'Father, we have put the box with your body into a hole in the burying hill. Oh, have you gone there for always?'

'No. I am the hollows in your mind that you must fill with pictures, which you must make into acts. This place and people were born in the minds of Havens and made real only by our acts. I came out of the woods, brought the starving burrow creatures here and made them into men and women.'

'All common things stripped away, we are pictures into acts? Must be?'

'If we stop, everything dies. The life of folk between swamp and forest is narrow and the two have an urge to come together. Go on, do as I did, make the people larger and larger.'

'Larger?'

'Push outward may be better. A house gives a man a solid coat against the winter. A ladder makes him ten paces tall, an arrow shot from a bow makes his arm a hundred paces long. But these are only child's things; from the little I know of it, the forefathers were giants. No larger in their bodies than we, but giants in the space around them.'

'And we can be such giants?'

'You are the third Haven. Your child will stand on your shoulders.

106

The tenth of us may be a giant. Or the twentieth.'

The settlement is made in the mind of Haven and the mind of Haven is the settlement. They partake of the same geometry. A wide, squared-off U of buildings facing a sandy clearing where a few trees have been left for shade. Behind the first row, a street and a second row of houses. Lines of white sisters: some of the buildings, the older ones, have overlapping clapboard sides and some are of squared logs, but all have the same faces—three steps leading to a door in the center, windows with solid wood shutters exactly on either side, a white lime wash covering all below, black roofs, gable-end stone chimneys. The stable is next to the storage barn and the common storehouse for foodstuff is alongside the common meal hall and the carpentry next to the smithy. Only the tannery is set at a distance, because of the smells.

You will build up your hearth fires, between frost time and thaw time, at early light, the first Haven said. At the sound of the bell, you will come to the hall for morning meal. Then, dressed for work, you will gather in the clearing by the middle post and the sheriff or the sheriff's first man will tell you your day's work. You will not laugh or talk here. At work, you will talk only when it's useful. Each work will be overlooked by a basman and you must do nothing else without his leave. The bell rings for mid meal, stop work and supper meal. The basman will note whether or not each man or woman has finished his or her work share for the day, and if not, he or she will work until darkness, until it is done. This had always been the order since the days of the first Haven.

By long tradition going back to forefather times, every tenth day is sun's day. You will come that morning to hear, to speak and to be judged. Standing next to the middle post, everyone in the settlement sitting on the ground around him, Haven recites the story that has long ago settled into the same formulas—how the man appeared out of the forest and saved the people from dying, how with Haven they built Haven—and finally, he raises his arms and they recite the promise with him, in a singsong of voices. 'Our father who is Haven, your name is good,' it begins. It goes on to pledge work, fair dealing and trust. Then Haven reads the law of ten things that are never to be done.

After that, there is the speaking out, when everybody is permitted to talk about his troubles and his disputes with another. And after each speaking out, Haven judges, sometimes setting a punishment or giving an order or a reproof. In the afternoon, no work is allowed and the people rest.

There should have been a marker stake here, but it was gone, and

107

Haven, guessing at darker water, turned the tiller to point them into the left-hand channel. After ten paces, he heard the scrape of roots against the hulls and the slippery sound of mud. As they shifted stance, trying to backpole, the boat came to a halt. Piet thumped his head with the heel of his hand—it had happened too many times. The whole channel would have to be traced out anew. But they'd both said that more than once this morning and so, wordlessly, they climbed over the side and, thigh deep in the water, began to shoulder the double canoe backward. As he worked, Haven's mind departed to another memory beginning.

In a way, the box had been the beginning. It was oblong, about a foot in length and rusted tight shut. Long years ago, some hand had put it on a shelf and there it had stayed, forgotten. Later, in the course of time, fire and destruction had come to the building where it lay, leaving shattered glass, fallen blocks and a half-collapsed roof. Then, after the clamor, came the silent years.

The winds of many autumns had swept a cover of sand over the ruin, almost hiding the broken stuff and the tilted roof, making a cave of it. Weeds and scrub bushes had taken a tenuous hold in the sand and vines had crept over the upthrust of walls still standing. But it was a dry place, well drained, and not much moisture got in. As the seasons changed and the years came and went namelessly, the box stayed on its shelf in the buried room.

Passing in front of the ruin was an old road, itself a ruin, its stone surface so widely cracked that lines of weeds and small bushes grew out of the cracks in a crazy pattern. At last, one morning in an eventual spring, three young men came down that road. They were not afraid of ruins. They were *looking* for ruins.

They walked over the site. Then they began to dig a sloping approach to one of the buried walls. They pounded and chiseled at the blocks until they had broken an entrance into the darkness. One holding a lantern, they crawled inside.

What they saw has had so many stories told about it that truth and tale can no longer be divided. In the middle of the shadowed cavern, two pits with things like low, flat railings on either side. A chain dangling from some kind of hoist. Odd shapes of rusty metal scattered around the floor or lying among the dust on waist-high benches at the far wall. Some round iron things like huge black drums from which a sticky black gum had leaked.

But the strangest—three rusty, dust-sheathed shapes that stood on wheels. According to the stories, they were about as long as a big canoe but bulkier, something like huts on wheels. A little scraping showed that they had glass windows in them on all sides. One of the men tried to pry an opening into a hut or wagon, or whatever it was, but though the rusty metal crumbled, he found no way.

The other two men called to him. They were already picking up what metal things they could use and stuffing them into their bags and throwing aside whatever looked outlandish or useless. Hammers of a strange shape, files, chisels, lever bars, a small anvil—yes. A long crane neck of metal with a tip on the end, a cylinder with a big handle and a snout, a bar with a six-sided hole in one end, a bar with jaws on it—no.

Just as they began to drag their sacks to the entrance hole, the tallest of the men put his hand on a shelf and felt the shape of the rusty box. He threw it in his bag with the rest.

A day or two later, when they were in the smithy, cleaning the tools they'd brought back, they came across the box again and pried it open and were disappointed. It held only some folded papers covered with patternless lines. But the one called Haven took them home with him.

During the next winter, in the evening when work was over, he looked long at these papers—which were all alike—and puzzled about them. He could read the words on the top fold—'Esso Road Map: The Northeastern States'—and he found many words written among the uneven lines on the face of the paper when it was opened out. The paper tantalized his curiosity and he began to feel that he held in his hands one of the secret devices of the forefathers.

One day, he discovered the name 'Haven' written on the map just at the edge of the part where the grayish paper gave way to blue. 'Grand Haven,' it said, and it struck him that the name of the place where he lived might have come down from forefather times—though now no one knew where it had come from or what it signified. Some time later, the thought came to him that the names on the paper might be the names of old settlements and the lines might be, as the words suggested, the tracing of ancient roads. A picture of the land made small enough to fit on a paper. The idea excited him. And dazed him: it must be wider land than he had ever dreamed. The bigger letters near the Haven spot read 'Michigan.' One morning, he went out and climbed to the top of the highest tree he could find and there in the wind, looking over the forest tops, he said the word many times: 'Michigan.'

He explained his notions to his two friends and they caught his fever. They decided that when spring planting was over, they'd set out through the woods to discover once and for all if there was in fact a broad land beyond the forest.

These were the three: Haven, a tall, big-headed man with arms like oak branches. He was a man never satisfied, raging after questions that seemed imaginary to others, a searcher, hunter, salvager, inquisitor, someone who almost always seemed to speak in orders.

Veen: Another troublesome one, an orphan, black-haired and rough-headed, surly often, his face striking you as vengeful under the black wings of eyebrows, but a greatly capable man as a rigger with ropes and pulleys and levers in building.

Cutters-son: He could climb like a cat, top a big tree, fell it exactly where he wanted it; he was yellow-headed, blue-eyed, stocky, smiling.

One morning early, they gathered in the village open with their packs on their backs. In each pack was a copy of the map, though only Haven believed he understood it. In their hands were short hunting bows—the wheel-and-ratchet kind old Haven had invented to replace the long bows. They were all happy to escape work for a hunting and roaming week; even Veen was in humor. And they had convinced themselves—they'd prove now and forever that there was a land beyond the narrow strip between forest and marsh.

They went inland, found the narrow, eroded forefather road that led south and ambled along for two days, enjoying themselves and the hunting. Then, one night around the fire, after some argument about what the maps showed, they had the notion of going in different directions for a few days. Haven wanted to go directly eastward through the woods because the map showed him the marks of many old settlements there; Veen chose to go straight on south for reasons he didn't explain; Cutters-son would go south and then angle to the east because his guess lay that way. And so they divided.

After another day and a half, Haven did come to one settlement, a ruin that daunted him with its tall, empty walls, sunken roofs and overgrown roadways. He stayed only one day in the ghostly place, looking over his shoulder a hundred times, finding not much to salvage because he felt unwilling to dig. In the night, in a burrow he'd made, he began to feel chills and fever and he had strange illusions of the ancient people walking softly all about where he lay. In the morning, he was worse; the fever kept on. And so he turned back and made his way through the forest to their first road and back to Haven settlement. Nobody believed him when he said that the lines on the map and the settlement names corresponded to roads and ruins.

Weeks passed and neither Veen nor Cutters-son returned. Haven went down the road several times in hopes that he might meet them returning.

Just before harvest, old Haven took sick. Before the leaves had stopped falling, he died. After the burial, the settlement, in meeting, called on young Haven to be the sheriff in place of his father.

The snow came, but the two did not appear. By the next snow time, their families had given them up. Everybody but Haven was satisfied that this proved the edge of the earth was over there, just beyond the forest, and Veen and Cutters-son had gone too close.

Closer inshore, the channel was much better; the markers had stood and there seemed to be no new treacheries. The sun was late in the west and, in clear stretches in front of them, the black water would go gilt. Over the massed bulrushes they caught glimpses of treeline. The afternoon buzz of the swamp was loud.

The reedtops parted as the boat slid through the last of them; one more turn of the channel and the slope of shore was in view. Two birds shot into the air across the bows, their shadows like bolts on the sun-tinged water. The prows slid alongside the landing dock and Piet sprang onto it with the rope in his hand. People were running down the patch from the clearing toward them and someone was shouting to Haven.

He felt very tired, sleepy, far away; he wanted no homecoming commotion. Leaving Piet to take care of the boat, he stepped up onto the landing dock, shut his ears and strode toward home.

But as he crossed the clearing, some of them followed and Kamp, his undersheriff and basman of the watch, was panting at his elbow. Annoyed, he turned to send him off, but then he saw import and trouble on the plump face. Kamp's lips were working but his voice lagged. 'Come on, then. Into my house and tell me whatever it is,' Haven growled.

He led through the door, crossed the room and, his mind on food and sleep, began unslinging pouch, canteen and map case and then taking off his shirt. 'Well?'

Kamp was saying something about his daughter, Glyn. Glyn? Haven realized with a twitch of conscience that he hadn't once thought about her for ten days. Why hadn't she come, as she usually did, to meet him at the landing? Not that he intended it, but she was usually out of his mind. He loved her and yet she had so many of her dead mother's ways that just her voice or expression could touch a wound that had taken him years to heal. 'Where is she, then?' he asked, half turning to look at Kamp.

And then what the man was saying began to come through. 'Carried off!' he said without believing it. He seized a chair and sat astraddle it, leaning his chin on the ladder back, and heard Kamp.

When the brief tale was over, Haven slapped his big hand on the table. 'A party of men on horses? From where? I'll take men and trail them; they're only a day away. And if they did take along the folk from River Place on foot, that's not far.'

Kamp, hands clasped behind him, shifted from foot to foot and looked like some fat rocking-horse toy. But his voice was level and sensible. 'Two hunters and I trailed them as far as a forefather road going south. There must be at least fifty horses. More horses than I've ever seen. No, Haven, it isn't just a few outlaw men from the woods as I thought first and maybe you were thinking. It's strange folk from far off and dangerous.'

Haven rose and strode up and down the length of the room, his face red even through the sunbrown.

'Did anyone see them at River Place? Or know for sure they took Glyn and Berk along?'

'We found her sandalprints mixed with hoofprints at the swamp edge, both going in and coming out. That's all. No one left to see them after they went.'

Haven got his map, spread it out on the table and leaned over it, frowning. 'I want Piet, five of the best hunters and you ready tomorrow at the first bell. We're going hunting.' His voice was low and tired.

'Eight of us?' asked Kamp. 'There aren't enough rifles to go round.' Haven said nothing but gave a sidewise motion with his hand, still staring at the map.

15

During the daytime, Greenberg lay in the brush lean-to Kinkaid had made, silent and rigid, his eyes in a motionless stare. Kinkaid left off trying to talk and came only to change the bandages—the burns were healing well—and to bring food and water to him. It was hard to tell if Greenberg knew he was there.

Kinkaid hunted a little, exercised the horses, mended straps and clothes, cleaned the rifles, found some berries and picked them, fished afternoon-long in a little stream he'd found at some distance from the hollow.

Every night, Greenberg again lived through his agony and carried on conversations with his dead. 'Is that the bell ringing? I said put two riflemen there and kill anything that comes into the road. I have been too kindly, Cochrane. But the blaze blinds me. Go and get him down—can't you see he's burning? Water, thanks. Answer me or I'll put out your eyes, do you hear? Your eyes! More men for the watch, more, more, and we have no more, old man, I tell you that. I can't breathe. . . .'

Kinkaid would get up, shivering, and put on his shirt. Then he would walk softly away across the grass as the voice dropped to a gentle, eerie tone, questioning. 'Is there milk for the child? Dress and go to, where you'll be safe, you'll remember, remember?'

Out of earshot, Kinkaid would walk for a long time in the splintered moonlight on the forefather road, sometimes lying down to sleep for a while on the ground and coming back to the hollow only when light began to break.

Fishing, sitting on his sun-warmed boulder by the stream, he had the thought that perhaps great trial and trouble made a kind of fire print within the blood of men. And it was passed down from mother and father to child, to grandchild, and lay invisible until some turn in the world made it stir memories far older than you, memories you never made but had given. In the fire of Erie Place and then in its ash he'd felt in constant company with an unremembered passage just the same; without knowing, he sensed each moment as something that had long ago occurred even while it was now occurring. This had led him directly to find Mary dead, to find Greenberg thereafter, to bring him blindly through the fire to safety. None of this had he calculated step by step.

And it had brought him directly to his most terrible unknown expectation—the black man burned against the wall. And he'd broken off and fled.

When he got back to camp one afternoon, Kinkaid noticed first that Greenberg was sitting up and sharpening his hunting knife on a flat stone. Then he saw that Greenberg had laid out on his blanket the few possessions he had left to him—water flask, ammunition pouch, neckerchief and the iron key to the storehouse door. He had washed his ragged, burnt shirt and breeches and they were hanging from a limb. He raised his hand in greeting.

'Kinkaid, how long have I been lying here?' It was the first time he had looked at Kinkaid or had spoken to him for ten days.

'Oh, a few days. But I was sure you'd heal.' Greenberg's eyebrows had grown back and a hedge of black beard covered his lower face, made it more agreeable now that the taut, bony line of the jaw was hidden.

He stuck the hunting knife into the ground. 'I've things to say, Kinkaid.'

'I know them. But let me fix supper and we'll eat and talk.'

Kinkaid made a kind of thick soup with deer meat, mushrooms and some wild onions. He used his cup and gave Greenberg the tin plate and spoon. They sat facing each other next to the fire as twilight came on.

Greenberg smiled slightly and said, 'What's my first thing, then?' In the half dark, with the small glint of white teeth showing in his black beard and the eyes sharp and intent again, he looked wolfish. He had recovered the dangerous part of his mind. Maybe all that came back from the dead, Kinkaid thought.

'*My* first thing. I asked you if you want to trail west with me. You've said no.'

Greenberg nodded.

'You've asked me if I would go backtrail with you to help find the ones you've lost. Hard as it is for me, I've had to say no.'

'True,' Greenberg said. 'And that brings us to the end of our conversation. There's only one other thing—I deeply feel it but I can't say it. Do you know what I mean?' He put the plate down and extended his hands to clasp Kinkaid's shoulders for a moment.

'Yes. There's no way of saying thanks for that aloud. But you've said them in your mind and I've heard in mine. Now—tomorrow I'll give you food and whatever else I can for the trail. You're healed enough to ride?'

Greenberg nodded.

That night, there were no dreams or voices. The sun, full on Kinkaid's face, awoke him at last, and looking across the hollow, he saw that Greenberg had already saddled the sheriff's horse and was bent over Kinkaid's map.

He raised his head, saw Kinkaid and, as if picking up a conversation from the day before, said, 'Look here. To the west of us lie ruins of a considerable settlement marked Cleve-land. I give you my advice as a salvager who has been in such places—keep away. Move to the south, around it.'

'The wars of the forefathers. And the black guard of plague they left behind to mind their burying places. And creatures that live in stone-sided underground rivers beneath the ruins. Well, I heard all those tales when I was a child. And don't believe them. Greenberg, are you a new man in a new time or are you pretending?'

Greenberg laughed. 'Then there's the story about how the old ones could build stars with the power to hear and see and shot them into the sky. My grandmother solemnly told me that the forefathers used to fly above the ground, like birds, in big baskets with wings on them. And there was the magical glass box where you could see pictures of something that was happening a long ways away. I believe in the ghost stories as much as I do these.

'But, friend, I'm trying to tell you about real things. The old ruins are a real enough treachery unless you're experienced there. One man took a torch into an underground room and suddenly it burst around him. We only found one of his boots and some shreds of flesh and cloth among the chunks of stone. Another man put his hand into a bottle of strange water and it ate the skin away. Some have been crushed by falling buildings and others have been lost in mazes.'

Kinkaid nodded. 'I'll circle, then.'

They were both silent, knowing nothing more to say. Greenberg handed the map to Kinkaid and got painfully onto the horse. Their casting together was over. Each to the other would always be an unfinished story. The friendly man, the clever and ambitious man, the foolishly cruel man, the unselfish man named Greenberg had all been burned away and nothing was left but iron.

Kinkaid felt that one human part of the future had turned backward into the past. Greenberg wheeled his horse, raised one hand in goodbye, slapped the reins, and man and horse slowly began to recede

115

among the trees until Kinkaid could see them no longer.

A little later, Kinkaid turned his face west. He had carefully erased all marks of the campsite as a means of telling himself that something had ended, that he would not pass this way again. He had to recover the habits of silence and loneliness. He led the horses out to the forefather road and began a steady pace. He would go as far as he could each day, driving himself into forgetful fatigue.

'Because you found a dead man, you are going to a place that may not even be?' Greenberg's question—it seemed to hang in the sunny silence. It was a hard question with a cloudy answer. There was an old land map with a faded line and an X marked by the words 'Grand Haven.' That might be a settlement much like Erie Place, or might be a ruin, or might be nothing. Where Haven stood there was the broad blue of another lake that time might have changed to another marsh.

But Haven was a real enough name, at least, a marker in the direction of the unnamed spectre that possessed his sleeping mind—the dream of cliffs, the shadowy room, the figure with the dark face that adducted him like an invisible muscle. All he could say was that he could go only in the direction of the sunset.

The air grew hotter as the morning passed. The tree walls would sometimes open up and he would walk in sunlight for a time but, even in the shady stretches, it was warm. Kinkaid took off his leather shirt and draped it over his saddle. He had no great liking for buckskin. Wearing it, he sweated under the sun and, when the rain came down, it seemed to coat his skin like slime. In the cold of winter, it was better than nothing, but not much. He wore it simply for brush country.

He tried to busy his mind with such small things, like choosing a straw of notion from a handful. He hummed and tried to recall the words of songs people sang in River Cross Place—that one about the dun cow and the ticklish bull. He took his mind back to episodes of life at home—the times he'd gone picking wild berries on the mountainside with other children long ago; market day in the settlement, with plank tables in the square ranged with bright vegetables, honeycombs, clay pots and woven things for barter; firelight in a cabin as he stood by a sickbed, helping the old doc and learning his homely art. With these, he tried to convince himself that his real life still existed solidly, though far away, and that one day he'd walk through its gate again.

The road he'd been following met and joined a wider one that he had noted on his map. Coming into it, he stared at something as monstrous as he'd ever seen. It was a broad gray belt stretching as far to the west as he could see. Then he noticed that it was, in fact, two roads separated by a strip of high brush and trees. A puzzle for his journey: Why did the ancient people build twin roads, side by side?

The country had changed body from the flatlands along the swamp's edge and had become low, forested hills on either hand, and Kinkaid noted that the roadbed cut through slopes and traversed filled gullies to maintain the same level always, as if obeying some mysterious law. The way was so wide that no trees overhung it and he kept to the shady right-hand edge. Unlike the cracked and broken forefather roads he'd walked before, this one seemed to have only occasional pits and eroded places and a few fallen trees; its general sweep was straight and clear.

Another oddness—most forefather roads appeared to lead from one settlement site to another, passing among the shells and vine-laced walls of ancient buildings, but except for one roofless cluster in a clearing of its own, Kinkaid saw no signs of past habitation.

At midmorning on the second day, he came upon the first of the crossings and he stopped to take it in. Across the broad roadway, another road had been borne on a bridge. Part of the bridge supports in the center had given way and large chunks of the porous paving stone lay under the span. Close by, there were long, broken poles of some metal that Kinkaid thought might have stood as a kind of framework above the roadway. To them were attached pieces of what seemed to be large, flat plates. Coming nearer, Kinkaid scraped the dirt and leaves from one of them and, on the flaking and mottled surface, saw a faint number 90 and the word 'West.' He knew that the dark line he'd singled out on his map also had the number 90 marked at intervals along it. The coincidence gave him a feeling of surety, a renewed confidence that he could go to the most remote places of the earth and return.

In the afternoon, as he rode for a while, Kinkaid pondered and tried to induce some sense of what he was observing. He could not imagine the magical means of making this great roadway, but its even width told him that it had been laid down to bear many riders and wagons at the same time. He narrowed his eyes and attempted to see backward into time, with the trees vanished, perhaps, and open fields bordering, a great throng of cattle, wheeled carts, flocks of sheep, horsemen and drovers in strange dress moving on the smooth stone track toward the horizon. He thought of the oft-told stories—and the picture he'd seen—of the boxlike, legendary wagon that was supposed to have rolled along awesomely, with no horse to pull it. But the picture could easily have been of something quite different and the story part of the tall lies made up by the fireside taletellers to amaze and amuse.

117

Where are they all going, those walking beasts and humans? Why are they so separated here from the villages where they might stop to rest and eat? What is it that they are carrying back and forth on this great stone river across the land? The scene was closed to Kinkaid and its meaning would not yield. He opened his eyes with the sense that his picture had been all wrong. We can't go to Other Time, he thought. We have to let it come to us.

Late that afternoon, the western sky grew heavy with clouds like immense boulders, gray and black, advancing like some slow avalanche. Kinkaid heard their far-off rumble, and before long, the wind began to plow the treetops above him. With his hatchet he cut a narrow lane into the roadside brush, then he built a branch-and-blanket lean-to and made a fire. He had no time to make a browse bed of fir branches and so he would sleep on a layer of ferns. Just at dark, the rain came and killed his fire. Before long, it had begun to come through his flimsy roof, and Kinkaid slept fitfully in an inch of water. But that was nothing new for him; on his rounds in the hill country of home, he'd slept in the saddle, in icy mud, on a flat-topped stone slab in a spring gale.

At first light, the rain still streamed from the leaves and Kinkaid sat patiently under his shelter and waited for clearing. That came on a western wind about midmorning. The rain faded to a mist, stopped, and the sun appeared in a thousand sparks on leaves and puddles. Kinkaid rose and took the trail again.

On the fifth day, he turned south. He found a narrow road that branched off the huge roadway and led into a hilly, thick-forested country. Now the going was much slower. In places, the surface had been washed out by floods and stands of saplings had taken over. There were no cuts through the hills and the track rose and fell with the contours of the land. Trees overbranched the road most of the time and often there were fallen trunks or long mats of fallen leaves. Then, from time to time, the tree wall would thin and Kinkaid would find himself coming to a ruinous forefather place of no great size and would pass along its old street, staring curiously. He saw empty windows, walls so roped and leaved with vines that they seemed to be strange growths, houses half engulfed by earth, with saplings growing in the rooms, fallen houses, and others whose fronts seemed almost untouched by time.

It was two days later, after he'd branched west again on another small roadway, that he felt a great urge to shelter for the night in one of these places. Dusk tinged the air gray-blue as he walked into the settlement street, and in the thickening light, the pale faces of the buildings were as if restored out of time. Kinkaid halted in the silence and let his mind look and listen. Once, he had been brought to treat a drowned man pulled from the river, and as he was trying to revive the hopeless body, he'd felt a slow, faint pulse begin. It was that way now. With no sound to touch his ear, he could perceive the voices of people coming and going in the twilight and in the shadowed street could almost catch the sudden glow of lamps at windows. Wood smoke in the air, the scent of cooking, the bark of a dog, the creak of a pump in some yard, all unreally present. And the sense that came to him was of friendly peace.

Yet that very feeling made him want to avoid the houses, as if he'd be a ghost from the future stepping across the threshold into the lamplight and the lamplight and the family would disappear at the moment of crossing, sent back. Kinkaid's attention was drawn down the street to one corner of the road crossing, where there was a yard thick with tall grass and bushes and, set back in it, a squarish building. Some part of a peaked roof was in silhouette behind what seemed to be a tower. It came to him that this was not a house and that there would be no presences within, and at the same time, he felt directed there in the spell that had come over him. He led the horses down the road, and finding a broken stone path through the brambles, brought them to the doorless entrance and tied them. He saw a dead pine tree there, and when he had knelt down with flint, steel and tinder to get a small fire going, he broke off limbs and made a pair of torches.

Their blaze revealed one great, open room, half unroofed. The floor was covered with piles of dead leaves, dirt, pieces of rotten plankwood and what appeared to be the wreckage of benches. As Kinkaid stepped forward, his boots grated on chunks of crumbling white stuff that had fallen from the walls.

Holding his torches away from his eyes, he walked carefully among the debris toward the shadowed far end of the place. The side walls were very high, with pointed window openings let in. A collection of tubes, like a strange raft, was hung on one wall. Then, by his light, he could see that the end of the room, overhung by the remaining roof, was a low platform, and in the middle of the platform there was a kind of cupboard crusted with bird droppings. Kinkaid found crevices where he could plant the torches and stood pondering for a few moments.

The place seemed to echo every step, but there were other resonances Kinkaid found hard to concert. If his fancy in the village street had been of soundless voices, here it was of sounding silence. It was the silence that comes just after the ring of a heavy hammer on an anvil and Kinkaid shook his head as if to clear it. Too many solitary days on the trail raised up notions, figments, dreams, delusions. But still there was the idea of a great sound that had ceased one instant before he could hear it.

He forced himself to business. With so much here that might burn, he hesitated to start his fire. He searched around among the rotten stuff and his hand touched something solid. He uncovered a huge, smooth stone that had been hollowed out to make a bowl shape. It seemed to have fallen from a stone stump that had once supported it. He cleared a space on the floor and dragged the bowl out to where he could set it up next to the edge of the low platform. In a little while, he had a good cooking fire going within the hollow of the bowl.

When he'd taken care of his horses and brought his saddlebags inside, he rigged a frame for his cooking pot and filled it with water from his canteen and the meat of a rabbit he'd killed that afternoon. Reaching again into one of the saddlebags, he came across something stowed away in a corner and he smiled as he drew it out; he had forgotten. There was a small leather bottle filled with the grape wine of Erie Place and with it a cloth-wrapped square of cornbread, given to him by the sheriff's wife the day before he'd departed. Supper would be more palatable tonight.

While the rabbit was stewing, he brought in more pine branches and began to explore. There was a great deal of the rotted wood that, he thought, might have been part of some sort of seats or benches. He had it in mind that this place would have been a meeting house. At River Cross Place, assembly was held in front of the granary, but Kinkaid had been in one easterly settlement rich enough to have built a barn just as a gathering place. There the sheriff (Kinkaid's memory produced a surly boar's head with gray bristles, but no name) sat once a week settling disputes, handing out punishments and repeating the laws.

Going into the dark corner on the left, Kinkaid stuck his torch through the doorway of a smaller room and gazed on tall shelves full of ruined books. A few covers remained, but the paper was reduced to scraps and fibrous dust. A startled mouse ran across the floor in front of him. He was turning away, when he caught a small glint from a bottom shelf, and pushing the litter aside, he found a thick square of glass with one corner broken off. By accident, it had fallen on the leaf of a book and had preserved part of it. Kinkaid took it with him to read later.

He'd grown tired of deer jerky and he relished this meal with its unexpected gifts. When he'd finished, he washed his hands and carefully held the small glass plate to the torchlight.

He read the words through once, understanding almost none, not knowing even how to say most. They seemed heavy and sorrowful, but to what purpose? Baffled and irritated, he decided to try them slowly and wring out their meaning. Guessing at their sounds, he began to read aloud.

' "Almighty God, Father of our Lord Jesus Christ, maker of all things, judge of all men—" '

He stopped. Except for the names, he did understand the words; it was the thought that bewildered him. Maker of all things? Judge of all men?

' "We acknowledge and bewail our manifold sins and wickedness, which we most grievously have committed by thought, word and deed against thy Divine Majesty—" '

'Sin'—he was familiar with that, though few used the word. It meant doing something wrong. We something and . . . wail for? . . . our sins, which we something have committed against something.

' "—provoking most justly Thy wrath and indignation against us." '

Provoking something and something against us. Was this the way the forefathers indeed spoke?

' "We do earnestly repent and are heartily sorry for these our misdoings." '

Heartily sorry for their mis-doings: Kinkaid understood that plea. But what were those doings that they were so sorry for? Nothing made sense. Kinkaid raised his head, shook it and laid the piece of glass on the platform. Dark and beyond reach as the meaning was, the words stirred something in him. They had a kind of vibration in his voice in this empty room.

He was still puzzling about them as he rolled in his blanket and slept by the diminishing fire.

Kinkaid got up with the earliest light, consumed the last piece of cornbread and a cup of herb tea, shaved staring into a triangular bit of mirror, and decided to look around outside before setting out. He'd expected an uneasy night full of dreams and visitants, but on the contrary, he'd slept deeply and in peace, awaking only once, when an owl hooted somewhere close by. The whispers he'd caught at twilight in the street he recognized as a sign within himself rather than anything heard. When he was younger, he'd chosen the healer's life because solitude made him free. He liked to ride alone. And dealing with the sick made for a certain solitude of another kind, because this most personal kind of attention was finally impersonal—the healer could act wholly outside himself while the ill were enclosed in their suffering.

But it was as if Erie Place had tumbled him into the life of other lives. Communion, friendship, love, revenge, death, however momentary, had tainted him with the unwished wish for engagement. He felt this without knowing it exactly and it made him hang back a little from the thought of the road and the long, unpeopled miles ahead.

He carried his saddlebags through the entrance and stood looking at the bushy field alongside the building. Suddenly, something caught his attention and he picked up a branch and swept aside a clump of tall weeds.

He finally uncovered an oblong shape, something that seemed to be a slab of gray stone lying tilted on the ground, and kneeling down, found a trace of some markings in one corner. With his hands, he scraped the dirt and slimy leaves from the surface and gradually revealed a pattern of worn letters carved on it. Another curious forefather object the like of which he'd never seen—and he traced the lettering with his forefinger in wonder.

R.I.P
Theresa Bond
1943–1977

A strange name and two numbers, the name in the old two-part forefather style, clearly the name of a woman long dead. But why was her name cut into the rock laid in this field—and were those special numbers that belonged to her? Did each forefather place a name stone of his own somewhere so that his own word would always remain in the world? He wondered about this woman; had she been young and pretty or old and fat?

There seemed to be more of the stones nearby and so he began to clear bushes, pull up clumps of long weeds and scrape moss from the hidden slabs. They lay in two rows, some still sharp-cut and others so cracked and weatherworn that their messages had gone into the ground with the rain and the melting ice. He went from one to another, trying to make them out: Beloved wife of . . . John Thompson, Requiescat in Pace; Memory of . . . Anne Davis, d. 1980; William Clark.

He was trying to recall something he'd heard a long time ago, but it seemed to escape him. The mysterious numbers all began with 19, he noted, and the biggest number was 1983. It might be that each ancient had a number group as well as a name. But why?

At last, he gave up and turned to go, thinking: It doesn't matter; they're many years dead now. He stopped. Of course—the years. There was an old notion sometimes figuring in forefather myths about the great wars and the starvation to the effect that they counted their years forward, from the beginning of time, that they'd counted nearly two thousand of them before their end.

He hadn't brought this to mind because it had always been considered an oddity—and not a very useful one. At home, years got their names from important events: the year the corn failed; the year lightning struck the hay barn; the year Parker chopped his foot off. And of course, thoughtful people kept track of the sum of their winters.

Thus, he reasoned, 1943–1977 must be a span of time and, probably, just the lifetime of that woman. And if the stone had been put here after her last year of life . . .

It took him a few minutes to accept the new thought. In all the settlements he knew, corpses were burned the first day after death. It was an old custom going back, some said, to the plague times. It was difficult to imagine bodies being sunk into the ground. But that was what the stones and the numbers said to him. The whispering voices he'd heard last night in the street—the ones who'd once walked and spoken there—were all here forever, laid under their separate stones.

That morning as he rode, he thought about time. A huge, changeable animal almost impossible to catch by the tail. For his people, it went about three lifetimes back and it was mainly the separate memories among families. But the forefathers, it seemed, could look back to any single point because it was marked by a number—and could look ahead to a time that already had a number? The last of those settlers in the small, nameless village had been laid in the ground in the year ticked off as 1983—and how much unnumbered time had gone by since then? Old men glibly said, 'Hundred years ago when the old ones were here,' or, 'Two hundred years back when forefathers were on earth.'

In this mood, he thought he knew the real danger of the ancient ruins. They made you long for things you couldn't comprehend. Even in disorder, they spoke silently about an order of time and space that had been lost. But all Kinkaid's dreams, waking or sleeping, had an insistence in them that no imagined thing was irrecoverable. Objects, whole structures, could vanish, but what was patterned in the mind once was always there, waiting in darkness to be patterned again in another.

It occurred to him that his people were without a past and so without a future. If a man with a map could know just where he was on the surface of the ground, a man with a measure for time could know why and where the present existed.

He was bearing due westward on the road, passing, as his map showed him, between the two old settlements of Cleve-land and

Akron. It was a country of ancient farmlands and the remains of villages spaced about an hour's walk apart on his route—Hudson, Peninsula, Brunswick, the map named them. He sheltered one night in an old barn that was slowly sagging to the ground, and looked at the stars through gaps in its roof as he was falling asleep. On this land, the forest was thinner and less frequent, so that he walked much of the time in the sunlight. The stone way was hot underfoot. Sometimes, he had to pass through clouds of flies, with the horses jigging and balking; then the woods overhung the trace for a few hundred yards, giving way again to bush-grown fields and long expanses of grass.

Time began to turn like a familiar wheel of dark and light, one day so much like the last that he no longer counted them. The four deer browsing at the wood's edge reappeared in a place that could have been the same as yesterday's; there was a wild pig he'd shot last week—was it?—or would shoot tomorrow as it ran into the same ditch. There was the barn with the sagging side, and seeing it from a distance, he knew he'd sleep there again tonight. And he seemed to have worn out every thought and every memory. Only the map kept him going, the tiny progress he saw on it every evening.

He'd looked hard for signs of living settlements and a few times he'd seen far away what he took to be cleared and plowed fields or a line of smoke from a chimney, but there was always some reason for not going there—from a little nearer, the fields took on the look of a swamp; at the next curve of the road, the smoke thread had disappeared and no track at all led into the thicket where he thought his sighting had been. He did not want to think about the possibility that River Cross Place and its little cluster of neighbor settlements, the few villages near Erie that Greenberg had spoken of and the place called Haven were the only places of man.

Following the roads that promised the easiest journeying, he'd gravitated southward. There would come a time when he'd have to turn his head to the right and bear north, but for the moment, he was content with straight roads and unhindered going in this flat country.

One day, the weather changed from its monotonous summer blaze and cheered him with a day-long fitfulness. When he arose in the morning, rain had begun to tap at the leaves, but a little later as he walked, the gray light suddenly dissolved and the air was spun with misty yellow. Over his left shoulder he caught the instant of a rainbow. The old road gleamed and the breeze gave a chill touch to his wet clothes. In a little while, it was hot again.

When he'd finished a brief nap in the shade at noon, ripe gray clouds came on a wind out of the western sky, and after a few hundred paces on his way, the rain came down like tacks and nails, as they'd used to say in River Cross Place.

And so it was all the day, sun chasing rain. He told himself he would halt early, in the best shelter he could find. At last, in the distance, through the blur of another shower, he could see what appeared to be the approach to an old settlement of considerable size, but he felt reluctant about chancing the ruins in the rain and dark. Then, to his left, he noticed, among a ragged growth of trees and brush, what must once have been a large farm place. He could see a tall stub of chimney and the angles of a house.

He found the vestiges of a lane, took his horses into it and, with the high grass on either side bowing in the wind, made his way toward the grove and the standing bones of a tall, peaked house. Most of its boards had fallen away, the windows were glassless and the low shelter along its front side had collapsed. No, he decided.

A little way off to his right and set back a dozen paces was a broken-backed barn with one wall gone and the exposed timbers charred by some long-ago fire. It seemed to balance perilously, waiting for the one drop of rain or gust of wind destined to bring it down in a heap.

Farther away, Kinkaid could see an odd framework structure, long and low, with a pitched roof—if there had been a roof. The whole thing, walls and roof, was composed of a regular pattern of open squares.

Trying his luck in that direction, Kinkaid moved to the far corner of the barn and there discovered his sound, dry place. It was a low, rectangular attached building with a stone floor and a tight roof. As he stood in the open doorway surveying in the dulled light, he saw a barren room with no more than a few cobwebbed pieces of tackle on the walls, some buckets and a line of stalls. The walls were of grainy stone blocks with a few scabs of whitewash still clinging to them. Because of the stalls, a place for animals—but it struck Kinkaid as neither a stable nor a cow barn. Even in the most ancient of those, there was the eternal ammoniac must of generations. He led his horses inside.

Just as he was falling asleep, the wind and rain sighed into stillness and the moon appeared among racing clouds. It frosted the treetops beyond his open doorway.

Next morning it happened, Kinkaid's awaited but unanticipated thing. He arose at false dawn, made a fire to heat tea and then, warmed by it, drowsed on his blankets for a time before urging himself to get up to saddle. It was still gray when he finally led the horses outside, but there was a tint of ocher at the eastern edge of the morning.

Sleepily, he passed through the grove with its skeletal house and turned into the lane. It had nearly disappeared in the tangle of rain-bent stalks and he made his way slowly, forearm in front of his face to ward off the drops. Then it struck him that he was better off mounted and so he swung onto the roan. The horse shook its head in annoyance and jogged forward. After a few moments, they broke into the road-way with a shower of drops and Kinkaid reined in.

Stock-still in the middle of the road about twelve paces off stood two figures. They had been approaching the lane entrance, but some movement in the grasses or the clack of a horse's hoof on stone must have astounded them into dead set, each with a foot stretched for the next step.

Kinkaid sat his horse motionless for a few moments, knowing what to do—first, a smile; then a slow raising of both hands, palms out (but not too far from the throwing knife sheathed just at the top of his right boot); then a calm greeting.

Under her gray head kerchief in the brightening day, the woman's face looked like a candle just put out. It was waxy white and thin, the mouth a downcurve, the black eyes staring. Her black hair hung to her shoulders. The sandy-haired boy was about fifteen. He wore brown breeches and a short homespun coat that was too big for him. His mouth had fallen open. He had a pack on his back and a bundle slung over one shoulder. His right hand held a heavy stick with a knob on it.

Kinkaid began—the smile, the raised hands, a quiet 'Don't be afraid; I'm not harmful.' At that, the roan snorted and did a nervous step sideways.

The woman screamed a sound of pure terror and dropped a small bag she was carrying. They whirled and ran back up the road, the woman hitching her skirts and the pack and bundle bouncing on the boy's shoulders. Kinkaid thought momentarily of going after them to have another try, but the sound of that scream was still in the air. He watched as they plunged off the road into some opening in the bush and, for a few minutes, saw the bushtops shudder as they blundered through.

He sat still and tried to look with their eyes. A stranger on horse-back, black-looking, no doubt, with the paling sky behind him, suddenly appears on the road. Enough for a recoil and a moment's scare. Not much more.

But the stranger carries no evident weapon; he is leading a pack-horse and seems to be riding alone. You must have seen riders before this, and unfamiliar ones. The stranger halts his horse and sits there, dark against the dawn. He is not menacing. He smiles. He raises his open hands and speaks in a quiet voice.

So you know that he will kill you and you run in desperation? Kinkaid shook his head.

The woman's bag—actually, he saw now, a big kerchief with the four corners knotted—had fallen open on the road and he slowly dismounted and went over to kneel by it. There was a half loaf of bread wrapped in a still-damp cloth, a piece of yellow cheese, an empty leather bottle, a bit of broken mirror, a small knife and a spoon, a tin cup, four chestnuts and a comb. He put them back into the kerchief, retied the knot and left the small bundle on the road.

Meditating, Kinkaid turned his horses' heads in the direction of the old settlement and let them walk at their own step. The woman and boy had been coming from some home place toward the ruins ahead. They carried food, blankets and clothes because they were going some distance. They had eyes out for danger, as if something had scared them badly. What? Kinkaid remembered that their panic had come when the horse had snorted and moved.

Thus, it seemed to point. His own lookout must be for another rider, a threatening presence. He touched the hilt of his throwing knife and unbuckled the strap that secured his rifle.

Passing a road border of heavy growth and coming into the open again, Kinkaid looked on a sight he could scarcely believe. About twenty paces back from the road was the half-fallen line of a woven metal fence. Behind it was a strange mountain, a monstrous heap of particolored shapes piled higher than the tallest house and stretching a hundred paces away. For an instant, it looked like a mound of gigantic rotting fish, but when he looked more narrowly, it was like nothing he'd ever seen or imagined.

As nearly as he could make out, it was a jumble of metal hulls of different strange shapes, some with patches of color showing or a few gleams of silvery strips, but most of them orange with rust. Their original forms were hard to discern because every one he could see appeared to have been smashed or partly crushed by some great force.

Kinkaid gaped. And studied. Here and there in the pile was the gleam of a glass plate—a window of sorts, it seemed, inset in the body of the hull. And the others showed empty window openings. He could see that the hulls had a kind of hollow rump and one close by had its rump lid sprung open. All this time, Kinkaid had been struggling with an old recollection and a disbelief. It was not possible. But there were the wheels—thousands of wheels.

He got slowly off the horse and cautiously went up to the fenceline. The picture in the old book—he struggled to bring it back. The dubious fireside legend of the forefather wagon that rolled itself along the ground by hidden force of its own, the thing some of the storytellers named a car. The old lies were real and here he'd discovered the last gathering ground of the ancient mechanical beasts? Kinkaid almost expected one of them to give a lurch. Then he smiled at himself. Wheels turned with wind or water or muscle, no other way.

He tried to peer inside some of the car shells and he could discern the outlines of interior wheels fixed on posts and something that might be a kind of bench, but rust, wreckage, dirt and the leaves of creeping vines obscured the hollow places.

Kinkaid searched along the edge of the great mound, hoping to find one of the hulls that was whole. He had a thought of hitching the horses to it, dragging it out to the roadway, giving it a push—He laughed. Then, someday, he'd be one of the old men telling stories around a fire at River Cross Place while the children listened with wide eyes and the older ones smiled and shook their heads. He wondered what he would say at the end of the story. A child would ask him how it was, if these big iron animals could move quickly by their own power, how it was that anything could catch them all and smash them and pile them in one place. That answer would take some mighty lying.

Finally, he mounted again and rode on amid new oddities. The way to the settlement was lined thickly with dilapidated buildings of various shapes and sizes. Blocklike ones; ones with wide, empty oblongs; some skeletons rising from heaps of broken glass; long, many-windowed ones, most with some outlines of lettering still clinging to their fronts: 'Ford,' 'Burger,' 'Wash-o-Mat,' 'Motel'—words unknown to Kinkaid.

He paced along a wall made of the brown, rectangular stones used so much by the forefathers. It contained a sort of big yard, at the end of which rose a tall projection something like a gigantic door. He tried to imagine its use. A battered, discolored signboard read simply: 'Starlite Drive-In,' and told him nothing.

To his right now was a low building with great, glassless windows. It was in the center of its own area of cracked paving and it once had had a kind of protective shelter stretching from its roof, though this was largely demolished. Along its front stood a row of large metal posts, chipped and weathered, from which a few tubular things dangled. A broken sign bore the letters XACO. Everywhere along the way were fallen poles, canted uprights and parts of framework that, Kinkaid judged, must have displayed other signboards.

Though he could make sense of little, everything here spoke to him of a confusion of life, an enormous noise of activity, crowds coming and going—doubtless riding the very cars he'd seen. The ancients, from every evidence he knew, looked outwardly like humans, but there was something grotesque and alien about how they had lived—that was the sense that lingered here.

Now he was approaching another wonder—a big open space of humped and potholed black paving stuff enclosed on three sides by an enormous, flat-roofed bracket of building. There were the usual window oblongs, a few with spears of glass still showing, spaced down the front and more signboards. 'Supermart,' he spelled out, and shook his head. Something defaced and then: 'Drugs,' 'Turntable,' 'Sporting Goods,' 'Milady Salon.' As he came closer, he knew for certain that these places had been emptied of all they contained long ago.

Still, he was curious enough to walk the horses across the yard and then follow along the building front, staring into one great, destroyed room after another until he began to tire of it. Suddenly, he reined.

Over his sound, the slow clopping of hoofs on the black surface, he'd caught another sound. It came again, from the far end of the building to his right—a rooster's crow. He listened for a few moments, but everything was silent again.

He found a doorway large enough and took his horses into one of the room-compartments where they'd be out of sight for the moment. Then, taking his rifle, he moved cautiously toward the right-hand wing of the building. In many places, he'd come across the wild horses, dogs, pigs, cats, even sheep, that must be the descendants of forefather domestic animals, but no chickens—they were too easy prey. A rooster sound meant a pen and a pen meant people.

He came at last to the far end and there he found something different. Some of the big, glassless windows had been covered with boards, fixed from the inside, and the doorways were closed by doors. Some letters clinging above one doorway read: 'Craftsman rdware.' He put his hand on the door and pushed, but it held fast. The rooster crow came again, louder now. It seemed to sound from the other side of the building.

When he had rounded the end, he came upon a yard with some chickens and the vocal rooster enclosed behind a low wire fence. There was a line with some washing—breeches, children's clothes and a few dresses—a pile of split firewood, a hoe with a broken handle, a bench in the shade with a bowl of berries on it. Next to the bench was an open door.

'Hello!' Kinkaid called. 'A friend here!' The rooster and the chickens answered, but there was no other reply. He waited a moment and then went to the doorway. Inside was a big room divided off into smaller sections by makeshift walls of boards and blankets. He saw several tables and some chairs of strange shapes. There was a squat iron thing with a pipe that led out through a hole in the wall, many shelves with vegetables piled on them and a large cupboard with doors ajar. At the opposite end he could see the boarded-over windows. He called again and again got no answer.

Being careful not to touch or disturb, Kinkaid walked around in the silence, trying to make sense of this. The screened-off parts all seemed to be bedrooms—some with wooden beds and some with nothing more than straw mattresses on the floor. The big table in the center of the room was made of a hard, shiny red stuff of a kind he'd never seen before and on it were dishes of the same kind of material. The dishes still had some food in them and there was a jug full of water. A doll—two sticks of wood, a piece of cloth and a painted knob—lay on the floor. Clothes were strewn here and there. Near one of the chairs, a little bag of buttons had been spilled on the floor.

As he turned away from one of the bedroom places, Kinkaid suddenly became aware of a distant buzzing of flies and, almost at once, a faint odor of spoiling flesh. A larder, he assumed, and turned to leave, but then a feeling made him turn back. He was at an anxious pitch to know why a woman would abandon her washing on the line, a family leave its meal uneaten, a child desert her doll. What had come so quickly into the midst of common life? Skirting the partitions, he began to walk silently toward the far interior wall and the fly noise.

The room was big and it was shadowy here. He had to make his way around various obstacles—a tall chest of drawers, a ceiling-suspended pole with clothes on it, a huge, agespotted mirror in which he caught a moment of himself as a gray ghost. The buzz grew louder; finally, he came to an open place and stepped cautiously out.

About five paces away, there was a doorway in the wall, and against the partly opened door, across the threshold, amid a whirl of flies, lay the putrefying body of a man.

He'd been wearing breeches, but he'd had no time to put on a shirt or boots. His feet, his torso and his outflung arms looked swollen and purplish in the minor light and his head was half black, half yellow hair. Kinkaid had seen dead men, ones worse off, but the chilling thing was always the thought of the moment before and so his own moment before, still waiting undisclosed. In bed, on a summer trail, in the winter woods? He was fixed for a moment, the man and himself merging.

Then he suddenly was struck with a curiosity to see what the man was trying to reach in the farther room. There seemed to be no other exit except for a small window high in the bare wall. Kinkaid held his breath and commanded himself to step through the fly cloud and over the body.

It was true—there was no escape way. The room was almost square and the walls were of the same grainy stone blocks as the rest of the building. Along them were broad shelves, but they gave no meaning to the tale. They were piled with all manner of bolts and bits of salvage—pieces of ironwork, broken tools, ragged cloth, a wheel, a basin, a lidless box and much else. In his last moment, the man was not hiding because here there was no place to hide. Nor was he trying to escape. Nor was he trying to protect someone or something, Kinkaid reasoned. But just the sprawl of the body—a man caught running—told a desperate purpose. Some other moment was trying to reach Kinkaid's mind.

He stood in the middle of the room and shut his eyes, but no scene realized itself behind the eyelids. He tried to drain his mind into darkness, to hear the sound of running feet, the door flung open—and the direction, the object of those sounds, as if the impulse persisted even after the man fell dead. Nothing.

And then, when he was just ready to give up, there was a graying and a form. Long, lateral lines along a wall, somehow suggested by the shelves here, but other shelves in another room, into which broad sunlight came from high up. And someone half seen was moving with no distinct steps toward one tier of laden shelves, reaching out silently, one hand catching something within the shelves. And the shelves began to swing outward.

Kinkaid opened his eyes. For one flash, the dead man's hand seemed to be superimposed, transparently, at an upright in the shelving, and then it was gone.

In a half daze, Kinkaid walked, reached out his hand, touched, pulled on a concealed bit of rope and saw the section of shelves coming slowly toward his eyes.

It was several moments before he could make himself lean and peer into the hidden hollow in the wall to find what he knew he would find.

The two rifles looked shiny and almost new. But they were of a strange pattern, clearly forefather rifles of a kind unknown. He took one in his hands and was surprised to find it very light. There was a straight-ended metal stock, an elaborate bolt mechanism that lay open and, beneath that, a grip like that of a handgun he'd once seen. In front of the grip was a trigger guard and trigger and, next, a hollow metal case that was socketed up into the body of the rifle. The barrel was three-quarters enclosed by a blackish tube and a strap was slung from the barrel to the grip. He looked closely at some lettering imprinted on the side: 'Auto,' 'semi,' 'safe.' On the grip was a small circle and incised within it the strange letters 'AR 18. Armalite.'

He put it back and took the other rifle. It was the same, except that the bolt opening was closed and the whole felt a little heavier. He stood motionless with the rifle in his hands. A queer, cold sense of power seemed to come out of it into his hands. It was not the familiar worn, wood-and-steel friend but a sharp-cut, coiled, alien thing that seemed almost to pulse against his fingers. He tried to imagine that man two moments ahead of reality, seizing it, turning it on whatever was coming at him through the doorway. But for that ending Kinkaid had no picture.

Beneath the rifles were two open wooden boxes filled with bullets and a few of the casings in which the bullets apparently fitted. He took everything out of the niche and pushed the shelves back into place.

Then he found a worn rug, wrapped it around the body and dragged the bundle outside, where he buried it in a shallow hole.

Coming back for the rifles and boxes, he paused a few moments to look at the collection of oddments on the shelves. All seemed to be remnants or objects collected from the forefather building with no special thought of usefulness. Pliable, transparent stuff, like glass but not glass. Metal shapes that had no meaning. He did pick up one metal bottle with a cap that would be handy to carry water, and a worn pair of gloves. Then, at the place where the shelves made a corner, something caught his attention and he halted. There was a coil of thin but stout-looking rope and beneath it a large square of some kind of thick paper. He drew it out and saw that it was actually two pieces of stiff paper that made a kind of pocket. Inside the pocket was a thin, round black plate with a small hole in the center. He ran his fingers across the surface and felt tiny ridges. The purpose seemed impossible to guess.

Then he looked at the square of papers, still a bit shiny beneath a coat of grime, and saw the words 'Louis Armstrong Plays.' But it was the picture that froze him.

The life-size face of a chunky man, but the wonder about the face was its color. The skin was burned black. Kinkaid, dazed, sat down on the floor and held the picture in his lap. It was the dark dream pursuer or pursued, the one who beckoned to him so often in the dark, the figure that had appeared—or his imagination had made to appear—flattened against the wall in the destroyed blockhouse. It came not only from dreams but from the legends of his childhood, when the lame man, tale teller, by the fireplace had spun the long-told fancy about how two brother peoples in the beginning of time were forefather men. How the white ones said it was against nature to be black and the black ones said the same about the white and how this had been the beginning of the war that lasted fifty summers and winters and had ruined everything on the earth. And how, finally, the last of the black kind had been killed and buried and the white ones left went to sleep and then, waking up the next morning, had forgotten all that they had ever known, and so had wandered off into the forest to starve.

But the black face in the picture did not look like that of an enemy. It looked gentle, humorous, a little weary. It did not match the story. Still, there was one thing true—such dark men had lived.

And one still lived in Kinkaid's sleep journeys—although he had no idea whether this was his face or not. If he were real, as the picture seemed to suggest, there might be a clue about the reality of the dream place. Kinkaid turned the square over and found a block of neat white letters printed on the black surface. But, when he tried to read, too many of the words bewildered him: 'Dixieland,' 'jazz cornet,' 'Hot Fives,' 'trumpet.' He looked for names that might be those of places and he found a few. 'New Orleans' and 'New York'—new settlements in the long ago time and named from older ones, he thought. There was another word, one that he remembered from his map: 'Chicago.' He unfolded his map and found the settlement at the foot of the big lake, around the curve from Haven. With excitement, he turned back to the white printing. But the words around it made the name obscure. 'When Louie came to the Lincoln Gardens in Chicago in 1922, he simply blew everybody out of the city.' Kinkaid re-read that several times and still no sense came out of it. But he kept the name in his mind.

At last, Kinkaid got up gingerly. Searching further, he found two stout bags in which he could stow his finds and some wrappings to protect the rifles. Now he was anxious to be away.

Before he brought his horses round, he went into the yard in the back of the quarters and, with the chickens clucking threats at him, scanned the ground carefully.

When he finally straightened up, he knew the course of the story. During or just after a rain many days ago, about ten horsemen had come out of the treeline about a half mile to the south. They had ridden their horses fast through the cornfield and had surprised this little settlement—probably just as it was at morning meal. They had killed the one man; why, Kinkaid did not know. The others they had formed in a line and had forced to walk off in the direction of the woods. There were several children and perhaps as many as twenty men and women, three cows and an unshod horse. If the later rains hadn't washed out most of the traces, he would have known even more.

Kinkaid sat on his roan and considered his choices. Over there, to his right, was the main roadway into the large settlement ruins. To his left, leading south and west, was the track of the horsemen among the broken cornstalks. The right choice was the roadway, more or less safe and aiming him, eventually, to the place called Haven, the wise choice.

He hesitated one moment longer, then he turned his horses in the direction of the cornfield.

16

The morning after they had come into the stockade, Glyn made a tour around the inside walls, looking for some chink or an upright that might have come loose; exactly what she wasn't sure. But the line of tree trunks seemed solid everywhere and, too, the idea of getting away now seemed hard to form in her imagination. It took her as far as finding some improbable gap but never took her through. She didn't know why.

She kept turning away from the wall to look at the people, entranced with them. It was as if a world full of people—more than she could have dreamed—had been made in one day. That was the strangest part of the new and so all the old was mistaken. As far back as memory went, Haven Place and the little marshside settlements had been all the human world that was. She felt dizzy with news.

The morning was in bright bloom and the day's heat was only a promise yet. The big enclosure was a hundred pictures. Over there, three women were giving some children a bath. One woman knelt by a wooden bucket with a cloth in her hand. An older woman, sleeves rolled up and a blue kerchief bound across her forehead, was taking each naked child in turn and bringing it forward to the bucket to be washed. One little boy, as soon as the cloth had gone over him, ran away, rolled in the dust and came back to stand grinning at the end of the line.

Off a way, four half-grown boys were teasing a blacksnake, each trying to catch it with a piece of shingle and to flip it at another. Some men were carrying a big basket full of split wood and distributing a few sticks to each shelter. Four or five older men squatted together and passed from hand to hand a little stick with a knob on it from which smoke came in a trickle. Each solemnly put the twig end in his mouth for a moment and then passed the thing on to another. Three young men were throwing a ball around a triangle. But there were more pictures than Glyn could take in.

Their faces were all somehow different from the faces she knew. The River Place people had faces with no thoughts in them, only animal suspicion or bewilderment. Her own people had a habit of straight faces and a blunt sameness. In these new ones she saw live messages she couldn't read.

She went up close and stood by the woman bathing the children, but no one paid attention to her. Finally, she spoke her own name. Then she didn't know how to go on, but after a pause, she said quickly, 'Will you talk to me?'

The woman looked up, squinting, and her narrow face was suddenly shuttered. From behind the cracks, she measured Glyn, muttered something and went back to swabbing the child with the gray water from the bucket.

She tried with other women, in other groups, three times more. She spoke to some playing children; they looked at her indifferently a moment and went back to their hopping game. Behind her, the kneeling woman at the bucket said something in words Glyn couldn't understand, but she was sure that they were about her.

She walked across the hard-worn, uneven ground and saw two young women who seemed to be bargaining over a leather bottle and a piece of cloth. The one in the ragged blue dress seemed to be using a kind of sign language and the one in the homespun long shirt kept shaking her head.

When Glyn looked up, she saw that she had come almost to the far corner of the field, where there was one small shelter roof apart from the others. Under it, there was a woman sitting all alone and sewing on a child's shirt. Something about that gave Glyn a little hope.

She looked like two fat saddlebags propped there, with a round, close-cut head on top and two plump legs with deerskin shoes crossed at the bottom.

Glyn tried timidly. 'It's a long time since I saw anybody sew. May I watch you?'

The woman raised her face and gave a little-girl smile, a quarter moon of upper teeth showing. 'Sure. Ain't much needlen thread around here. I had mine on me when they come.' She went back to her work.

Glyn squatted in front of her. 'I wanted to find some to mend my sandal strap.'

The needle moved quickly in and out. 'They drug you a long ways?'

'All the way from Haven Place.' She asked hopefully, 'Do you know where Haven Place is? I'm Glyn Havensdotter.'

'Bet Waltsdotter here.' She bit off the thread, tied a knot and

136

reached out for the sandal. 'No idee. A far ways? They kill any of yours?'

'Not any I saw.' Glyn, with a hundred questions hanging, paused and held back. She mustn't lose this woman, the only friendly creature in this unnatural place. Finally, she tried: 'How did you—I mean, what happened in your settlement?'

'Now, *that's* a story.' The woman suddenly snorted and wagged her head from side to side. Glyn watched her carefully and decided that it might be a kind of laugh. Bet sewed on for a while.

'Welsir, them buggers came treaden their horses acrost the ford at first light, mean and about to swoop. And was we ready forem even if sheriff chickenhead well knew how they'd been round the country at sowing time year last? Welsir, did he build a log wall? And three rifles ain't so many, so did he go out to trade for some more? Nope, not called for, he said. What he did figger was to put Ham up top of the stable at night to watch the trail acrost the ford.' She stopped and gave the strange laugh-snort again. 'Ham! Anyways, when Ham sees a sight of strangers, he's to shoot his gun and us are to run out and hide in the woods. Like mice in a tubful of cats.'

Glyn remembered the horsemen scouring the swamp, but she thought better of breaking into the story. 'Then what?'

Bet dropped the mending into her lap and leaned forward, gazing directly at Glyn. She went on slowly: 'Welsir, Ham, he heard splashes and I guess he stopped dreamen and sat up. *Thought I heard somethin noisy in the crick. Can't be. Look over there and think I see about fifty dark men on fifty dark horses bustin right on toward the settlement.* Welsir, when Ham saw what he saw, he got so exercised that he fell right off the roof into the stableyard.' She clucked her tongue twice and paused.

'Oh!' said Glyn.

'Now, sheriff bughead had a big, mangy watchdog name of Tooth, equal as smart as Ham. So when Tooth saw Ham plump down like a shot duck, first thing he did was to run over and bite him. Ham yelled like to call the hogs, rolled over, upped with the rifle and blew a hole in Tooth.' She gave her snort again. 'Them two's what sheriff called our eyes and ears.

'So just when every soul come boilin out into the road, the horsemen come trottin in and there's all of Ripple Ford neat surrounded in three shakes. Except me and my kids.'

'You ran to the woods?' Glyn remembered running in the dunes.

'Nope. Long before, I'd dug a little root cellar under a brush heap out behind the shithouse'—she pinched her nose between thumb and forefinger—'so's the smell would amaze their dogs when they come

137

lookin.' She sighed. 'They found us anyways and we was all drug off with our horsen cattle, three days march. Been here since.'

All this she told with such wags of the head and such plump middle shakings, in such an undismayed voice, that Glyn began to feel a little more assurance.

'Who are they? Where do they come from? What do they want with us?'

'Now, dearie, don't fret. Them one-eyed buggers're humankind even if they smell like horses and talk like dogs and are meanern snakes. Hear tell they're Southrons, that means from miles south of here. Wisht I knew the other answers.'

'Why do they wear that thing over one eye?'

'That's the eye that sours milk, gives calves colic and brings on warts, maybe—don't know. Could be they're born that way. What they want with us, all I ken calclate is they can't keep us here all winter, so one day they'll start walkin us south.'

'No!' Glyn said violently. 'I'm not going. I'm going to escape.'

'That's an idee, dearie. Sounds good now you say it. If you ken turn black as the killer people in the old stories, you ken get past the lookouts at night. If you got no smell on your body, well, then, their dogs can't track you. And if you ken run fastern horses, then you're halfway home. I guess I thought about the same thing once or twicet, but I got two young ones with short legs.' Glyn watched her needle stitching and noticed that it was one of the old kind, not iron but thin and silvery.

Glyn suddenly saw a cracked stone road under the hot sun stretching away to the end of her life. 'I'll die if I don't get away,' she said in despair.

'Welsir, it just might strike you that the way to do it is to hide hereabouts in a hole inside the stockade.' Bet shook her head and pointed her thumb downward. 'Then when they march us out, you'd be left free and alone. It might strike you to try that if you've never seen a dog at a badger hole.' She paused and then said softly, 'Don't cry, dearie.'

Glyn had put her hands over her face, the momentary cheer all gone.

'Don't cry. I want to, as bad as you. I want to slip out too. But quick gone, fast caught. We got to study.'

'What study?' she asked. The word had always meant learning to read in a book.

'Gettin to know their ways. Watch and learn how they figger. See what they do common day in day out.'

'But how can I know how they figure? Or know anything about

them?' It seemed to be getting more hopeless.

'Welsir, first out, there's three kinds of em. There's the lot that're horsemen. Young and raw and not too clever. Then the few that're sarjints, who tellem where to go and how to do—ones with the white three-points on their sleeves. Now, the chief one of those is the stout belly with the bird's nest on his face, name of Hurt.'

'Yes, I know that one.'

'Proud as old punch of his own self, but mean as a pregnant bear. I seen him looken in a little pond to comb his beard, like a mother with a baby. And nother time saw him smash—'

'I know,' Glyn said quickly. 'I've seen it too. He must have named himself.'

'Then there's the one they call Cunel, tall and ugly, with a beard like the ass end of a crow. He's the chief man and the rest are scared of him. Cracked in the head, my guess—if you ever seen him set by himself and stare into the fire.' She laughed. 'That's not what I call a study, but it's a beginnin.'

'I have to go,' Glyn said, 'but will you talk to me again? And thank you for the sandals.'

'You come anytime, dearie. Lay low, take heart, and don't tell a single body what we said. We got time.'

But she was wrong, as signs began to tell. That afternoon, small parties of the horsemen began to go everywhere over the field, examining feet. They made the River Place people sit down in a row and two men passed along it. Whenever they found a swollen or infected foot, one put a poultice on it and wrapped it in bandages. It was all done wordlessly, with no more than a few orders in sign language, and then the horsemen went on to another group.

That night, there were a chunk of meat, carrots and a bowlful of dried peas for each of the cooking kettles. Glyn boiled it all for soup and took the plenty as another sign. After this supper, she tried to find Bet again, but she had disappeared from her shelter place.

Campfires, like scattered candles in a dark room, pointed the little plain. A long way off, a woman's voice began to sing a mournful tune without words. It was the wind over the bare dunes in the dead of the year and, like the wind, it rose, held a few moments and then suddenly died.

Berk and Glyn sat close together, arms across each other's shoulders. He said, 'They were loading wagons today.' People moved around the fire, settling for the night.

He said, 'Glyn?' and paused. 'Glyn, I've found a burrow in the woodpile against the south wall. We could slip away in the dark and hide there. Then, if they all go tomorrow, we could wait for a while and come out.'

'They'd find us. No.'

'How do you know that?' His voice was abrupt and angry.

'I know. You have to trust me that I know.'

'I think you're just afraid.'

'Yes; afraid with reason.'

'*You've given up*,' he whispered. 'And I can't do it or they'd make you tell on me.' He sounded like a small boy who'd lost a game. He got up and went away to find a sleeping place apart from her.

At first light, the camp was in turmoil. First there were shrill whistles, and then the mounted men, controlling their horses in a line, herded everyone into a crowd near the blockhouse. There were shouts when the people moved too slowly, and the crack of a whip.

Then, suddenly, everyone could see six men with dogs on leashes scouring the empty field, the lean, long-eared animals yelping as they dug into piles of grass that had been beds or worried an abandoned rag of clothing. The dogs moved quickly, going straight to certain spots they seemed to have noted, ransacking whatever might give cover, then racing on.

Berk's breathing was like a bellows close to Glyn's ear and his fingers tightened on her hand. One of the men had unleashed his three dogs close to the woodpile on the south wall and they were already yelping and scrambling into it. Several more men ran up and began throwing aside the billets of wood.

The first full yellow of morning had come onto the ground and the silent crowd could see everything clearly. The men had made an opening and the dogs went in; then they were dragging two figures into the light.

The man was tall and thin and he wore a loose brown shirt that fell to his hips. His face was bleeding. The woman wore a ragged dress and her hair was woven in a long black braid. She got to her feet and took three running steps before they caught her.

Suddenly, they were naked and their ripped clothes were on the ground. The men took them by the arms and forced them to walk to the nearest shelter roof, and there they tied them hand and foot and stretched their arms above them to be roped to a beam. One of the horsemen took a pole and knocked the thatching from the roof so that the two bodies, brown as bark on the arms and legs, pale as milk on the backs and buttocks, hung upright in the sun. The crowd murmured and shifted uneasily.

The men whistled to their dogs and moved toward the gate. Riders came along and started herding people through onto the roadway. Behind them, Glyn could hear the creak of wagon wheels beginning to turn.

That march ended each night like death and began a new long dying with the break of day. Most of the time, Glyn was lost in a daze of heat and dust and empty motion. One foot raised itself and then the other followed; she was reduced entirely to this one mechanism. Days died into the miles behind them and she could not remember having one thought or saying one thing. Life was bright heat, then dark, then heat again.

A few times were real enough, as though her head and eyes had cleared for a little while: a grassy slope, tree branches overhead, a creeper-covered wall a little way off, she and Berk and Bet resting there, away from the others. It must have been noon, though they'd had no food and just a drink of water from a bucket passed round. Berk's head was bowed and his arms rested on his knees.

'I'm going out,' he said. 'Whether or not you go with me. I mean tonight.'

'Berk, Berk, you know the reasons why not,' Glyn said. 'They have a lesson every little while. They want somebody to try it and they want us to see him die after he's caught.'

Bet had been staring at her two children, who had fallen asleep on the grass. Now she said, '*Where* is what makes *when*. Pick your own where and you got a chance on the flip. So this here where is flatland and if you got a better horse'n they, that makes it a good when. But you ain't. Now, you told me about the try you made in that swamp by your place. You ken swim fast and far and under the water?'

Berk raised his head and looked at her. 'Yes, but the only water around here is little ponds or runs.'

'Don't signify,' Bet said. 'Now, when them buggers was after you in the swamp, did any em get into the water and swim?'

'No. They stayed on horseback. They seemed a little scared of the swamp—and if I'd been able to get to the deeper part, I'd've shook em.'

She nodded. 'On the march, I seen them washen theirselves. Dassent get in over their hips. Settlement boys I know would've been paddlen and diven in that little baby river.'

'I don't know what you're talking about,' Glyn said wearily. 'This is the driest land I've ever seen.'

'Welsir,' Bet said, 'they's a river at the end of it. Many a time a hunter or a trader has told of a giant river to the southwards. Where

141

there's enough water, that's when they can't catch you on horses or with dogs.'

'How will I do it?' Berk asked. He looked more cheerful now.

'We see where, then we'll know when, and by that time I'll figger how.'

One of the horsemen was coming up behind them with cries of 'Git! Git!' and now they had to rise and begin to walk again.

There were other moments Glyn remembered. Some of the people were digging a shallow grave by the roadside with their hands and she helped. They laid a woman in it and none of the others dared close her eyes and so, fingers trembling, Glyn did that.

Coming along the road to a little woods, they startled a herd of wild pigs and she remembered the halloo and clatter as the horsemen went after them, the cracking sounds of the rifles, and then the greasy smoke from the fires that night and the good taste of the roast meat.

She remembered carrying Bet's small daughter, Sue, on her back until she was so tired she stumbled and all the while the child slept, cheek against Glyn's shoulder.

She remembered two River Place men fighting over a piece of dried meat and one of them biting the other's arm until it bled.

One night she woke because her legs ached and she saw a small fire in a clearing. She crept toward it, thinking she might warm herself, but then she saw that the blackbeard horseman chief was sitting there alone on a log. She could see his face in the shuddering light, eyes like thin skins full of blood under the black wings and the face above the beard like ridges of bone. In his hands he was holding a large, much-creased paper and she noticed the scrawl of red and black lines on it.

This was the paper her father had at home, the one he stared at so often. In her daze, she thought that she heard herself saying coldly, 'Then Haven is dead.' In the morning, she remembered this as a bad dream.

In the end, they came to the banks of that broad river. They saw it shining in the distance and just the promise seemed to awaken them. Glyn had a hazy recollection of approaching it and then the column wound westward, following it. And then they must have arrived, finally, at another camp. Glyn had no true memory of this, but it was there when she awoke lying in a pile of dry grass with the sun high in the sky.

She saw a haphazard collection of shelters and lean-tos on the shore of a river. A great number of people were sitting or wandering among them and there were many more of the horsemen in butternut brown.

But what astonished her was the work going on at the river's edge. There men were busy building four log rafts so huge that they seemed hopeful of covering the river with a floor.

In Haven Place, boys made rafts of a few saplings bound together for swamp fishing. But the ones here were constructed of the tallest trees, and they were so long and wide that one of them might carry a whole settlement. In fact, there were big cabins in the middle of the rafts and Glyn saw a line of men crossing a plank bridge from shore, carrying kegs and sacks into the cabins. Scattered around on the wooden acres there were conical shelters made of poles with skins for covering. And there were stacks of firewood and slabs of stone where fires smoldered.

She walked down to the river and stood staring. How could they paddle these great things? Then she saw something that looked liked paddles. They were enormous shapes fixed between stout posts and sloping from the ends of the rafts into the water.

One of the butternut men had halted to rest a minute near her. 'What are those things?' she asked, pointing.

'Them's the sweeps,' he said, and spat a brown juice onto the ground.

On one of the rafts, workmen were just finishing rows of stalls and already other men were leading horses down toward the plank bridge. She guessed they would be moving soon and the thought froze her. She had never gone over water more than a few dozen paces—but more than that, going on the river seemed a final parting from all hope of return to the place she knew. What was real you could walk to and walk back from. Reality ended here.

The next morning early, after a quick handing out of food, the horsemen began to crowd the people onto the muddy shore. Then, with shouts and prods of the whip butts, they made them file across the planks and aboard the rafts. The horses were already stalled. Men stood at the sweeps. Other men stood by the ropes that tethered the rafts to trees on the shore. In all the yelling and confusion, a plan was being carried out.

The black-bearded horseman leader was standing a little apart from the crowd; he seemed to be giving orders to the men around him, who then passed those orders on. Strangely, at that moment, she remembered how he had once spoken to her in her own speech and then had spoken to the horsemen in theirs.

She felt a hand on her back; she was being pushed along to follow the woman ahead of her.

Once on the raft, she began to be aware of the slow rise and fall of the river so close beneath her feet. The other people stood in a crowd, bewildered, looking down at the great tree platform, then looking up as if wondering how to get ashore again. One woman, with a broom of gray hair and wild eyes, suddenly grew aware of the movement under her—she was walking on water. She screamed and ran blindly to the raft edge nearest shore and threw herself into the shallow water. One of the horsemen waded into the water, laughing. He seized her head and held it under the water until she had stopped thrashing. Then he picked her up easily and tossed her aboard again. She lay on the logs, gasping and vomiting muddy water.

The men ashore had loosed the ropes and now they threw them, with a long, looping throw, onto the rafts. Then they waded into the water and scrambled over the edge. Glyn saw the shore moving slowly backward. The men at the sweeps strained and shouted. There was a small shudder underfoot; the logs rubbed up and down against one another. Then the current caught the ponderous craft, like freed islands, and gradually brought them into the stream.

That afternoon was the first time of stillness and pleasure Glyn had known since Haven Place. The raft moved with a kindly undulation; the sun-shot water spread all about them; the timbered shores went through slow changes of thicket, clearing, mudbank, forest. The western breeze was soft and cool on her face. She sat with some of the children and trailed her legs over the edge, soothed by the warm fluidity.

Late in the afternoon, they passed through a series of bends in the river that brought into view shattered walls and vine-grown buildings of an ancient settlement. At one point near the shore, there was an open place with many grassy mounds and near that was a field, gone to high weeds, where some large structures of extraordinary shape lay roofless and crumbling. This was the closest she had ever come to a forefather settlement and she stared intently at everything—the fallen stonework along the water, the roadways among the broken buildings, the stone fingers that stuck into the sky.

If she half closed her eyes, perhaps she could bring it to life, with the sun shining on its windows, people and horses crowding the streets, smoke drifting up from the chimneys, a host of canoes at the landing. She tried, but it was not quite there.

The remains of the settlement gave way to more forested shoreline as the rafts drifted around a big bend and approached an island. There was a shout from the lead raft, and on each of the others, men ran to the sweeps and hauled them at an angle with the course. Slowly, the rafts answered, rounded the island and, late in the day, swung into shallows near the shore and were secured. The cooking fires for the evening meal were already started.

In the night, she dreamed that the horsemen had loosed their dogs and that she and Berk were running along an endless log stockade, trying to find an opening, but there was none. She awoke for a moment, to hear wild dogs howling somewhere in the woods near the shore.

The days that followed were as easy and sleepy as the first afternoon. Glyn stripped off her dress and washed herself in the river water, letting it cascade down from the bucket to dissolve the dirt and fatigue of weeks. Then she washed the dress as best she could and let it dry on her body. The people looked at her curiously while she was doing this and whispered among themselves, but no one imitated her.

Her sore feet began to heal. She ate well; food was now more plentiful and every day there was a thick soup with meat and vegetables in it. The sun warmed the raft timbers and they gave off the sweet smell of new-cut wood. The river swept in broad turns and soon they were drifting along a shore of unbroken forest on the southern side.

At the departure, Berk and Bet and her children had been put aboard another raft, but one evening when the rafts were moored for the night and the general confusion of cooking time was in progress, Bet had persuaded a family to change places with them and so now the three were sitting together.

'We all look alike to em,' Bet said. 'They can't tell me from you, but they do a lot of countin heads.' She paused and looked up at the sky, where a pale, smoky blue still lingered. 'Talk quiet, now. Tomorrow when we lay up along shore, that's Berk's night. You and me'll have to be patient a spell longer.'

Near dusk, the steersmen always tried to find some sheltered shoreline behind a point and they'd bring the ponderous floats to within about ten or fifteen paces from the shore for mooring.

'I been watchen,' Bet said, 'and I know what they do common every night. There's always one guard awake on each raft. He stands near them steerin oars and watches so's nobody slips off and paddles to dry ground. Then—what we can't see—there's always some of em lurken in the dark on shore. They change the watch four times evry night.' She leaned forward and cupped her hand around her mouth.

'Now picture this. It's late in the night and the watchman is standen there.' One finger pointed momentarily. 'Of a sudden, whoops! He goes ass over ears into the water. Yells, splashes. The rest of em come runnin and pull him out. They look for who done it. Meantime, Berk has slipped off on the river side, swims out, not in. Time to see what his braggin's worth.'

145

'Damn you, I can swim five miles with that current,' Berk whispered. 'You'll see.'

'Nosir, nobody'll see—that's the trick. You get downstream fast as you can ahead of the rafts, find yourself a good, flat shore to pull up on and make as many miles as you can before morning. All the while, they're pokin around the shallows here, sayen, I swear, who pulled Goggle-eye into the pond?'

'Who did?' Glyn asked sharply. The whole notion suddenly seemed preposterous to her and she had a prevision of Berk's drowned, pale face beneath the running water. 'We can't just wait for the watchman to fall over.'

'This,' Bet said, and from her sleeve she brought out a little knife and showed it momentarily. It had a short blade that had been honed to a good edge; its end was bound into the split end of a piece of wood. 'And this.' She unbuttoned the middle button of her shirt and they could glimpse, wound about her torso, a thin strong line about twice as thick as a fishing line. 'Stole it from their supplies,' she said, 'and it don't help sleepen much. Wait, dearie, I'll show you tomorrow how you'll take part in the fun.' Buttoning again, she gave them a small crack of smile and wink

'Just give me ten counts for a start,' Berk said, 'and I'm out of sight, Glyn. And then I'll bring all the men in Haven if needs be and we'll set you free. ' He said it with such boy's innocence that Glyn felt heartbroken.

All the next morning, Bet sat on the same spot with a blanket over her knees. She was about ten paces away from the end of the raft and on a direct line with the three-legged stool where the watchman always sat at night. But she faced in the opposite direction, forward.

'Sit here and talk with me low like,' she had told Glyn, and Glyn had dutifully sat. 'Now, you may have noticed that my hand is doin somethen under this blanket.' Glyn saw a small up-and-down movement. 'What it is doin is maken a good, smooth groove tween these two logs with my knife. Big enough to slide the end of the line through, with a chip of wood tied to it.' She looked around, but the few horsemen on board were either tending the sweeps or in a group at the other end of the raft, playing some sort of game on a board. Two small boys nearby were trying to fish with a length of yarn and a bent nail.

'Now, the line pays through the groove. It has a slip knot on the end of it and it slides easy like right to the end of the raft, where the chip bobs it up to the surface. I tie this end to a little peg. D'you see?'

146

Glyn said that yes, she did.

'Welsir, the uneasy part. You and me sort of wander back to them men by the sweeps and you start talken to em. Keep their eyes on you.' She smiled. 'Mebbe you could start getten ready to take another bath.'

'I don't understand,' Glyn said.

'Well, just makem talk to you, then. An next me, all thumbs, I drop my blanket right by that stool, almost into the water. So I stoop down, pick it up and perty soon we go away. Now, what happened?'

Glyn shook her head. 'What you said, I guess.'

Bet gave her cluck. 'Nosir. What happened is that I scooped that little chip out of the water when I was grabben for the blanket an then I put the slip knot round one leg of the stool, low down where nobody'll pause to look.'

'And next?'

'Tonight you and I make our beds right here. Berk is down there at the front of the raft, near to the edge. When all's asleep, we give a monstrous tug on the line. Splash! Berk hears it, slips over the edge an underwater. Some amount of runnen and yellen then, an while they're up to that, we keep tuggen till the stool pulls up under our little groove here, when we cut the line and let it go driften downstream.' She covered her mouth to stop a laugh. 'Watchman stands up all night from now on an all of em are goen to be skittish.'

A little later, just as Bet was dropping her blanket, Glyn suddenly leaned forward toward the man at the sweeps she'd been talking with and said, 'Why do you wear that thing over your eye?' She made a gesture as if to snatch it.

He knocked her hand away with his fist and said, 'Don't never do thet agin! Now git!' But he did not seem angry. A minute later, as she and Bet were going back to their place, he said something in a low voice to the other sweepsman and then Glyn could hear them laughing.

'Fast an neat,' Bet said, 'but you didn't tell me you was—'

'I just thought of it,' Glyn said. 'Now I hope that line doesn't snag on the logs somewhere.'

'I spent half a night greasen it. Now, when the time comes, we'll tie these little pegs into it fer handles. An now we wait.'

For Glyn, it seemed an endless time to sundown. At last, as the afternoon light began to darken over the river, the rafts were worked out of midstream to make their long slant to the right bank. Luck to begin with, Glyn thought, because the southern bank would have meant another day of waiting, at least. And when at last they were slowed to the mooring, the shoreline itself looked favorable. It ran straight for a considerable stretch, with a flat, muddy bank and a treeline close beyond. Downstream, there was the outthrust of a wooded point, at which Berk stared until she made him turn away.

'I can get there before they can rub their eyes,' he whispered. She knew that, in his mind, he was already crawling ashore and starting for the cover of the woods. He had the look of absence already, as if nothing here mattered, and Glyn suddenly felt abandoned.

The people were getting the evening cook fires going and there was much moving about. In the woods, the tree toads had begun their monotony and frogs sounded along the banks. Glyn had a fragile feeling, meditating that all the next turn of life depended on a few pegs, a greased line, a sudden pull and the luck of the swimmer. She tried to make herself be calm and eat the food from the little square of shingle and to say something to amuse Bet's children, who always asked her for a story at this time in the evening.

Then there was a long time just lying in patience. Berk had gone off to make his bed at the forward corner of the raft. There were low voices in the darkness and then they died away and the frogs and tree toads took over the night, with the hoot of a lone owl coming now and then. Listening to them, Glyn had dozed when Bet woke her.

She felt two pegs put into her hand. Being careful not to raise her head very much, she looked to the rear of the raft, and by the light of a cooking fire that had been left to glow, she saw the outline of the watchman sitting on the stool. She knew—because Bet had told her this—that he had a little, hooded candle lantern beside him. When the candle had burned down to its first mark, he would make a round of the raft to see that all was in order and then he would wake another man for the next watch. He seemed perfectly still and she hoped that he was half asleep.

They slowly pulled the line taut. It slid easily. Glyn braced herself with her toes wedged between logs. Bet gave three almost inaudible hisses. On the third one, they pulled.

It must have been true that the watchman was dozing, because his yell came late and was cut off at once by the water. Glyn had expected an enormous splashing sound, but what she heard was noise no louder than that of a small branch falling.

Silence for a moment, and then there were voices. Someone came out of the cabin at the center of the raft, holding a lantern in his hand. He began to walk back toward the sweeps, stumbling over sleepers and mumbling something. Then they all could hear his voice: 'Bileh, yo thar?'

When there was no answer, he said, 'Gitout the way,' and began to run, an awkward run among the people who were beginning to sit up. Glyn and Bet were hauling in the line as fast as they could, but Glyn could see the running man. Now there was a commotion of voices. The watchman had changed his course to go along the edge of the raft, which was clear of people.

Suddenly, man and lantern seemed to be lifted into the air. For an instant, she saw his astonished eyes and his open mouth before he sprawled over the side with a splash louder than the first. In the lantern's last wink before it hit the water, she saw the arms that had thrown him.

And then, everywhere on the raft, people were crawling to the shoreside and dropping into the water. The raft tilted a little under her. She heard moans and cries in the dark and the sounds of people in the water.

'Bet! They're all trying to escape,' she said.

'Hush. Now hold this line tight while I cut it.' Bet seemed to be sawing with her little knife. 'Stay right here and don't be sorry.' The line parted and Glyn let it slide through the groove. There was the sound of a rifle shot from the shore. Then there was a horseman's whoop. Men were running on the raft. Orange fires suddenly bloomed in three places along the shore.

Glyn twisted around and looked toward the front of the raft, and in the dim, reddish light, she could see that it was deserted. She turned back quickly, in fear that someone might see her staring in that direction.

Then there were several more shots, splashing as people in the water came back to the raft's edge and crawled onto it, horses' whinnying, cries from the shore.

Quickly, it seemed to her, this was over. The rest of the night, the horsemen kept the fires alight and the raft lay in a red haze. All around her, she could hear wakeful breathing, a moan now and then, the dripping of water, until sleep took her.

As she opened her eyes in the morning, Bet said, 'Look tords the river, dearie. The shore ain't pretty today.'

Glyn did not look but she said, 'Tell me. I have to know. Is Berk there?'

'Not a sign. But four bodies hangen from the trees. When the shouten started, all them buggers come down like hornets on this spot. Berk's away clean and hid up by now.'

A little later, a party of the riders came through the woods to the shore. Their horses were sweaty and winded and the men were silent. They dismounted and walked down to the river's edge to

149

stoop and drink. They had brought no one with them.

Late in the morning the rafts were cast off and began again their sluggish course out toward midstream.

The happenings of that night seemed to unloose some drawstring and the raft people began to talk as Glyn had never heard them do before. Around the cooking fires, everybody had a story of how he'd awakened, what he'd supposed, where he'd been in the water or on shore when he was caught. There was an undertone of pride. They'd seen the horsemen panic and they said that three—no, seven—no, ten—had got away. Some of the women stared at Glyn and she knew that they knew. They had seen Berk with her too often. But they said nothing.

Then there were tales about the horsemen's coming to their settlements—the usual one about the riders appearing at first light, a futile defense with a shot or two fired, the rounding up of people and cattle. One story—told in many different forms—related that a certain settlement, variously named, had been forewarned and had made a plan. Lookouts had caught sight of the horsemen making camp one evening. The next morning, when they came out of the darkness and rode into the little stockade, the gates were silently shut and barred behind them. The place was empty of people. As the horsemen began to search, the village began to blaze. 'Reckon moren a few of em was burnt up,' was the usual ending. Glyn could see in their eyes that they wanted to believe it.

One day, she sat at the edge of the raft with some women from Cornmill Place. Theirs had been one of the bigger settlements, with a mill and a barter market, and they seemed to her to know more about the world than the others.

'Has anybody ever come back again?' she asked.

'Nary.'

'Why do the horsemen take people?'

They looked at her and shook their heads.

'Where will they take us—does anybody know?'

No one spoke. Then one woman, a gaunt woman with an old scar traced down one side of her face, said, 'River end.' She sighed. 'I guess.'

There were many floating branches and sometimes whole trees on the water's surface and, at twilight, Glyn stared at them, thinking of Berk and wishing. At those times, she imagined slipping over the side, catching a log large enough to float her to shore. But once or twice, she had seen the bloated body of a wild dog in the river and another time a dead deer. She had the thought of being touched by one of these corpses and she turned away.

Some days before, they had passed the point where another stream joined theirs and now the combined river was broader and swifter. The landscape along the shores had changed, with profuse bush and stunted trees at a distance from the low, flat banks. No songs of birds sounded in the air, no pleasant scents, no moving lights and shadows from passing clouds. Hour after hour, the changeless glare of the hot, unwinking sky shone upon the same monotonous objects. Hour after hour, the river rolled along, as wearily and slowly as time itself.

At last one morning, they came to another junction of rivers, the new one flowing from the north. A ruined settlement lay rotting in a swamp, teeming with rank vegetation, at the point where the streams came together and, becoming a greater one, turned on a southern course, a slimy monster now.

It was like an enormous ditch, sometimes two or three miles wide, running liquid mud. The strong and frothy current was choked everywhere by huge logs and whole forest trees, sometimes twining themselves into great rafts through whose fissures a sedgy foam worked up to float on the water's top. Some rolled past like monstrous bodies, their tangled roots showing like matted hair, some glanced by like giant leeches, others rolled round and round in the vortex of a small whirlpool, like wounded snakes.

The marshes along the shore swarmed with frogs, and in the airless heat, mosquitoes penetrated everywhere on the rafts. There was mud and slime on everything. Only the sundowns had a kind of beauty, a fierce beauty Glyn had never seen before. With the day's decline, the sky was tinged deeply with red and gold and the dying light on the western bank seemed to make the slightest blade of grass distinctly visible, like veins in the skeleton of a leaf. As the sun slowly sank, the red and golden bars upon the water grew dimmer and dimmer until all the colors of day paled to somber night and there remained only the glow of cooking fires on the rafts and the harmless lightning that flickered now and then on the dark horizon.

In the night, the raft constantly struck against floating timber. A lookout stationed at the head of each raft kept watch for the ripples of water that were the signs of hidden snags. When he caught sight of something like this, or saw that the raft was running toward a shoal, he would ring a bell to signal the men at the sweeps and then, ponderously, the raft would change course.

Through long bends and turns, the river made its way southward, sometimes passing along ruined embankments or the vestiges of forefather towns in the distance. Once or twice they came to the great pilings and wreckage of forefather bridges that must have spanned the whole stream, and here the rafts had to be slowed by drags thrown out behind and the sweeps had to be maneuvered skillfully to steer through a free channel.

A kind of apathy had come over Glyn with all the idleness. She lost count of the days they had been on the river. Then suddenly one afternoon, as they rounded another of the interminable bends, a call drifted back from the lookout on the lead raft and was taken up by the lookout on theirs. Men jumped to the sweeps and hauled until the rafts, keeping still in line, began a long angle toward the eastern shore. She ran forward, and standing among a crowd of people there, she could make out some sort of landing place in the distance.

The call came again from the lookout, the words hanging slow and drawn-out in the humid air: 'No-o-o-o M-e-f-f-i-s-s.'

17

Six rifles would be aimed the moment he came in, from the block-house, from behind a woodpile, from the stable windows. And that left the other three to take him—no shot to be fired unless they failed.

Maybe he was no more than a wandering trader, countryman, or lone hunter, but Haven and the others were sure that he wasn't any of these. As they waited in the heat of the morning, they had a gingerly feeling, as if something from an unknown race, with uncanny powers, would come through the open gateway.

One of the hunters, out for game, had sighted him at nightfall the previous day, watering his horses at a creek and then taking them into cover on a wooded rise. He had moved silently; he had disappeared quickly; he had made no fire for cooking. A young man, tall, wearing buckskin and homespun—that was the glimpse of him.

The morning passed and the noon sun burned overhead and they were growing afraid that he'd passed them by, but Haven was sure in his heart that the horseman would come at his chosen time. Still, he was uneasy at the signs of caution. A man going to his home place would have ridden directly in last night. Haven shifted and sweated as he lay on the board floor of the lookout platform atop the blockhouse, but he lay stubborn.

It was late in the afternoon, with the shadows long on the field, when Haven wiped his eyes again with his damp kerchief and looked to verify what had appeared as a triangular brown spot wobbling in the far distance of the road. As it began to sharpen a little in the heat shimmer, the spot took on its horse-and-rider outline and Haven called hoarsely, 'He's coming!'

The men, who had some time ago left their places to lounge in the shade, picked up their rifles and went back to their ambush. The waiting seemed to have dulled them, as if all things in the heat of this long afternoon were bound to be unsurprising. Haven had listened to their somnolent voices coming from below him and had heard mention only of home, families, crops.

They had started off with him nimbly enough, as if this were no more than a bear hunt. Horsemen, they agreed, would be unhandy when they were hemmed in by the forest. They talked about getting ahead of them and setting a trap on the road. Haven could scarcely keep them to the steady hundred paces walking and then a hundred running he had designated for the march.

Haven had been fearful. He knew that these young hunters of his had no powers to imagine a man enemy, let alone a strong party of them, armed. Once or twice, an outlaw man had been captured in the woods, but that was all. No strangers had ever appeared in the few miles of woods where they hunted and even the thought of it seemed unreal. 'Off' was the word they used to speak about any possible place beyond those limits, and when, as it sometimes happened, a man or boy ran away from the settlements, he had 'gone off'. It also meant to die.

The first days, they'd made good progress, but then there was change of luck and spirit. They'd found the body of a child by the roadside, wrapped in a ragged cloth and half covered with dry flowers and grasses. As they were burying it, Haven saw several of the men look anxiously back in the direction of Haven Place and he knew that they were thinking of their own children, though they said nothing. There was less quickness in the pace that afternoon.

On the fourth day, toward nightfall, a heavy rain had come and next morning they had found that the trail was no longer so plain. The downpour had washed out any signs on the road and had erased any hoofprints near its edges. When they came to another forefather road that joined or crossed, they had to explore for signs in either direction.

When they had got to the open country, still going south, Haven was a wild figure in the sun. His pack on his back, his clothes stripped down to a rag around his loins, a sweat cloth knotted around his head and a stick in his hand, he moved far ahead of them. Through the heat waves, they saw him always diminishing in the distance.

When, at last, they'd come to the stockade, Haven was waiting for them. He'd already buried the two sun-blackened bodies he'd discovered strung up to a beam in the open place. It was later on that day when they'd heard of the horseman.

Now Haven strained to watch him approach, an incalculable silhouette against the sun-blank distance, enlarging very slowly. In a few moments, he would be at the place where the road ran through the treeline for about twenty paces, and passing through that, into the sun once more and near enough to see clearly.

154

Haven wiped the sweat from his eyes again, blinked and looked up. In that instant, the rider's shape had merged with the ragged shadows of the leaves and Haven had lost him. He waited, fixing his eyes on the place where the horseman must emerge before long and listening. Then he began to count, thinking that a slow twenty counts would be about right.

At thirty counts, the road in front of the gateway was still empty. Haven squinted and tried to search among the trees for a clue, but the man and the horses had vanished. He must be there, perhaps lying in the undergrowth and examining the stockade with its open gate. That wariness disturbed Haven. The man must have expected to see a sentry, some activity, and by their absence, he'd been cautioned. Then, among the green confusion, Haven caught the gleam of sun on a roan horse's flank and a movement as the horse raised its head.

Nothing more happened for a time and then, not far from the horse, Haven saw a little gray smoke, rising above the treetops and dusty in the sky.

He hitched around and crawled to the back of the platform. He cupped his hands and said in a low voice, 'Piet, he's stopping in the woods. Hitched the horses and has a fire going.'

Piet stepped out from behind the gate, shaking his head. 'Shall we slip into the woods then and circle him?'

Now all the men came a little way out of their hiding places, looking up at Haven for the next order.

'Or better wait for dark,' Kamp said.

'He may be gone by then,' one of the hunters said.

Haven felt drugged by the heat and thoughts seemed to come very slowly. The man had sensed or seen them and now he was trying to draw them out? Were there other horsemen coming along the road behind him? Or already waiting in the woods? Haven closed his eyes and tried to sift the chances.

Suddenly, he heard a scraping sound and then a slight thump on the platform behind him. He twisted around. There, crouched, facing him, was the man. He was dressed in buckskin and homespun; his dusty black hair was tied, settlement fashion, in a queue behind his neck. His face showed no expression; in his right hand he held a stout throwing knife. 'Who are you?' Haven asked calmly. If he could waste a few moments. Piet might see and have time for a shot.

The knife hand rose a few inches. 'Tell them to throw their rifles in the open space and then stand back by the wall.' It was the voice of a man who ordered things and had them done. 'And then we'll go down the ladder, you first.'

155

Haven called to Piet and told him to have the men throw their rifles out.

'Haven!' Piet shouted from below. 'Haven, what's going on?'

The stranger dropped his right hand and shook his head. 'Haven?' he asked in a puzzled way. 'Haven . . . but this isn't the place. It's far north on the map.'

'I am Van Haven and my settlement is Haven. It is north on the map. But how can you know what is written on my map?' For the first time, Haven had a good look at the man's strange gray eyes and he had a hint of the answer.

'I've come a long way to find you, not to kill you,' the stranger said. He put the knife into a sheath at the top of his boot. 'I'm called Kinkaid.' He held out his hand and helped Haven to his feet.

A great deal had been told and they were getting used to some of the wonders of it. They had built a fire near the blockhouse and had fed on roast pig and cakes made from some cornmeal Piet had found in a bag in a woodpile. Now, Haven was pacing up and down and Kinkaid was sitting cross-legged on the opposite side of the fire, watching him.

'Unhandy of you, Kinkaid, to be a friend! I longed for an enemy I could stretch on a rope in the sun until he answered the whole riddle. Especially the how and whereto of their going away. Why I'll leave for later.' He stopped to kick some embers back into the fire and then stomped ahead. Kinkaid found it hard to think of this fierce, disorderly old man as a sheriff. Still, there was a power about everything he did and said.

'Your Haven Place,' Kinkaid said, 'is it cliffy, with narrow roads among tall peaks?'

'Hah!' said Haven. 'It's flat marshside. Log houses, shingle houses, sand dunes, pasture, a cornfield.' Then he paused and came walking back toward Kinkaid. 'But there *is* a settlement of tall towers like peaks in the sky. I've been there for salvage. Do you know of it? Have you been there?'

'No. A tale that I heard. What was it called?'

'On the map, Chicago.'

Haven ran his fingers through his tousled hair and turned away. 'Of that, later. Now we should plan. You've come from the east and we from the north—and in both places they've come and gone. So, it's south or west for them, and I think south. We'll look for tracks tomorrow. They're slow on the road with their gaggle, and we can rest one day and catch them in three. I wish I knew how many days to their settlement.' He halted and stood staring into the fire.

156

'These Haven men of mine are good hunters—but a shooting match with fifty horsemen? With six slow-loading, smithy rifles true for about a hundred paces? Kinkaid, it's a joke with a poor ending.'

'Yes,' Kinkaid said. 'Forget the blood spilling. That's only for desperation. Now, what's the first aim in your mind?' Kinkaid was beginning to enjoy this. He liked to apply his thoughts to a hurt or a danger—as he applied splints, a poultice, a herbal emetic. 'The one thing we can't go back without doing?'

Haven poked at the burning logs with a stick. 'To bring my daughter back, of course. Then, somehow to wring those horsemen so they'll let free the other folk.'

'Those are different things. The first means patience, trailing, lying low, watching—then a quick move of the hand to snatch her away before they know. The second means surprise, blood spilled and, as you say, a poor shooting match for us.'

Haven stretched, threw back his shoulders, then began to pace again. 'That shooting match will have to come someday soon. I won't run away from it.' He camp up to where Kinkaid sat. 'But you're right—a time when we're stronger and can choose the place for it. Even saving Glyn is risky enough.' He paused and looked into Kinkaid's face. 'A moment ago, you said "we" and "us"? I hope that's not a slip.'

'No,' said Kinkaid. 'I came looking for a place called Haven; now I find that it's less a place that it is a man. I'll follow the man awhile, until my road branches off. Can you show me the way to this Chicago place?'

'In the spring, I'll take you there in my double canoe.'

'Good. Now, in the meantime, I have a makeweight to add to your six rifles.' Kinkaid raised his arm and pointed toward the stables where his horses were. 'You see, I chanced on two forefather rifles in good repair. They're a strange pattern and ugly as rattlers, but they can weigh on our side. That is, if one of you understands more gunsmithy than I do.'

'Piet and I made the first Haven Place rifle out of salvage and proved the old tale of mixing saltpeter, sulfur and charcoal. He'll study them and find out their workings.'

Haven picked up his blanket and slipped his head through an opening cut in the center. Because he slept little, he had taken the first night watch. Staring fiercely through the firesmoke, he said in a low voice, 'Kinkaid, I still don't know if I believe you exist. You say when you were a boy you saw my old friend Cutters-son die and you took his map and because of that map years later you've come ten hundred miles to find me. And now you're going with us on the

157

most crackbrained hardship hunting a man could find. But I have to think you exist because you believe I exist.'

Kinkaid laughed. 'Let's say I dreamed you and you dreamed me.' He lay back and settled his head on his saddle. 'But there's a purpose in it, I think, after this hunting is over. We have a great deal to do to make a world.'

'Make a world? Your words have an odd fit to each other. "World" I've seen in the books and I thought it meant—Never mind what I thought it meant. If I take your meaning, it's the same as mine.'

Coming back from their separate surveys, Kinkaid and Haven found two neighbor stumps on the riverbank and sat down on them.

'All this cutting but no sign of a palisade. Yet here's where they came with all their great drove.'

'No,' said Kinkaid. 'Rafts. Great floors of logs with all the folk on them floating downstream.'

Haven hawked. 'Rafts? You've seen them?' He spat. 'This must be the biggest river of all. It must flow into a spread of water somewhere as big as mine at home. Would you try to ride it on a bundle of logs?'

'I haven't seen them, but I can see them,' Kinkiad said. 'I see the woods, yonder, where they were timbered, the creek that brought the logs to the shore, the posts in the water where they were roped together and made rafts. All shows they knew what they were about. These men have rafted before. Well, Haven, do we make our own and follow?'

Haven slapped a mosquito on his cheek. 'I wish I had my double canoe. It takes time to build another and there aren't tools.'

Piet was coming down the slope toward them, in the cradle of his arm one of the forefather rifles Kinkaid had found in the storeroom. The other men came along behind him at a wary distance. 'I've never seen a puzzle that fit smoother,' he said fondly, looking at the rifle. 'The shrewdest work of a man's hand you could ever dream.'

'You've solved its mechanics, then?' Haven asked.

'I've even stripped it partway and put it together again.' He raised it to his shoulder. 'And had a shoot with it.'

The men following stepped back a few paces. 'Fearful thing,' Haven said. 'Care with it, Piet.'

Piet turned toward the river. 'D'you see that lone post in the water, out a dozen paces?' He squinted along the barrel toward the post. There was a sudden, explosive rattle. The top of the post was a cloud of dust and flying splinters, while shining bits spewed from the side of the rifle and fell to the ground.

Haven shook his head to get his hearing back and held out his hand for the rifle.

'That would cut a deer into shreds,' one of the men said disgustedly.

Haven destroyed another post, a little farther out from the bank. The whole shore rang with the shots and they could see birds everywhere springing from the trees into the air. Haven handed the rifle back to Piet. 'It rides up some after the first shot. You have to hold it down,' he said.

Then he turned to Kinkaid. 'I know you know the lesson of that. I think you must have guessed something of it long before now.' Kinkaid nodded. 'And I thank you that you didn't walk into the stockade against us with the thing cocked.'

'Ten to fifty,' Kinkaid said. 'The odds have just gone down to fifty-fifty.'

'But a hundred to one against if we trust our bones to any raft.' Haven looked around the littered shore. 'I see some axes with broken hafts and a rusty saw somebody left behind and plenty of rough-hewn planking they used for walkways. There must be some old buildings nearby with iron in them for nails. Pitch in the pines back yonder if we can't find some tar.' He was drawing in the dirt at his feet with a twig. 'Piet, come here and look at this plan.'

It took the better part of six days, but at the end, the boat rode in the shallows, tied to the old mooring posts. It was about thirty paces in length and wide enough to carry stalls for the horses and a plank lean-to shelter. The rudder was hewn from a single log and the tiller post had a space for three men to heave against it in a strong current. It was a long box with plank sides hip high and a canted, shovel-shaped bow where riflemen could lie and aim downstream. In the middle of the craft was a stubby mast and yard and on it a sail that disgusted Piet. He'd done his best to sew it together from blankets and sacking cloth, all the while groaning at it and saying that the first baby wind would tear it to rags. But, the first days out, they found that the current was strong, the wind was from the west and the boat answered the rudder well. In the late afternoon, they would come alongshore and hunt a little. At night, they built a great fire on the flats and did their cooking. The men played like small boys, rigged fishlines, made bets on everything. The endless miles of shore unrolled like a sunny new world for them.

Haven, too, watched the miles. He sat near the tiller and said very little. Kinkaid knew that, in his mind, he was counting miles backward. In Haven's mind it was snowing and the long road home lay ahead.

18

In front of the gate there was a ditch about five paces deep and five paces wide, and on the far side of it was a sloping earthwork. Both the ditch and the slope were so covered with knee-high grass that they had an absent-minded look, as if the original diggers had been unconvinced by their efforts and had never been quite sure whether they were closing themselves in or walling something out. Across the ditch lay a plank drawbridge that creaked and complained as man or beast crossed it. It seemed never to have been raised, because its draw ropes were slack and rotten.

The gateway had been built with a somewhat more formidable thought in mind. It was, in fact, a passage through a big, squared-log, pointed-roof blockhouse that straddled the road. The heavy wooden shutters of one of the upper windows were open and a guard leaned out, joking with some men below. He had white soap on his face and in his hand he was holding a razor. Though the words couldn't be heard clearly, he seemed to be saying that he was too busy—they should go away. The three men waited with their horses and mules—evidently laden with barter goods—for the gate to be opened, yelling back at the man in the window. One of them called good-naturedly, '. . . en comen up theh an taken yo razor an shaven off yo balls!' Just then, another man began to open the gate from the inside and the traders, with their animals, passed through. Glyn noticed everything with enormous curiosity.

On either side of her, between the earthwork and the woods, stretched broad acres of cleared land where people, scattered here and there in the distance, were working among neat rows of plants—not corn, as she'd expected, but a low, bushy kind of thing. She tried to make a guess as to how long it would take to cross the earth wall and the ditch and run to the woods.

The horseman at the head of their column raised his arm and made a lazy forward gesture and then she could hear the planks of the bridge rumble under his horse's hoofs. The line began to move.

Then she was walking across the bridge, into the shadow of the gateway passage and beyond to the sunlight again. There were two sentries, leaning on rifles, no expression on their bony faces, chewing steadily. One of them spat a stream of brown juice onto the ground. Glyn tried to see what their eyes were seeing, the succession of starved, woeful faces, matted hair, ragged clothes. But whatever they did see stirred no twitch or change in their faces.

Now they had passed through the gate and were coming into a long, straight road lined with slope-roofed, low-lying buildings. The walls were made of grainy stone blocks, and in the old time when they were built, they must have been windowless. Now they were broken with squarish holes covered by wooden shutters. Many of the old roofs had been repaired with a patchwork of wood and metal. A horseman came trotting down the length of the column, saying impatiently, 'Giton, giton!'

Though the sun was hot and the day stifling, the streets were full of people. There were two-wheeled carts drawn by mules and men with whips walking alongside; there were women, barefooted and dressed in long, dirty-white cloth gowns, coming and going with bundles. A few of the buildings had low porches attached to the front of them and other women were sitting there, talking idly and watching the walkers go by with no particular interest. Glyn was bewildered by the noise, the dust and the congress of people but she kept noting two things. First, these settlers seemed hardly different from the people at home in Haven Place—the faces were much the same, they had two eyes— and there was nothing much different about their daily work. Then, they were used to seeing lines of captured people in their streets, a common thing that raised no curiosity.

At the end of the street, the column emerged into an open square faced by two-storey buildings. Along one side was a row of carts without horses but with cloth sunshades raised on poles above them. People seemed to be bartering goods. One woman was filling a bag with shelled peas; at another cart there were green melons and a shirtless man was weighing one on a scale; beyond that, a boy was reaching into a cage of squawking chickens.

On the square's opposite side, Glyn noticed a tall T-beam of timber with a rope hanging from the forward arm. Beneath it was a low wooden platform. There were more new things than she could take in, a coming and going in the square that bewildered her. Sunburned men, wearing a kind of woolly hat even in this heat, led burdened horses and mules past the column. A boy with two goats on a lead rope pushed his way through it. There were many voices, the creak

161

of wheels, the rumble of carts.

One of the riders sat his horse and waved the column into a side road. There was another turning to the right, then past a row of stables and finally into a big, fenced enclosure in front of a building with wide doors. And here they were halted.

They sat in the sun and waited; nothing happened for some time. Finally, men came into the yard carrying two big tubs of what turned out to be a whitish kind of porridge with some lumps of meat and fat in it. They put the tubs down on a plank table where there was a pile of shingles and, alongside, a big skin full of water suspended from a tripod. Most of the people seemed too dazed to move, but Glyn went to get herself a shingle and a scoop of the food. She looked around to try to find Bet, but she had no luck.

A little later, there was some stirring over near the big doorway and Glyn saw that some horsemen had come into the yard. One of them sat on a stool behind a little table. The others dragged a wooden tank of water from inside the building. Then they began forcing the people into a line.

There was a commotion and confusion and Glyn craned to see what was happening. The horsemen had just taken a woman at the head of the line and had made her strip off her rages. She was naked now and she threw back her head and screamed toward the sky. It was a thin, hopeless sound, as if even her fright was exhausted. The two horsemen laughed. They took her by the arms and pitched her into the tank, and when her agonized face reappeared, one of them pushed her head below the surface again.

They let her get out. Then the man at the table got up and tied something around her neck. Another man handed her a long, gray-white shirtlike thing and made her put it on and nudged her through the doorway into the building with his stick. The other horsemen were already pushing the man next in line into the tank.

Glyn loosened her clothes. When it came her turn in line, she pulled them off quickly, before the horsemen could touch her, and jumped into the tank. The water had some bitter-smelling stuff in it that stung her eyes. When she climbed out, the horsemen were standing back a pace or two and staring at her. She turned to the man at the table and snatched the little thong of rawhide from his hand, saying in a low voice, 'Don't touch me!' The man had a fat, pink-splotched face and his mouth hung partly open.

Glyn looked at the thong. It was strung through two holes in a little square of wood and on the wood was burned a number.

'Forty-six,' she said. 'Is that what I'm called now?'

'Yew kin read numbas?' the man asked, squinting at her.

162

'Yes, and I can cipher too. And read.'

The man turned his head to look at the other horsemen, as if to make sure that they, too, had heard the animal talk. Glyn twisted her head to look down at the paper on the table in front of him.

'*Y-u-n-g* is wrong,' she said. 'It's *y-o-u-n-g*. And the other word should be *f-e-m-a-l-e*. And I have a name, so I don't need a number. It's Glyn Havensdotter. Write it down, if you can.' She stooped and picked up her discarded shirt and with it tried to wipe the stinging sensation from her eyes. She felt a hand on her elbow but she shook it off. She reached out and took the long, sleeveless shirt and slipped it on over her head. As she was going through the doorway, she looked back and saw the pink-splotched man making a painful attempt on his paper with his pen. She hoped that he would put the *o* in the right place. She thought that the rest was beyond his capacity.

Inside, it was half dark and slightly cooler. The building was all one open room, with pallets of straw lined along the walls. The people who had come before her squatted in little groups, talking in grunts and whispers and fingering the strange woven stuff of their new shirts. The first thing Glyn did was to throw away her number. The second thing was to find a pallet close to the door.

She watched and waited a long time for Bet to come through the doorway. But when she did, she was kicked through it by an angry horseman, who threw the shirt in after her. She sat up looking pleased, nodded at Glyn and slipped the shirt over her head.

'Figger he needed a bath bad as I did, so he got one,' she said. 'Pew! That's some kind of stink they've got in the water here.'

'Bet, why are they doing this? What will happen next?'

She came over and sat down beside Glyn. 'I don't know what they mind will happen next; it's what we do next bothers me. First thing, we keep close together. Then we learn to talk that whiny way they do. But don't talk to em. Dearie, you made a mistake tellen that one you could read an cipher; I heard you. No matter now. Wait an watch an keep still.'

Bet's children finally appeared, and soon after, the last of the people were pushed into the room. The doors were slid shut and they were left in heat and darkness.

That night, in her sleep, Glyn seemed to be carried backward. First, she felt the low rocking motion of the raft and the whisper of the water beneath it. Then she was lying on grassy ground in a clearing with Berk breathing beside her. Suddenly, she was in her bed at Haven Place, the breeze from the marsh blowing through the window, the tree toads making their buzz outside and an owl sounding like a ghost lost in the woods.

There was a creak, a widening bar of yellow, then a dazzling rectangle of sun. A man in butternut brown stepped into the room with a whistle. He shrilled it twice and then he yelled, 'Gitup, yawl! Upen out!'

The sleepers stirred and sat up. A few children were already wandering in the aisles between the pallets. Bright slivers and specks of sunlight were apparent through the cracks in the roof. Glyn sighed as the dream slipped from her mind, and she was back again.

When they had slowly made their way into the yard, they found the same tubs filled with the gray-white porridge and they sat on the ground and ate as they had the afternoon before. But this morning, there was to be no waiting afterward. The fence gates were swung back and a dozen men with long staves in their hands came into the yard. Quickly, without any lost motions, they began to form the crowd into a column of twos, as if they were much used to herding cattle. A sarjint, with a switch in his hand, stood by the gate, looking on until it was done. Then he turned on his heel and led on.

They passed through the roadways by which they had come. Here and there, a cart driver pulled his horses aside to let them go by and a few faces of children appeared at windows, but as before, the settlement was indifferent.

The square, when they came to it, had a new look. Wooden barricades, head high, had been placed across the streets, leaving only a narrow opening where two guards stood. Several of the men in wool hats that Glyn had seen yesterday were just being admitted and the line halted momentarily. Then it moved again and they filed into the square.

Inside, there were other changes. The market carts were gone and their litter had been swept up. Benches had been placed in rows in front of the wooden platform and there the wool-hatted men were gathering, some seated, some with a boot perched on a bench, talking and spitting in a kind of rhythm. The early sun whitened the housefronts and glared on the awning shades hung out above the windows.

Ambling from a doorway across the square came a big man with a forward-borne belly and a rare-beef face under one of those broad hats some of the horsemen wore. On his sleeve was the white arrowhead, bigger than the others Glyn had seen. The men with the staves all turned to pay him attention and he seemed to prolong his parade until all eyes were on him. Then he halted, waited, raised his

164

chin and,' in a kind of howl, said, 'Obrine-gettem-ovaya-n-makemt'sit-down-ena-shade.' He turned around ponderously and made his way back toward the doorway.

The stave men began punching at the crowd and hurrying it forward. When it finally reached the shade of the buildings, the stave men ordered it into uneven ranks and made the people sit. Glyn was in the third row, separated by three from Bet and the children.

She had quite a long time to wonder and notice. She saw the crowd of men in buckskin or butternut brown grow thicker in front of the platform. Now and then, one of them would come over and stroll the length of the seated lines, staring with narrow eyes, then shake his head and walk back to the others. She tried to read something from their looks, but their faces were like closed fists. They walked with a kind of deliberate laziness and seemed to take care not to pause over any one figure along the rows, though, once or twice, she seemed to catch a momentary measuring glance on her.

She realized now that, waiting, at last she had time to be afraid. All during the strange happenings of the march, she'd been fearful of the near dangers—failing exhausted or being struck with a whip —but the great fear that came to her now was the fear of meaninglessness. Every move the horsemen made was one of purpose and she'd always supposed that what was methodical must come from method and method from some further design. Now she had a dizzy feeling that she must have fallen through some gap in real life and time into another space—like Berk's notion of a forefather world beneath the swamp—where the endless busyness was for nothing. She tried to comprehend that: A place where everyone knew exactly what he was doing but no one knew why.

There was some activity on the platform. A boy carried a little table and a chair onto it and set them down; on the opposite side, another boy was standing with a drum. The whole space in front of the platform was filled now with men standing or sitting on benches. The boy began to beat the drum in a sharp rhythm and the drone of voices died down.

Through the barrier opening and into the square came three men. Two of them were booted, broad-hatted horsemen, but the other was strange. Everyone turned to watch.

He was very tall and the sunlight glanced on his hair as if he were wearing some kind of silvery cap that flared behind his head and he shone all in white. He wore a long, skirted white coat that flowed backward from his stride, white shirt, white breeches and low boots. He looked at the sky, stepping out as though he thought himself all

165

alone in some empty place, with the other two almost trotting at his elbows. He swung his arms in a pumping motion that reached chest high ahead of him. Glyn watched in fascination.

The instant he reached the platform, the drum stopped. The two horsemen caught him by the elbows and helped him onto the platform, where he turned quickly, then stood still in the silence, looking at the crowd. Glyn could see him in profile. He was staring at the men gathered in front of him as if astonished to see them there.

At last, one of the horsemen stepped close and whispered something in his ear. He nodded and raised his arms in an open-handed gesture. He began to speak in a clear, round, raised tone, as if he were addressing not the ground but the sky.

But though Glyn heard the tone, the words themselves all seemed to be lofted into the air like mysterious birds. '... welcome ... New Mefis ... mah-kit ... an most numerous ... ample ... willin hands ... Ah say't you ... new acres ... an blessins of the harvest ...' Glyn looked at the crowd and saw that, just as the speaker seemed unaware of them, none looked up at him. They were spitting or glancing around and a few of them were shaking their heads.

The two horsemen stepped forward and took the speaker gently by the elbows. He looked from side to side in surprise. Gently, they turned him around and marched him off the platform. One of the men with a stave, near Glyn, covered his mouth with his hand and laughed into it.

Before Glyn had time to puzzle at this, a stringy old man in a white shirt and homespun, a man with a mouth like an open boat and a voice like a rattle, stepped to the front of the platform and began calling something.

Two of the stave men took sudden hold of the man seated at the head of the first row and ran him toward the platform. The sleeveless shirt flapped, his bald head tossed from side to side and he made one long wail before a rap with the stave silenced him.

Sarjint Hurt had arisen joyful and early from his feather bed and now, standing naked in the yellow gridiron of sunlight, he prepared for momentous matters. He was trying to fit his head's image into the irregular piece of broken mirror nailed to the wall and was contemplating the thicket of his lower face. Yesterday, at the end of the long trail, he'd soaked in the wooden tub of hot water while the barber had cut his hair. But the beard, no—that was his private place and only he could shape it into the smooth crescent, like a rich fruit, that set him off from the common. Turning and craning, he took a long survey, plotting out tactics of snip and trim. During the long run downriver, he'd had two things held in his mind, two sweats in the night, and the beard was the first of them. He raised the scissors, switching them open and shut and then, with immense delicacy, cut off the hairy outshoot that had thrust toward his right ear.

It was quiet in his three rooms and it was good to be home. As ranking sarjint of horse, he'd had his pick of quarters and he'd taken this small house on the edge of the settlement, near the earthworks and far away from the dust and noise of the town square. It felt good to be here, good that the raid was over. He made two artistic snips.

Some of the time on those raids was likable enough—there was a tang to it when he sat his horse at the edge of some nameless woods away up yonder, waiting in the cool air as first light gradually tinted the rooflines of some lonely village. He enjoyed thinking of them in there—like rabbits in a burrow—not knowing they were about to be scared out of their skulls.

But the long days on the backtrail, on foot or in the saddle; the half-burnt, half-raw campfire meat; the dazzling heat one day and the soaking storm the next; the hard nights on the ground in the everlasting northern woodland—those were bad on a man who wasn't young any longer.

He stroked gently downward with his comb and then made a series of dainty slices along the left side. On parade, in the field, the beard was his badge, a better sign to the men than the triangle on his sleeve. Only officers and senior sarjints could wear them and his was the most powerful-looking in the troop, when it was trimmed. Better a lot than the nasty patch on Cunel Veen—hooked out in front to make him look like a big-ass bird. He held the scissors away from his face and thought about that outlander. A kick in the balls was what he was planning for *Cunel* Veen.

Now that the left side was smooth as a bowl, he turned his care to the mustache. Dust, sweat, hot winds and bacon grease had made it ropy, and now that it was washed, it bloomed like thistles. Disgustedly, he cocked an eye at the mirror and began a foray of small clips around the borders. He wanted people to look at him and think of bears, smooth-furred, quiet, containing danger.

Fur; she used to call it that when she rubbed her fingers in it, that whore. One of the kindly moments—and there had been some of those—when he'd come back from the north and she'd meet him in fresh cotton, smelling pretty and clean, laughing, a ribbon in her hair. Never a bird to tell him that with the first cry of rafts sighted on the river, she'd got up from another man's bed to hurry here and change herself from night sweat to morning sunshine. He still couldn't understand how women did that, slipping so easily into another thought.

He put the scissors down and gently combed out the loose hairs. He did miss the woman at the door to meet him, at the table, in the bed. The girls he could bring home from the town square were new-come from the eastern hills. They fucked like rattlesnakes. And smelled like wet dogs. And that girl—after he'd caught her stealing his blanket and had begun squeezing on her wrist, for just a minute he'd seen the rattlesnake in her eyes and the excitement had been in him ever since. But Veen had stopped it. He'd dreamed about what would have happened next if Veen hadn't been there.

He'd watched for her a lot on the backtrail, but he hadn't seen that again—just had seen her taking care of the sick ones, helping at the cook fires, sitting together with the fat woman and her children. Under the dirt and rags, she was a pretty one. Under the gentleness, she was a snake.

The thought inspired him to snip along the lower mustache edge with infinite care. He'd watched her always walking with that yellow-headed boy and thought he was her brother until one night he'd seen them sleeping together, just sleeping, arms around each other. But the way they held wasn't brother-and-sister, or shouldn't be. And that was why he'd disobeyed an order from Veen for the first time.

He'd been ashore that night when Snodgrass fell asleep on watch and plopped into the river. Then there was all the uproar when the bounden people hit out for the banks, and in the middle of that, it had come to him that a good swimmer could have used the chance to go off the river side of the raft and get downstream. Just a few minutes later, he'd seen the girl, still on the raft, without the boy, and he'd known. That was why when Veen had said 'downstream,' he'd taken his men on a kind of aimless circle, walked them for a while through the brush and brought them back. He hadn't quite thought out why he did that, but he'd been moved to do it.

He jerked his hand back. When his attention had wavered, he'd trimmed off more than he intended beneath the nose and now he bent close to the mirror and squinted at the damage. A bare body in the sunlight had flashed into his mind for an instant.

After the boy had gone away, she'd been chopfallen for days—on the raft his eyes had kept returning to her like a tongue to a broken tooth, and not being able to stop the turn of his head had made him sour with himself. He raised the scissors again and began an evening around the hollow he'd cut unawares.

There was something between Veen and the girl, something he'd caught in the blink of an eye the one time he'd seen them talking together. It wasn't a look or a smile between them, he thought, but a sound he'd heard and couldn't place. The sound of a passage back and forth. He stopped and stared at his scissors for a moment, then blew the small hairs away.

Veen, long ago when he'd first walked into New Mefis, a gaunt, ragged, ugly man who couldn't talk plain words; drifted downstream on three tied logs, from nowhere; a sorrow he hadn't drowned. Then, unbelievably, Veen over the years coming up lucky again and again, winning fights when he should have been killed, building, soft-talking the old sheriff, getting the horse troop trained, leading the raids. Now he was the second man in New Mefis and, in effect, the first. Hurt suddenly felt clipped hair on his lips and he spat.

Had he cut the right side too close? He turned his head and tried to judge. The face in the mirror had a black scowl.

He raised his chin so that only the beard would show and, gradually, a good feeling came back. The shape was there, almost as he wanted it; the sun was shining; this morning he was going to make his own raid. He picked up his soft brush and began to stroke the whole expanse.

That second day on the raft when she'd taken off her clothes to wash herself. Almost all the bounden women were she-goats or cows to him, scabby, sunburnt, withered or big-assed. He'd gasped when the girl suddenly shone bare in the sun and his mind hurt. He seemed to see the lines of the bay colt his father had given him when he was a boy; the forefather gun, curled lines drawn in its metal and its polished stock, that once he'd owned; the white-winged birds he'd seen sailing one morning in the northern sky. He didn't know why these things came to him. The colt had died; his father had traded the gun; the birds had flown away.

Her neck was slender, small and long through the fall of brown hair. Young breasts like plums, nipples like berries, her bush an arrowhead. She was thin from the march and he could see the rack of her ribs, but her legs and hips had that easy curve. Then she was wet, so that the brown of the body shone like syrup and the white of it like cream.

The men seemed to suspect that Veen wanted her—there was even a joke about the cunel riding a new filly. At first, Hurt had ignored that as the usual kind of pissing talk. Veen was a man without company, alone in the field, in the town, solitary in bed. Then, in the nights he'd had to think about it, the little signs came back to him. Veen had never before talked to one of the bounden people, let alone given one of them a favor—but he had talked to the girl and had given her a favor. And Hurt had seen him watching her at times. In one of those night sweats, the idea had come to him. Now he was convinced that Veen did prize her and so he'd test Veen.

He gave his beard a finishing stroke with the brush; it was as nearly perfect as he could make it. He put on his clean breeches and his cotton shirt and tugged his boots on. From the table he took a short piece of rope. Then, with his wide-brimmed hat on his head, he went into the road.

At the barrier, the guard grinned at him and stepped aside. He could hear the drone of a voice in the square.

'How long they statid?'

'Jist begun. The sheriff give his *re*marks and they done lock him up again.'

Hurt strolled across the open space toward the crowd in front of the platform, watching the guards as they plucked a man from the seated rows of bounden, haled him to the platform and made him stand straight. One of the guards—it was Obrine, Hurt noticed—seized the long shirt and pulled it off over the man's head. A skinny one, Hurt thought, likely dead at the end of the season.

The auctioneer began his high singing: 'Howmy-bid-fo-thisyer-strongun-thutty-two-summer-ole-an . . .' Hurt had now reached the edge of the crowd. The naked body was shivering in the hot sun and the man's head drooped. The traders were spitting and talking indifferently. A mistake to begin with this one.

In a few minutes, the auctioneer would have to bring out his customary joke. He would squint at his paper and make a show of studying it. The creature on the block might be a fat, half-bald, bewildered man. The auctioneer would begin to chant, 'Howmy-bid-fo-thisyer-sweet-purty-virgin-gal-no-chillen-kin-cook-sew-ex-setra . . . .' At which, he'd take a glance toward the block and then, with eyes wide, jaw dropped, hand to forehead, would bend to the paper again.

The traders always roared at that, yelled they were being cheated, pretended they'd drag the auctioneer down and beat his head in.

Hurt took a twig from his pocket and chewed on it patiently. Obrine was making the thin man turn around slowly, the plucked-fowl thing up there, skin-bound bones, sores and bruises ugly in the bright sun. There was no bid.

'Mosta-his-teeth-good-eyes-strongen-willen-fo-hyad-field-work . . .' A trader in the back row raised his hand lazily and made a sign with his fingers. 'Goen-goen-gone-fo-one-shoat.'

As the first dozen passed onto and off the block, Hurt moved around restlessly. He scanned the seated rows and, among the bony shoulders and collapsed breasts of the others, he found her, sitting with her head bowed and her face hidden. He stared, then looked back at the traders. Veen was not here.

Hurt wondered if he'd misjudged. Veen lived like a wolf in a lair, in one room, owning nothing but his clothes and his rifle. Even his horse was borrowed from the common stock. And a woman is the most troublesome of all possessions. But, with the doubt, Hurt had an overpowering sense that Veen's man was here somewhere. According to the sheriff's rule, the girl would have to be sold with the others. But someone had spoken to the auctioneer. At the last moment, only one bid would be seen; men would step forward and quietly take her away. Hurt looked from face to face among the traders, trying to guess.

The auctioneer was just finishing the sale of three together—slouching man, squat wife and a half-grown boy. They clung together, trying to hide in each other, and the guards had to pull them apart to stuff the sacklike shirts on again. A planter's man prodded them off the platform with a stick.

And now she was being brought up to the block. She stood awkwardly as hands took the shirt at her shoulders; just at that moment, a man stepped in front to Hurt and blocked his view. The auctioneer began his singsong in a changed voice, almost as if he expected an interruption at once. Hurt shoved and elbowed into the front row, raising his hand to make the barter signs. But something had not happened—the girl was still dressed in the shirt and she'd been given a kind of cap that half hid her face. There was a murmur, but Hurt's hand was the only one in the air. The auctioneer turned his head away and seemed to search among the crowd. Hurt's guess was no guess now.

A man had come into the square and was hurrying across the open space, a red-faced, big-bellied planter with dark sweat patches on his white shirt. He gestured toward the platform.

Hurt yelled at the auctioneer, 'Ova-eyah, ova-eyah!'

The auctioneer pointed toward the fat man and swung into, 'Bid-one-mule-one-mule-one-mule-en-fo-sacksa-cone.' The man came to a stop near the crowd and nodded.

Hurt vaulted onto the platform and made a bowlegged run to the other end. He caught the auctioneer by the arm and stood face to face with him. The auctioneer, bewildered, looked up at the sarjint, like an old child. Hurt's fingers pressed through the pulp to the bone. 'Cunel done change his mine,' he said. 'Ahl taker.' The auctioneer's mouth was opening with pain. 'Bid one mule an five sacks.' The man nodded.

As Hurt's fingers relaxed, he turned and saw that the planter had pushed up to the edge of the platform. Hurt stood over him like a tower ready to fall.

'Mah bid,' the man said. He stared up at Hurt.

'Too late'.

'Hit's mah bid.' The red face was greased with sweat.

Hurt put his hand on the man's shoulder and the fingers were like iron tongs again. 'It ain't,' Hurt said. He wondered if he could make the bone crumble. He thought he could. He increased the grasp. The man bowed his head and slowly sank to his knees, and the crowd, in silence, could hear him panting.

Then the pain was too much; the fat man gave a small, ludicrous cry and bobbed his head. Hurt left him with his face flat on the boards of the platform.

Quickly, he tied her hands behind her and led the girl off the platform and through the square, half hearing the whistles and whoo-ee sounds among the traders. In his mind, his hand was still closing powerfully and the bone was beginning to break like chalk in his fingers and the planter was rearing an agonized face—Veen's face now—upward to him. He had a dizzy, joyful sense then that he could break anyone—that feeling in his hands and in his genitals.

In the street, he strode fast, shouldering people aside and cutting in front of slow-paced horses. He could hear her hard breathing as she ran to keep up and he pulled the rope taut.

At last, they came to the lumberyard and turned into his small byway. From the great stacks of cut logs came a sweet wood smell; chips and pieces of bark covered the road. He pulled her along faster, past the row of plank fronts, to his own door. Just as he was changing the rope end to his left hand and reaching for the latch with his right, she broke.

He felt the rope whip from his fingers and turned to see her twist away from him and begin to run down the byway. Astonished, he watched her for an instant. Then he laughed. He flexed his fingers with pleasure and started to run.

She had a ten-pace lead, but all things were against her—the hard mud surface was rutted; the fence on one side and the housefronts on the other gave no opening; at the end of the lane, a horse and cart, led by a shaggy figure, were just rounding the corner. With her bound hands, she hitched the shirt higher and gained a little speed.

Hurt, grinning, kept close behind, not yet ready to spring. He was trying to judge at what point she would dodge to the left among

172

the piled timbers. His boots pounded on the cracked ground. In his mind, he already felt the touch of her flesh.

She swerved sooner than he thought she would and he had to lunge, off balance, between two banks of logs. But there he caught her.

The shirt ripped in his hand and she tried to spin away, but his other hand came down between her roped wrists and jerked her back so that her hair brushed against his face. And in the next moment, he had taken her by the thighs and heaved her onto his right shoulder. She gave a cry and a great gasp and he knew that he'd knocked the wind from her, though her hands still beat on his back as he carried her into the lane again.

The shaggy man, with a toothless smile, was standing there by his horse and cart. 'Was betten on her,' he said. 'She don like home life?'

'Fuckyew,' said Hurt.

'Ain't me yew gotten mine, reckon,' he said and laughed a phlegmy laugh.

Panting a little, Hurt carried her back down the lane and into his house. He kicked the door shut with his heel, strode into the bedroom and dropped her on the bed. She lay there gasping and trying to cover her face with her hands. He stood over her for a moment, looking, looking, feeling the blood-beat in his head. She made no sound now, but her eyes seemed to moan and it was as if he heard his own long-ago moans as the shoveled dirt slowly covered the glossy colt's hide; the walls of the room seemed to circle. He reached down and pulled the torn shirt from her body with one rip.

He saw his hands take a piece of rope from the shelf and tie her hands to the headbar of the bed. When he did this, she tried to kick him, but he was quicker. He grasped both feet and tied each one to opposite corners of the footboard. Legs splayed out, belly heaving, gasping, she looked like a thin, fearful, trapped young animal.

He would like to hear her scream; in a minute, he would make her scream. His fingers were slowly unbuttoning his breeches. He was surprised to find that his cock was hard. Surprised that he was surprised.

He came down between her legs, chest to hard breastbone, and he suddenly felt her body twist partly free. He heard a scraping noise—she'd pulled the rope loose from the headbar.

As he grasped for her hands, faster than he could take in, she rolled sidewise and he felt her frantic fingers in the midst of his beard.

Before he could catch her wrists, the pain came—a fire in his face, a wrench as if his jaw had been sprung.

So strong a pain that all sight turned into a white smear; he sank across her legs and put both hands blindly to his chin. There was a raw, wet emptiness under his fingers. He groaned as the blood slowly flooded his hands. Then he could see dimly and what he saw was a nest of bloody hair in her clutch.

And now he had to kill her.

He raised himself to his knees, grasped at the table beside the bed and closed his fingers on something round and hard, as if it had been given to him—his brass candlestick. Dizzily, he brought it high, looking down, trying to keep her forehead in his sights.

Then he heard the sound of quick bootsteps on the floor behind him.

Veen had suffered one of his headaches all night long. In the field, with actions and duties to plan for, he was free of them. They only came when he'd returned to New Mefis—and they usually lasted in spells of a night and a day, a paralysis of pain when he'd lock himself in and lie in his darkened room with a wet cloth on his head, dying. He could not eat or sleep or move except with enormous effort. The feeling was that of lying in some desolate wilderness gully while an immensely slow-falling avalanche crashed onto his skull. Boulder piled on boulder, slowly crushing his head. After the terrible hours, he'd awake, or come to, weak, terrified, his bed sweat-soaked and foul with urine.

And then, as he lay tender as a wound, the memories invaded his mind. He reached now for a cup of corn liquor on the candlestand beside his bed and took a sip of the warm stuff. Better, just a little.

A ragged boy running down the road in Haven Place, behind him the yells of other boys. A stone thumped into the middle of his back and he began to cry.

They said he had no father because his father was an outlaw man who had taken his mother in the woods one day. She had died when Veen was born; that was all he knew.

He slept in Muller's lean-to, bitter cold in winter and stifling in summer. He did the chores for Muller Cow-man—never right, it seemed—and Muller beat him with an oak stick. He heard Muller-wife screaming at him, 'Wild, savage thing, you.'

Someday, I'll kill them all. I'll watch them drown in their own blood.

Better later on when he'd learned to rig ropes and pulleys for the building. They needed him. He saw a timber swing up into the air on a rope hoist as he and the men pulled and he saw the builders take it and ease it into place at the top of the wall. 'Good, Veen. Done well.' Young Haven's voice. Young Haven was friendly, always dealt with him well. He hated Haven for that. It reminded him of all the rest of it. One child came into life all alone, another child was born the sheriff's son.

Veen took another sip of the pale, burning liquor.

And that was why he'd worked hard at the salvaging. There were stories about a thing like a stick that could kill a deer at long distances—a rifle, though he had never heard the name then. He wanted to uncover one of those things, steal a knapsack and supplies and set off into the forest on his own. But Haven had saved him the trouble of that, had even given him leave and a map and had wished him well. So, one day, he and the two others had walked away from Haven Place.

He sat up now, feeling a little stronger. He wished he could rid himself of those memories, but they were like a spike driven through his mind. And they made him do all that he did.

The long walk—except for the recollection of pain and heat—he didn't remember much. He supposed he'd been close to dying a few times. And, on the river, drowning. The logs of his makeshift raft had come loose more times than he could remember. One night, on a mud flat, kept awake by clouds of mosquitoes, his raft half wrecked, he'd started into the water to let the river do with him what it would, in time wash his swollen corpse up on some other mudbank far downstream.

But something had preserved him, and he'd walked into New Mefis like an animal, nearly naked and nearly mad.

Veen rose with painful care and went to the washbasin and doused his head and the upper part of his body in water. He sat down again to let the coolness seep into him.

They'd put him on a work gang, clearing stumps. Then one day Markus, the sheriff, had noticed him and talked with him. Before the first frost, he was in charge of the work gang. Markus liked him because he never let up on the men, because he won a fight when it came to that.

Later, Markus had given him a uniform and a place in the horse. Veen had watched the sheriff carefully, a model. He'd learned to read letters, to deal with bigger problems than rigging, to command a company of horse. When the raids north had begun, he'd made his name. He'd lost no more than one man and he'd always come back with captives. The collecting stockade and the plan for the wider raids had been his. In his mind, he'd always kept a picture of Haven Place afire and the people driven off.

Now he suddenly began to wonder what was keeping Jessip so long. He should have been rapping at the door by this time. Veen reached for his shirt and slowly began to put it on.

Burning. He'd had that picture again not very long ago when his horsemen had made camp in the forest no more than an hour's ride away from Haven Place. The dream of fire was in his head all night and he had arisen just at sun-break to walk in the woods and think. The fog had been knee-high so that all the trees and bushtops seemed to be floating on a pale flood.

But, he'd found, in the chill of that early morning, the picture had gone. No longer could he see himself riding into Haven Place. Something in his mind closed it off.

And angry with himself, that day he had led his men a mile or two farther north, to come down on the little settlement of huts by the river.

Jessip must be very slow—or the auction longer than usual. He stood up and drew his breeches on. When he tried to button the buttons, his fingers trembled.

In the little oak opening, there'd been a flood of sunlight. It was hot, even in the trees' shade, and it would be a labor to get them started on the trail again. Everything was clearly outlined—the rag-and-bone figures lying on the ground, the flank of a brown horse with the sunshine making it tawny, the butternut, sweat-marked back of the sarjint, who was just tightening the saddle cinch. Then the girl, walking quickly across the clearing, yellow hair, short breeches, torn shirt, legs and arms sunbrowned. She was different from the rest of them.

She'd come up behind the horse sarjint and apparently had said something to him. The man turned slowly and gazed at her and then turned silently back to his horse. Veen had seen this from a long way off and, for some reason, his attention was held.

The girl hesitated. Then she took a few little running steps and stooped for the rolled-up blanket that lay a few paces in front of the horse. The sarjint was on her in an instant, catching her outstretched wrist in his big hand. Veen felt himself striding forward. He saw the fingers around the thin wrist and he felt the sarjint think that he would break it. Veen spoke.

He saw the hand on the wrist relax and the bearded face turn toward him, the eyes angry. Then the sarjint seemed to be out of his view and the girl's lips were moving.

It was as if something about her face and the intonation of her voice came back to him from a dream.

Again, a few days later, she'd spoken to him from a roadside somewhere on the route. And then he was sure of the voice and the face. From dreams, but from memory before that.

He walked stiffly to the window and looked out, seeing that the sun must be at midmorning, and the thought bothered him. He picked up his boots and put them on, dreading the notion of going out into the heat.

As he opened the door, the hot wind struck his face and he felt faint for a moment; his knees hinged and he had to put his hand on the doorpost. But just then he saw Jessip hurrying down the road from the market direction and he staightened. Jessip's belly jigged as he trotted and his face, under the hat brim, was redder than usual. He slowed as he caught sight of Veen and came on at a walk, wiping his sleeve across his forehead.

'Welsir,' Veen said, 'you're alone?'

'Cunel, done the best ah could, sweah. But theter sarjint major done beat me out. Bid higheren me en wooden quit.'

'Who?' Veen asked, astounded. 'You mean Hurt? But I told you to bid as high as necessary.'

'Ah know, but, Cunel, ah cooden hep . . .'

'He threatened you, then?' Veen thought of the little episode in the forest clearing. And Hurt had kept a grudge smoldering since then? 'He faced you down, Jessip?'

'Wal, yo might say . . .'

Veen shoved him aside and began to run. Strength came back into his body with the swing of his arms and the beat of his boots on the ground. He had no impression of the roads down which he ran, just a series of startled faces moving sidewise from his path, mule-drawn carts that appeared and disappeared, a woman with a bundle balanced on her head suddenly squawking and shying away, the bundle falling.

After a long time, he was rounding a corner into a narrow byway; he was aware of some huge piles of logs to the right of him, the little clapboard housefront halfway down the road.

He reached its door and, heels skidding, came to a stop. He panted and listened. There was a low cry from inside. He drew back his foot and kicked the door open, then strode in, through one empty room and into the next.

The girl was half sitting up on a bed, her legs tied in a wide V; her face was terrified. A naked man clutching his bloody chin was just rising up alongside the bed. Hurt. In his other hand was a brass candlestick, rising to strike. Veen swung his boot with all the force he had left.

He was surprised to see the man flung so far. He slid backward against the wall and slumped, his head on his chest. Veen turned and took his knife from his sheath and cut the ropes. She brushed her hair back from her face. They were silent for a minute.

'Haven?' he asked.

'Havensdotter,' she said.

19

'How many days have we been on the river?'

'I've lost the count. Days and nights wash away. Time flows through your fingers. Is this a real river or are we drifting on some forever-never?'

'I'd say real enough—you've seen for yourself the signs of old settlements along the shores and the river walls and the hulks of what must have been boats. Then those broken bridges across it, five by my tally. How many must have sailed here; it was full of life!'

'Vanished. Walked into emptiness one fine day. I can prove there was life, but that doesn't make me know it. We haven't seen a boat or a raft or a man fishing or a cabin. Woods full of birds, endless deserted shores.'

'A few times I've seen cows on the west shore a long way off and now and again the smoke from chimneys. Even signs of tree cuttings in the woods. But you can see how the river floods over its edges when it's high. Not a place I'd sow a farm.'

'I know that's reasonable. But I wake in the night with a terrible thought of the ground we walk on split in two by a great stream of nothing. It sucks everything on it at last into nothing. I think that when you close your eyes to die you may board a little boat and float onto such a river.'

'Haven! We'll steer to the shore and spend a day hunting. We'll find an old settlement and salvage something useful. You have to sleep on earth a night or two. I'm a doc, a healer, and I tell you that.'

'You're saying I'm moody. I'm letting my mind drown in the river. No, we keep on. Kinkaid, take the watch and wake me if there's any change.'

That night, the wind gusted from the west and it rained in sharp spells. They found a little shelter in the lee of a brush-grown mud island close to the western shore. At first light, the men had hard work to pole the boat off the shelf where it had grounded. Haven lay on a blanket in the lean-to most of that day and Piet and Kinkaid alternated at the lookout watch and the tiller.

During that gray and clouded morning, Kinkaid began to notice more signs. Far in the eastern distance, he saw smoke tingeing the air above the river-edge forest; he sighted a narrow roadway cut through the trees down to the bank, with what might be the flank of a small boat half hidden in green growth; he saw a floating log with an ax-hewn end. He took the tiller at noon and kept the flatboat in the slow, shoreward current, watching ahead where he could steer to shore if he must.

The afternoon passed and the sun lazed toward the western rim. Half dark fell on the river like a film, while the now cloudless sky gleamed blue one last hour. He craned his neck and saw the moon—half a dough cake—already visible. On the lowlands to the west, the river had overflowed in a great watery, dusky sheet almost as far as he could see; then the banks rose again and the stream bent again in one of its great whims until they seemed to move straight north, then in a gradual curve west, and at last bore south in another long curve. Here the river kept to its channel.

Scanning hard through the day's-end dimness, Kinkaid suddenly caught sight, on the eastern bank ahead, of what he'd almost begun to disbelieve. But it was there, just as he'd placed it in the future the day they'd first launched their flat-boat on the shallows. A landing with a long, low pier; mooring posts and alongside the posts the broad rafts. One or more of them had already been dismantled and dragged from the river—there were stacks of logs on the higher ground.

He motioned Piet to steer even closer to the western shore—they'd be in the best shadow there. Then he noticed a slow-floating mass of branches and flotsam and he went back to help Piet bend the tiller to take the boat behind its screen.

There was no hail from the farther shore as they drifted by, no shot, no sign of life. But the great rafts, one of them still with its log house and horse stalls, told all that need be. Kinkaid roused Haven and made him look.

He stood at the last inch of the stern and stared until they were beyond sight of the landing. He turned and took Kinkaid's shoulder in his grasp. He smiled and shook his head as if to show it was clear again.

The stretch of water ahead of them now was fairly straight, and before long, the moon made it a silvery-sleek roadway.

'Turn us to the near shore wherever it seems likely now,' Haven said to Piet. 'Tomorrow we'll find a way to cross and then we'll scout

179

them from the south, where they won't expect us.'

Just then, they began to hear a low, mumbling sound in the waters, a sound they'd heard before. Kinkaid, who was at the prow post on lookout, turned and said, 'Another bridge, that must be,' but before he'd finished, they could all see it—a long span that had once crossed the width of the river, now half standing, part buckled, the rest long since swept away. The part of it that still jutted from the eastern bank rested on huge slabs spaced out into the water and it was topped with a great, curving rise and fall of what seemed a kind of trellis. From a distance, in the clear moonlight, it looked like needlework in the air.

The river swept through a wide gap where there were points of white water and Kinkaid yelled to the men to take poles to the forward sides and be ready to fend off from any underwater wreckage.

But in a few minutes, they had passed cleanly between two stumps of the old bridge base and were in the open water again.

'I'm glad that's—' Kinkaid began to say, and stopped. There was a strange, new noise from the water ahead. It was an enormous, throaty complaint, as if the river had found a voice, and the boat hitched and half swung in a sharper current. They looked ahead and were astonished.

About a mile downstream, they could see an enormous, grotesque barrier stretched from bank to bank, the full width of the river. It seemed to be heaped and tangled and bristling with spiky growth, towering above the surface where the stream narrowed. One moment in the moonlight it seemed to be a gigantic thicket, the next moment it seemed a solider black, like the collapse of some great wall.

But it was not solid. In several gaps, large and small, the water swirled, whipped white and coursed through. Kinkaid saw what must have been a heavy tree trunk enter the white, rear and upend, and then shoot forward to disappear.

The men stood watching with hands on hips, amazed, not even seeming to notice the rougher motion of the boat. Kinkaid ran back to the tiller and yelled at them.

'Stop gawping, you lumps! Help on this tiller or we'll get et by that thing! Here—we'll swing her to the right bank.'

The western bank, as the moon showed it, was low-lying, flat and treeless. With four men heaving against the tiller and Kinkaid and Piet pulling from the other side, the boat gradually began to swerve in that direction. The bow jerked and slapped the water; the rudder creaked under the strain.

The shore was an almost unbroken curve, but Haven, standing on the lip of the bow, made out a small indentation. 'There!' he called. 'I think we can catch hold there. Head for it. Otherwise, we'll be swept right along the bank.' For a few moments, it seemed that they might overshoot the place, but Haven made his way back and added his strength to the match with the tiller and gradually the boat swung toward the half-moon break in the shoreline.

As they neared it, Haven said, 'Look what luck and a hard pull will do!' It was the only place along the whole stretch where the riverbank, in one small place, had crumbled and fallen in a gradual slope to the water. And here it was that at last, drenched with sweat and aching, they grounded their boat on the mud and made it fast.

They climbed to the field at the top of the bank. Haven and the others started across it to find some sheltered place where they might build a fire that wouldn't be seen. But Kinkaid stayed near the boat, resting on the ground and staring at a new surprise.

On the opposite side of the river there were bluffs and all along the bluffs lay a vast forefather place in sharp-cut black and white under the moon. Kinkaid could think only of an unearthly woodland whose tall, bare, oblong trunks forested the sky. It seemed impossible that anything could be raised so high by men, but if that was true, why? Did the ancient builders reach so far upward from some old, heart-deep longing for the treeland they had once come from? Did they have some belief that made them want to live in the upper air? On the moon-whitened fronts he could see regular rows of small perforations that must be windows and he longed to climb up inside one of the buildings and, looking down on the land, put himself in the place of one of those vanished men.

He tried to imagine living there—like living in a high nest in a hollow tree, hanging dizzily in the wind, sometimes strangely among the clouds and lightning, sometimes in the very eye of the sun. It might take half a day to climb to the top. Hauling a bucket up from the well would take hours, and as for firewood . . . He stopped and shook his head. No, the familiar rules of things, of course, didn't apply. There would be means he couldn't imagine, reasons that his reason could not recover.

There was the chance, he thought, that this might be the refuge place of the forefathers he'd often pictured in his mind and that there might be sleeping people of the old race over there as he watched. But the sense that came to him from the silent towers was one of emptiness. There was no light except for the moon's and no sound came over the water and no smells of life—only the river smell. The great place almost seemed to speak of its death.

Mysteries. Kinkaid looked again toward the tumbled barrier stretching across the river and wondered what its purpose had been. But he was too weary to plague his head with more answerless questions, and so he turned inland, walking through the knee-high grass to a line of low trees and, before long, toward the flicker of the fire.

On the river's edge the next morning, in the first glint of the sun, they walked through the mint-smelling grass toward the bridge end. Kinkaid could not keep his eyes from the great, notched silhouettes across on the bluffs of the far shore, just as mysterious in the backlight of the early day as they had been the night before.

But the others had glanced at the settlement and had turned quickly to the river barrier, Piet and Haven talking in low voices. Piet was carrying loops of light line over his shoulder.

'You see now, it's the wreck of three bridge roads. Look there at the place where they cross onto the shore. Three of them built close together, but why?'

'No saying, but there stands our only way of crossing, if it is a way.' Haven was squinting, calculating. He had not shaved for the past three or four days on the raft and his face, burned brown by the sun, was half covered by a gunpowder beard with sprouts of gray.

They came along the curve of the shore toward this strangest of sights. The fallen bridges had made a monstrous hedge, over the years hoarding from the river every kind of drifting wreckage. It rose far above their heads, a wild, tangled, briery confusion of masses and spikes. There were nightmare forests where whole dead trees had swept to rest; broken shapes that might once have been parts of hulls; flat, boarded planes that could have been sides of barns or houses; fence posts with wire still clinging to them; long, twisted strands of what seemed to be metal; parts of roofs; slabs of stony stuff from the destroyed bridges. But the whole impression was bristly, branchy, a great inert porcupine.

In seven places that Kinkaid could count, the river had cut through, but there were probably other, smaller channels he could not see. In each of them, the water reared and glistened like a thick snake, endlessly slipping through its escape hole. In the near stream, branches and other floating oddments would bob, then suddenly pitch forward to disappear into the flow.

'I see our boat swallowed like that branch,' Haven said

Piet was crouched on the edge of the bank, running his eyes along the length of the barrier. He did not speak for a long time.

At last, he said, 'Going careful, we can work it out about two hundred paces, just before the first gap comes. Tie it hard then we need ropes. Every settlement I've ever salvaged has ropes.'

'All the fiber ones are rotten dust,' one of the men said.

'Some. But there are ones that aren't.' Piet didn't bother to look at

182

the man who had spoken.

'To rig a rope bridge across, that's work for six weeks, even if we find the rope,' Haven said.

Piet shook his head. 'There're long stretches with good footholds for a path—that needs one rope. Over the gaps we need three, two for handholds, one for walking. Three tight-strung.'

'And your ropes swim themselves across?' asked the skeptical man. He was a thin, reddish-faced, reddish-haired man who sometimes seemed to speak up for what the others were thinking. Kinkaid had never heard his full name, but he was always called Kip or Kippo.

Piet rose, swung over the bank and climbed down agilely. They all watched in silence as he began to scramble along the very edge of the barrier, sometimes on sure footing, sometimes using a branch to swing out over the water until his foot found another sure spot. It was tricky going, but Piet moved steadily forward. They held their breaths for a mis-step. The noise of the water was a monotone of danger.

Far off now, Piet slipped and fell to armpits in the water. But he rose again easily, ran the length of a beam, jumped to a stony slab, and at last had worked his way to the lip of the barrier. There he took the line from his shoulder, crouched down and seemed to be tying it to something. Kinkaid knew that it was a line of the thin but very strong kind made of some variety of fiber that never seemed to be affected by damp or rot. It was sometimes found in the salvaging searches and it was much prized. But Piet had only one length of it.

Piet was standing now, whirling a small chunk of stone above his head at the end of the rope. He threw once, missed his aim and had to pull the weight back from the flood. On his second try, the chunk arced across the ten paces of water, the white line trailing from it, and fell among angles of beams from the old bridge, and there it caught fast.

Piet tested it, then tied the other end on his side. In a moment, he was swinging hand over hand out over the gap, his feet barely dipping into the surface now and then. Twisting from side to side, he was like a strange dancer above the flood. He reached the far side and, standing there, raised his arms in a signal.

'Proven, then,' said Haven. He slowly scanned the opposite shore as far upriver as he could see. 'Today we strike inland for salvaging. Rope, as much as we can find. Anything else good for spanning. Axes and useful tools. Horses. There should be some wild ones loose hereabouts—and, Kinkaid, you can use yours for decoys.'

Seven days later, Kinkaid sat on the far shore at last, his nerves still twitching from the perilous traverse. The midmorning sun felt good on his body and he waited for his sodden breeches to dry. Unbuckling his pack, he took his shirt from it. Then he unwound the wrapping from his rifle and, with his shirttail, dried it carefully.

Beneath him lay the treacherous path they had sweated for a week to weave along the skirt of the barrier. From here, it looked like a child's amusement of sticks and string, a precarious line of logs here, there a stretch of rope walkway strung through a cutting in the branch heaps to angle across one river gully. And beyond that, other strange devices of Piet's improvisation. Kinkaid had volunteered to try it first. He would spy out the far shore.

The boat lay like a little shuttle, tied to the barrier just beyond the final gap. He could see two of the men moving around on it. Closer, he noted the series of resting places at intervals along the path, slabs or logs for a platform, big enough for two or three people to halt for breath and solid enough to give a rifleman good footing. The nearest one had a breastwork of planks and mud on the side toward him.

Kinkaid shook his head at this long cat's cradle. He had managed it without much difficulty on a clear, windless day, but it would be otherwise in wind, dark, or rising water.

He turned around and looked again at the array of buildings, now only a little distance away from him.

The moment he had reached this side, he had realized that his senses on the first night had been true—there was no buzz or stir or odor of life in this place; it was as empty and desolate as all other forefather places.

Off to his right, he could see a number of very large white things protruding from the bush-grown land. Like enormous, perfectly circular white jugs, they shone in the sun. In front of him, curving inland from the barrier to the north, was one of the queer roadways he'd come across now and then in his travels—big iron bars about two paces apart that ran in a continuous line as far as the eye could follow. Directly inland from him, there were roads and many low buildings. But none of these things interested him.

What drew him were the great towers off to the north. Rising above the jumble of lower roofs, they seemed to finger the clouds in the sky.

Kinkaid shouldered his pack and rifle and set off to follow the shoreline. He found first a path and then a stone forefather roadway that ran along the rim of the bluffs. A belt of trees screened the settlement from him now, but he could look down on the expansive bend of the river and see, far ahead, the bridge they had passed at dusk on the day of their arrival. It spanned a channel and a spit of land before it projected out above the water.

As he walked, it struck Kinkaid to wonder why, without thinking, he had chosen to take this route rather than go among the ruins. Fear, some trace of the childhood awe? He had grown up among a natural way of behaving that he had only later recognized as total fear. Diseases, poisons, traps, suddenly collapsing walls, vast underground passages full of strange vermin; the legend of the former people who lived too richly and were cursed.

No; Kinkaid knew that he'd outgrown all that. He knew that the buried secrets had to be searched for, found again—or else grand-children's grandchildren would still live their small lives, fearful and laborious, in the little clearings of the world. It came to him that he would have to settle in one of the vast ruined places and be another kind of hunter.

As for now, he had a longing to go very high up. He had come to the place where the channel split the narrow island from the shore and just to his right now, a little inland among roads, were the upthrusts of the tallest monoliths. He stood in awe and tried to choose one. His head frozen in an upward tilt, he walked and stared.

It was true that the holes he'd noticed before were windows, rank on rank of them. Some of the glass from them crunched on the ground underneath his boots, but some of it remained in place, reflecting like scattered flakes of sun. He tried to count the rows and he grew dizzy, there were so many and they mounted so high.

He went down a road, turned at random, picked another, still staring. Around him, there were other sights—an iron stump at the side of the road, rooms with wide openings that had once held an enormous glass, iron poles with some kind of empty basket at the top and litter, broken pieces of things, everywhere.

He came to a great white slab, even more toplofty than the other buildings, and in a kind of daze, walked through its open door.

Beyond the entrance, there was a room that told him nothing except a story of long-ago destruction and then a long decay. The place, dimly lighted from the sun in the street, was piled knee deep with more fragments, dust, rotten wood and slivers of glass. He wandered around and looked into similar rooms. Some of the door-ways still had their doors and he opened these, finding nothing worth looking at.

Finally, tired of the effort, he was turning to go when he saw a metal door that had been left wedged open a little way. He forced it farther and found what he had been looking for—a stairway leading upward. Here there was a thin daylight from some window he could not see.

He put one foot on the metal step and tested it. It was solid enough.

He tested others, farther up. At last, he began a slow climb because he knew that he was going a long way into the sky.

At each landing in the stairs, there was a door, but he was not interested in exploring beyond and he did not even try to see if any would open. On one landing he came across a heap of dusty cloth that must have once been clothes, with the bones and skull of their wearer. He'd often come across human bones in forefather places, but always they'd been broken and scattered by animals. This was the first time he'd found what was recognizably the remains of one person. A woman, he thought; the cloth must have been a dress. Was she fleeing higher? How did death catch her on these lonely stairs?

In general, there was not much dust, and the stairs, ever doubling on themselves to rise, were monotonously the same. He lost track of how many landing doors he'd passed and how often he'd sat down to rest. He thought that the day must have gone and night come—but the dim light remained unchanged. He thought that he had fooled himself and had imagined a top to the building when there was none. It would go up forever. He could not understand the fact of the stairs. They were shiny and scarcely worn. Reason told him that no one could make this climb every day. There must have been wonderful ways of transporting people and things up and down.

He sweated and his leg muscles began to pain him. He blamed himself for wasting all this time when he should be on his way to do the task Haven had asked him to do. Each time he rested, it was harder to get up again.

Suddenly he'd arrived. He came to a place where the stairs ended and an iron ladder led up to a closed door. He opened it and stepped out onto a level roof in the bright afternoon sunshine and was struck blind.

After moments, when his eyes could accept the light again, he saw that he was on a flat surface with some kind of structure still looming above him. Greatly careful, he took half steps out to the parapet wall and looked down.

He was shocked, overwhelmed with terror. He closed his eyes and he felt his hands trembling. He could not believe that any man had been so high without dying. It was like dying—that dizzy fall of the sight through the air down to strange squares and dots below. He wanted to sink and clutch the floor under his feet.

He realized that even his eyelids were trembling as he made himself open them again. He had expected somehow to find everything upside down, but there were the clouds still sleeping in the blue and the parapet wall still solid under his fingers. Cautiously, he peered down again and this time the view did not drop suddenly away from him, began to make a kind of sense. He made himself look and, gradually, he grew calmer.

Bewildering planes of roofs—off to his left, the biggest, two broad ones in the form of a fat T. Straight ahead from right to left, a great, white seam of roadway passing through the buildings to the bridge. The island where the bridge crossed not really an island at all but a spear of land between a channel and the river. The bridge reaching out into the river, with its lacy upperwork shadowed on the stream, then the bridge split off like a broken willow stick, the rest of its former course shown by stumps of the supports and a white confusion under the water.

He admired the river for some lost space of time, having never imagined that he would look down upon it. At this place, it ran almost straight from the north, then took an ambling curve and narrowed to where the old bridge barrier lay. The surface gleamed in a million points of light. Kinkaid could almost believe what Haven had said— that it halved the earth and went on forever.

On the other side, the land was open and flat except for white streaks of roadways. One of them led northward and he followed that with his gaze as far as he could.

He turned back to his own shore then and began to stare at the enormous puzzle of roads and roofs everywhere below him, noting here and there a detail that stood out—a building shaped like a rimless, unfinished wheel, a place where the roads ran in two graceful loops for no reason he could think of. But the endless, rectangular intricacy baffled him.

The works of ancient men were made to cover whole landscapes and to drive into the sky. Kinkaid sensed a great, forceful impatience here, a lust to overlay ground, water and air with a structure that made the land landless, the water floodless and the sky stormless. And, abruptly, that impatient force had vanished. The emptiness between past and present seemed like centuries of night.

At last, Kinkaid remembered his excuse for climbing to this height. He concentrated his gaze, searching to the north. There he saw two parallel, smaller rivers cutting through the landscape to the bigger one, beyond both a belt of trees and, on the hazy horizon, open fields with what seemed to be the faint traces of smoke from the chimneys of living men. The settlement of the horsemen. Reluctantly, he turned back toward the long stairway.

They are not very different from us, except in the small things. They walk with a careless roll, like men used to flat places, unlike men who have to walk on narrow forest paths. Many of them ride.

Their horses are fine, nimble beasts, better bred and taller grown than any in Pennsylvan-land. Cared for well. And on the roads everywhere.

Dress not much different, but the homespun is a kind of clayey brown. Baggy-sleeved white or gray shirts of some other stuff than wool. And an odd kind of hat with a shade all round it. Like a collection of roofs when they lean together.

They are quarrelsomelike in their humor. When they seem most to be jibing and stiffening for a fight, they are playing up to a joke. One of them talks, storytelling, and the others listen, then they laugh, but in the laugh there is meanness.

Once, they expected attacks from outside and they built this wall, ditch, gate. But the grass overgrows the ditch now and the rain washes gaps in the wall and the gate guards turn their backs on the men and animals passing through.

When a snatch of words is hearable, it's not much different—except for one or two. But there's another, slower tune. The voices have a slide in them.

Abundance of everything here, food and manufactures, with traders in a stream through the gate with their creatures laden.

The men are clean-shaven, except for some of the older traders; many wear a patch over one eye.

This village was a forefather place long ago. Many of the long, smooth-stone buildings forefathers used for storage, perhaps.

As in Erie Place, there are the two kinds, the horsemen and the others, who labor for them. These others must be the people brought on the rafts. They would know each other and know where Havensdotter is.

There are so many folk in the village, in the fields, traders coming and going to other parts, that one more stranger would not stand out. If he was quiet. Round hat, long-ear beast with a pack, road dust on me. I can find or steal those things. To go in tomorrow early when the guards are still sleepy.

Kinkaid had made the long walk and had slept overnight in a ditch in the woods, bothered only once, by a curious dog. When it was light, he had crawled to some bushes about fifty paces away from the gate, hidden himself well, and had spent the day watching and listening. As he watched, he knew that Haven's half-formed idea of a raid on the settlement and a freeing of all the raft people was not possible. But it would be possible for one man to slip inside, with luck to find the girl called Glyn, and to bring her away.

20

Glyn moved softly in the ashy light, washing and dressing. She had been in New Mefis a bare fourteen days, but even in that time the hours from sunrise to sunset seemed to shorten visibly. It gave her a feeling of time closing down, the possibilities narrowing with a briefer sun. She hurried.

At night, she had planned the moves of morning to be as silent as possible. She had filled her washing bowl from the pump in the yard and had rubbed grease on the hinges of the gate. Now she opened her door and looked outside. The place that Veen had given her was a low-roofed, dirt-floored room that might have been a storage shed once. It had a straw mattress on the floor, a three-legged stool and a shelf jutting from the wall.

She walked softly, in bare feet, across the yard and peered in at Veen's cabin window. His one room was no more than twice the size of her own and the chief difference in comfort was that he had a board floor and a low, wooden bed. There he lay.

He was half covered by a blanket and his face was hidden under a cloth. A bowl of water, which served to keep the cloth wet and cool, and a stone jug rested on the shelf beside his bed. It was the second jug she had brought him from the lean-to last night and she knew that it had been full of a clear, burning liquid that people here called 'cone.' They seemed to drink it a lot. Veen talked little to her, explained almost nothing, and so she had no idea why he lay for long hours with no more than mechanical moves between cloth and jug. But she knew that it would be midmorning before he'd rise and call for her to bring him some food. He called for food or water, told her to sweep his room, sent her to the market or on other errands, but he never spoke of the day he'd brought her here or of anything else. He almost never looked directly at her.

Glyn picked up a sack she had filled partly with rags and put it over her shoulder and went out the gate into the narrow street. In the early morning, only the household bounden people were seen in the streets, hauling kindling, carrying clothes to the wash pond, going to market. At the corner of the street, she met one of them she knew, a man who had been on the march and on the rafts with her. She had never known his name then, but now she knew where he lived and knew that he was called Simson's Sam, just as she was now called Veen's Glyn. He had a face sanded with freckles and an open smile with no teeth to show. He was a builder, at home used to saw and hammer.

They stopped close to each other for a moment. 'Mornin,' he said. 'Six ladders ready and hid in the grass. Four kegs cottonseed oil buried under my steps.'

Glyn nodded. 'Your folks are ready?'

'They know how to do,' he said.

They side-stepped quickly and went opposite ways.

Glyn turned into a narrow byway, a gray shaft between long walls. No sun fell into it yet and all the surfaces were differences of pebbled shadow stretching ahead to where at last an angled bulk blocked the way. Then it moved with a creak of wheels and from that and the stench she now smelled she knew that it was the morning slop cart. On another morning, she would have turned and gone by the longer way, but today she kept on, walking close to the left-hand wall.

Shadowed and hooded figures, dun and charcoal, pushed the cart along. Other figures, flat in the gray light, came from doorways hauling pots and bowls, lifting them for the muffled splash that seemed to raise the stench higher for a moment or two—the household bounden people doing the first chore of the morning.

Glyn got within a few paces of the cart and flattened herself against the wall to let it pass. She felt faint; the odors in her nostrils were strong and rotten.

One of the hooded people saw her and turned. He was wearing a cloth over his lower face and she caught a faint whiff of some herb smell from it. Under the hood, his eyes looked like two pale, oval bones; she knew that other eyes were studying her. She tried to stand as firm, look as directly as possible into the muffled face.

'We expect you to have the carts ready before the signal is passed. Can you stop up the lanes and streets we talked about?'

There was no answer from beneath the cloth. The bone eyes were still on her. Slowly the man's head dipped forward; then he turned with a loud 'Ho!' and heaved the cart forward, leaving Glyn behind.

She came to the end of the lane and then to a dumping ground behind buildings, where she made her way through low bushes and around piles of refuse until she reached the straight path that led,

190

through lines of trees, to the horse troop parade and the troop buildings.

Across the hoof-trodden, red field, sallowed by the rising sun, they looked like stale and hardened loaves—the stables, timbered across the place where there had been two huge doors, the storehouse, the blacksmithy, the shot tower, the guardroom where the horsemen congregated. Glyn tasted bile on her tongue. It seemed to her that all anger and hatred and desolation on her earth came from this one place. The spectral, single-eyed horsemen loomed over the dune again for an instant. Even now that she had seen them close for a long time, even now that she knew that the lost eyes were no strangeness of nature but the mark of the fights they had among themselves, in which thumb to eye was the main object—even now a voice or a hoof fall could make her shudder. Her mind made a huge hand come out of the sky and crush the blocky buildings flat.

She found herself nearly crying with anger. She shook her head to clear it and walked on. Beyond the buildings and to the right of them were wide fields where figures were already at work cutting the cornstalks for fodder. Here and there, far in the distance, shreds of smoke rose from farm chimneys.

When she reached the stable building, she tapped at the door. After a few moments and a second knock, it was opened and the night guard, a man she knew by sight but not by name, a brawny smith's helper, dressed in gray breeches and a buckskin vest, let her in. In one hand he held a mug of steaming soup and he was yawning. The passageway behind him was dimly lit by a lantern.

He smiled when he saw her, a fat and simple smile with three tooth gaps in it. He put the mug down on a ledge and stood lazily in front of her, feet apart, hands on hips, belly advanced. His brown hair stood up on his head like forkfuls of hay.

'I came to get the cunel's boots and some things he wants from his saddlebags,' Glyn said in a small voice.

The man stared. Finally, he said, 'Reckin so, honey. But ah kin give yo somethin better.'

'Please let me go by.'

'Not till yawl answer a question.'

Glyn felt a chill. 'What question?'

'Ifn ah get offn duty raht-smat, will yawl lay down in ma bunk with me for a spell?'

She was afraid to speak; she shook her head.

He grinned again and put one big arm around her. She could feel his fingers between her buttocks and the other hand, under her shirt, squeezing her right breast and pinching her nipple.

She dropped the bag and butted her head under his chin as she kicked wildly at his shins.

He held her struggling for a moment, then he laughed and let her go. 'Reckin yawl ain't sleepy,' he said as she pushed past him down the passage. 'Hea,' he said, and threw the bag after her.

She went through the door into the stables and walked down the long row of stalls with the straw rustling under her feet and the sharp, briny smell tingling her nostrils. Except for an occasional snort or the stamping of a hoof, the horses were quiet. She recognized the shiny rump of Veen's new black, its tail switching. Later in the morning, when he had dragged himself from whatever gulf he descended into at night, he would come to exercise it, riding as far from the settlement as he could go in an hour.

She felt gratitude and a little sorrow for Veen, but it was almost the sorrow and gratitude of looking backward, because for her he had the mark of the soon-dead. Every word he spoke, every gesture he made, had the sense of dying.

She went into the tackle room and found Jos waiting for her. He was standing alone at the big table cluttered with a variety of reins, girths, stirrups, and bits and curbs spread out in front of him for inspection or mending, but he was only pretending to work. He wagged his bald head at her and held up a forefinger; then he pointed to a pallet off in the corner where one of the horsemen was noisily asleep.

Jos had been taken and brought to New Mefis more than three years ago and what he knew and what he'd learned about horses and horse sickness were vast. In time, he had become the bounden man in charge of the stable, under the orders of the sarjint of horse—whom he hated.

He crooked the finger and turned. Glyn followed him to the outside door and into a little blind walkway between two buildings. He led along a windowless wall and they came to another door, which Jos slid open quietly and closed behind them.

They were in one of the unused buildings—Glyn could tell that from the dust everywhere and the musty smell. The roof was a high, round arch, and just below it, rows of windows let in a grimy light. At first, she was aware only of shapes, then a bigger shape that bulked in the center of the space.

'Stay here a minute,' Jos said, and went off.

She began to look curiously at the extraordinary apparatus in front of her. It had the body of an enormous fish, about ten paces long. The end near where she stood was a tall blade, half oval in shape, and two more blades of much the same shape jutted out on either side, almost parallel with the floor.

From the body, two thirds of the way along, projected an even huger blade, so far outstretched that she wondered why it did not tip or bend. She walked slowly around to the other end, beginning to realize that this was a machine of some sort. She saw a long blade on the other side to balance the one on this, two big, podlike things with heavy sticks attached to their fronts and—when she stooped down to look—legs with wheeled feet on which the whole affair rested.

She examined the blunt fish nose and saw small windows in the front and windows at the sides. There seemed to be doors in the body just under the wide blades. She stepped close and peered in, wiped off the dust and peered again, but what she saw only confused her—a board with strange circles on it, chairs and a half wheel. She stood there, almost expecting something to happen in the interior, and she felt timid.

Then she walked out and stood in front of the thing, half closing her eyes and trying as hard as she could to imagine what it was.

And suddenly the form of it came to her. She remembered the children at Haven Place running down a steep dune and shrilling, 'I can fly, I can fly!' The forward-leaning nose of the thing and its widespread arms said, 'I can fly!'

Of course, she had heard all the fanciful forefather tales about sails that carried people and goods through the air, but that was only a story. Now the sail was real, in front of her. She saw herself step forward, open the door of the thing, climb inside, and pull the string that made it start. The building doors opened to let it jump into the air; then she was sailing over the trees and the river, in the blue, toward home.

'Come on now,' Jos said in a low voice behind her. He led on through an aisle between piles of crates and big cylinder shapes to a little iron staircase at the far side of the building and finally to a landing and a peeling green door.

Sitting at an old table in the half-lit room, Bet studied a paper in front of her. She smiled at Glyn and then cast her eyes down to the paper again. It had many lines and squares on it.

Pictures. They were a thing Glyn had never seen much of and her own few she had nearly memorized; Robin Hood and his merry men shooting arrows was the best. Here there were dusty pictures on every wall: a man's face, one of the air-going machines with three people standing by it, tall hills, a dog. On the wall behind Bet was a yellow oblong of papers with big printed letters that Glyn read slowly and did not understand: 'EARTH MOVER CORP.' Then

another line: 'Heavy Equipment For All Construction Jobs.''
Smaller letters said: 'Memphis, Tenn.'

Below the words there was another line that read: 'June 1989,'
and beneath that there was an oblong lined off in many squares,
with each square containing a number from 1 to 30. There must be
a sense to this, but it was hardly clear how the forefathers could
make the earth move with a set of numbers.

Bet suddenly raised her head again. 'Child, there's things to tell
you. Sit down on that chair.'

Glyn sat. Jos stood by the door, one ear close to the crack.

'I brought the messages,' Glyn began. 'Oak is ready for the gate-
house, but they need more axes, three at least. Beech and Chestnut
have the tunnel mostly dug, but last night they found it's still ten
paces short—another day and a night, they say. Hemlock snaked two
trade rifles out of the gun smithy but there'll be a count before makit
day. One man in Buckeye died yesterday and two more are sick—can
they get others? Hickory did what you said and hid the oil kegs and
torches in other places. I think that's all.'

Bet nodded and looked at Jos.

'My tens are ready,' he said. 'Ready now for days, two from in
and two from out.'

Bet turned back to look at Glyn. 'There's something.' She
stopped and tapped her knuckles on the table. 'Something wry. A
stranger come into the settlement and he asks for you. He knows
your name.'

With a jump in her heart, Glyn said, 'My father!'

Bet shook her head. 'A young man with the look of a trader. He
came through the gate with a mule at first light, didn't go to the
makit, tried to talk on the sly with what boundens he could find.
Found one and asked where Glyn Havensdotter could be. He don't
talk like any Southron.'

'He could be a Haven Place man my father sent—'

'You know them all by sight?'

'Yes.'

'Then come back here past dark, just at suppertime. We'll fetch
him. Jos will show you a side door where you can slip in. Better go
now before some nosy begins wonderin.'

Glyn wanted to ask Bet if she had learned how to read the
numbers of June 1989, and so could move the earth, but Bet said,
'Now hurry. Jos, show her the slip-out door.'

There were three candles on the table. The little window in the wall
had been covered with a blanket and scantlings. Glyn was standing

hidden in the shadows while Jos with two of the men stood with their backs against the wall by the door. Each held a bushcutter.

Glyn liked the look of the stranger; he was tall and easy. Back straight, feet apart, hands clasped behind him, he stood in front of the desk and looked at Bet. He was not smiling, but his face had the sense of a man ready to smile. He seemed untroubled by being brought to a secret room in the night by men with long knives. He wore hunter's buckskins and much-traveled hide boots.

Bet finally looked up at him and spoke. 'Name? Where from?'

'Kinkaid, from River Cross Place in Pennsylvan-land. But that's no matter.'

Bet nodded as if she knew what all that meant. 'Welsir, and what do you come for?'

'To take away Glyn Havensdotter to her father. He's waiting.'

Glyn wanted to believe. She had known that Haven would not give her up. But Bet had told her not to speak until she was asked.

'No one hereabouts carries that name. Glyn is it?' Bet paused. Then she began to speak in a quick, harsh voice. 'You wear the patch on your eye? You came into the settlement with a mule an barter goods? You got on a trader's hat and a trader's coat? I think you came to find us out.'

The stranger looked puzzled and then amused. 'Find you? No, only the girl.' He raised one hand and took off the eye patch. 'It was just to look like one of them. I see from both eyes. The clothes came with me from River Cross Place. For the hat and the mule—well, last night a trader had an uncommon meeting with a stranger in the dark. His hat and his mule came along with me and he's tied up in a cellar a ways from here. The truth is that I came down the river on a boat with Haven and the Haven Place men.'

Glyn spoke suddenly. 'Where did Haven come from before that?'

'Across the big lake Michigan in a double-canoe boat.'

'Alone?'

'With Piet.'

'And how did he know the direction to come here?'

'From a map he found long ago.'

'I believe you now,' Glyn said. 'Bet! I believe him! Tell me where my father is!'

The stranger turned toward Glyn's shadowy corner. 'So here you are,' he said. 'And your father is at a place near the big ruins downstream. Will you go with me tonight, then?'

There was silence for some moments. 'How many rifles are you?' Bet asked at last.

'Nine all told.'

Bet considered that. 'Nine.' She waited again before she said slowly, 'Would you and yours help in a fight to make all the bounden free?'

Slower still, the man called Kinkaid shook his head. 'I think there are too many horsemen. I can't speak for Haven.'

'We can't let you go now,' Bet said. 'The horsemen would catch you and you'd talk to em.' A bushcutter clinked against the wall. For the first time, Kinkaid looked troubled.

'Bet, tell him!' Glyn pleaded. 'Kinkaid, listen to her. We are bounden people, just like the people from your own settlement. Someday, the horsemen may come to your home place and take the folk away.'

Bet waited a moment more. Then she seemed to make up her mind. She stood up. 'Three nights from now, we're goin to surprise the Southrons in their sleep and set afire this settlement. It's all laid, all schemed out to block the roads, stifle the guards, an hand out the guns. There's a tunnel—' She paused. 'Well, I needen say. Nine rifles comin at em from outside the walls would make a go of it.' She looked at him from under her eyebrows.

There was a disturbance in Kinkaid's face. A muscle twitched in his jaw and he bit his lower lip. He put one hand up and covered his eyes for a moment, saying something in a voice so low that Glyn could not understand.

'The girl kin go with you if you swear to bring back your eight. Not unless.'

He lowered his hand. 'You'd trust me?'

'I trust her. And her father, to do right.'

Kinkaid was thinking. After some time, he sighed and nodded his head. 'Yes, then.'

He spent that night in the cellar of an outlying house near the town hall, distressed and wakeful. A dozen times during the hours he got up and stood in the dark near the cellar door, listening for sounds outside. He had fallen into a sweating sleep when Glyn came just before daylight and roused him.

She brought his mule—he'd learned the name of his animal from Bet—and his rifle. Then she led the way to a place where the mound wall had slid away into the dry ditch over the years and where they could cross it without being seen.

She brought him through some woods to a dirt track, little traveled, that led southward. That day, they met only a bounden boy driving a cow, a man who looked incuriously at a trader leading a bounden woman behind his mule and went on cutting wood, and two old women on a path to a cabin in the distance.

Late in the afternoon, when Kinkaid judged that they had passed by the last of the settlement farms, they let the mule loose in a pasture, took the saddlebags on their own backs, and went on into the twilight.

The house they found for the night was a forefather place, almost lost in weeds and bushes. Its roof had slumped, but by the light from a candle stump, they found a room that was at least covered and dry.

Kinkaid had spoken seldom during the day. As they shared a little meat and bread from the saddlebag, he was still silent and Glyn hesitated to try talking. Very soon, he twitched out the candle flame with his fingers and they lay down, a pace apart, on the littered and musty floor.

21

There were two sounds in the dark—the steady slurring of the rain outside the walls and the irregular plop-plink-plink of a leak somewhere in the room. Kinkaid woke and tried to put the fragments of reality back together—no, he was not awakened from his dream in Erie Place, nor was he in the place of the graves, nor was he in the cellar in the settlement of New Mefis. He reached out a hand, felt a body beneath a blanket and heard Glyn softly moan, and was back in his present. He let his hand rest on the blanket for a moment, thinking about the deceit he had entered into and today would have to confess. There was his promise to Haven, first among promises. Weighing deceit against trust in the scales troubled him because he could not remember ever breaking a trust before, and he knew that this would be his hardest day.

He pressed her shoulder and she sighed as she awoke. He wanted to put his arms around her and say, 'I have told you a lie to save you from a horror. And likely, death.' But instead, he said gently, 'Come; it's morning and we have far to go. We'll eat a corn cake and hope for the rain to slow. Then we start.'

He could hear her sitting up, sensed she was rubbing her eyes, felt the blanket pushed aside.

Kinkaid groped his way to the door and filled a cup with rain water. They sat in the dark, sharing the cup and the cake, their fingers meeting and touching.

'They'll be on the hunt for us today,' she said. 'They never forget and never give up.'

'When do you think they knew you were gone?'

'Late, I think. The cunel would have looked for me at noon. Then he would have gone to the training.' She paused. 'In the late afternoon, I think.'

'And been riled?'

'He's a queer man, kindly sometimes, cruel others.' Kinkaid felt

198

her hand on his arm. 'As a bounden girl, I'm not much. But run away, I'm a sliver under their skin.'

'Yes,' he said. 'In the rain, their dogs can't scent a trail, at least. D'you know how they hunt runaways?'

'One of the field men tried the day after we came. He ran north, but the dogs found him in the morning. I think he was dead, or might as well be, when they hanged him.' He could see just a faint tracing of her face in profile in the edge of day. He wanted to forget the rain and the running and hold her under the blanket close to him until he could bring himself to tell her.

'They send out hunting parties, a dozen horsemen to each,' she said. 'Every one has its own roads and trails. They know the country.' She stopped and turned to him, but she did not ask her question. He liked the quiet, steady sound of her voice.

'Yes, we have a chance,' he answered. 'Our chance first and theirs second. We know what we're going to do and they don't—and have wasted time finding out.'

'Do you always know what you're going to do next?'

'I'm still alive. I reckon what others—man or beast—think I'm going to do and don't do it. One pace ahead. I reckon what they'll do when they find they're wrong—two paces ahead.'

'And the paces now?'

'They thought we were heading north; wrong. The next most possible is that we'll hide in the big warren of the settlement ruins. And for the twists and turns of that, they need their dogs. And so we have slim time, but time enough.'

While they had been talking, she had risen and packed their few things in the saddlebags. He went to the window and looked out. The light outside was the thinnest of skim milks; they could see shapes in the room. Kinkaid went into another part of the house and rummaged, coming back finally with two pieces of rumpled, slippery stuff, like cloth but not cloth.

'What is it?'

'You find it in forefather places a lot. I don't know—but it never seems to rot and the water rolls off it.' He shook the dust from the two pieces of material and they were dully translucent. He wrapped one around her, as a kind of cape with a cone over her head, and tied it with a string. She did the same for him and they strapped the saddlebags on their backs and went out into the road.

The rain was stubborn but not heavy. The light came grudgingly. They walked for a long time in silence. Kinkaid was calculating times and distances, working out their route by the features he remembered from his approach, stopping to peer for the distant tall buildings through the gray rain. They had two smaller rivers to cross, both running through belts of forest and both with still-standing bridges.

He decided to risk those bridges. Better caught in the open than struggling in the water. Then, keeping always south and west, they could angle through the thickness of the settlement to the way he'd come by, the one that led to the riverbank, and finally, there would be the road along the bluffs to the barrier.

They marched a long time after the rivers were passed, the morning like a greenish scum in the eastern sky. There was no sound except for the splash of the rain and the squelch of their boots. They moved through road after road of dilapidated small houses. Kinkaid was beginning to feel that his nerves had relaxed one notch. 'No!' he said suddenly.

'What?' asked Glyn. She had been following a few steps behind him, but now she caught up. 'No riders? Are we safe?'

'By all rights; we're in the roads now. If I were a horseman, I'd give up on this maze. It's so big it would take a day to walk across. I saw it all from one of the high towers.'

'But?'

They had come to the crossing of two roads. In the space where they met, a big, blocky, rusted form made of metal rested at a tilt. It had a row of wheels along the side and a kind of long, cleated belt was looped under them and over. Atop the body there was a squat tower with a long tube pointing from it.

'But I remember my grandfather's old saying. He's dead years, but it's as if he reminds me sometimes. He used to say, "Winning positions are the most dangerous ones." '

'And the sense of that? Winning positions?'

'You have to think of—' Kinkaid suddenly stopped and put his hand up.

The only noise was the slither of the rain. They were standing in a road lined on either side by rows of small, close-set houses, some sagging, some with roofs fallen, some half carpeted with creeper.

He pointed to the nearest house and began to walk up the overgrown path, while she followed. They found a place where they could crouch behind a tangle of chest-high bushes and waited while slow time passed.

Finally, in the distance, there was the echoing clop of hoofs on the roadway, moving deliberately. Kinkaid risked a brief look and saw three riders coming along in single file, their hats streaming water and their leather capes black with rain. They looked routinely from side to side, but the shoulders had a weary bow and the eyes had seen too many empty roads since daybreak. They were headed north.

200

After they had waited awhile, the two set out again. 'Did your grandfather whisper they were coming?' Glyn asked.

Kinkaid smiled. 'Call it a quiver in the air,' he said. 'I sometimes seem to have a hearing a little beyond hearing.'

As they came to the roadway approaches to the upriver bridge span, the rainfall lifted and fell inconstantly. The tall towers, with their thousands of oblong punctures, were clear at the lower levels but grew indistinct in their upper reaches. Glyn lagged and stared at them. 'Are they real?' she asked. 'I can't believe in them.'

At last, they arrived at the bluff-edge road that Kinkaid had followed the first day. Through the gloomy mists that hung over the river, they could get a view of the tumbled barrier. From this distance, it looked like some natural growth on the waters. Kinkaid pointed out the tiny fleck of the boat riding at the far end, the several mouths where the river flowed through the barrier, and he tried to explain about the precarious path across.

They walked the length of the road in silence, gazing at the river and then at the clouds in hopes that the sky would clear. When they finally came to the field and the triple bridgehead lay just a hundred or so paces beyond, they stopped to rest and took the saddlebags from their backs. Glyn sat down and Kinkaid squatted on his heels.

'We'll climb down to the starting point,' he said, 'and find some shelter if there is any. It's death to try to cross now. But the rain's less and less. It may dwindle off.'

'Will they know we're here?'

'There's a man on lookout and I'll signal. I told Haven to watch for me on the morning of the second day, with or without. But he knew it would be with.'

She was tracing a circle on the muddy ground with a twig. 'And tomorrow we take the Haven men with us to New Mefis. To set the others free.' It was not a question.

And so Kinkaid had arrived at the bleak moment. He hesitated awhile, wishing that he had something more than plain and simple speech to command, wishing that he could speak in colors. The color of fire gnawing through wood, color of black smoke rising in the sky, bright color of blood, pale color of a dead face, color of ashes. He said softly, 'I lied to you. There's no going back.'

She looked at him and half smiled, as if waiting for him to explain another oddity.

'Yes, and I'm ashamed. But I had a promise to Haven to bring you back, and so I had to lie. From here, with luck, we go north to home.'

He saw that she was biting her lower lip and that a band of color had spread across her cheekbones. She was staring at him. He said,

'Yes, and I'm sorry for it. But we're too few—a few rifles and the bounden people with their bare hands. The rising is damned, with us or without us. Some of theirs and a lot of yours will die and all will be worse for it.' He heard the unnatural sound of his own voice, like the hollow sound of a voice in a well.

She looked furiously at him and stood up. 'I'll go alone, then.' She turned her back. A gust of wind drove cold rain between them.

'I saw a great killing once,' he said. She took a step.

Then, above the heavy monotone of the river, they heard something. Again. The hunting whoop of the horsemen, faint and far off. They were gathering.

Kinkaid straightened from his crouch and peered down the bluff road behind them. Away in the distance he could see miniature black figures in the midst of side-splaying water as a group of horsemen came on at a gallop. How had they divined that he and Glyn would be here? Some trace they had left or some chance sighting? He thought of what he'd said about the winning point.

He ran and caught Glyn by the shoulders and turned her toward the bridgehead. 'Leave the bags. Run!' He gave her a push, then he was unwrapping his rifle to fire one unaimed signal shot. It had a muffled sound and a soft echo in the watery air.

Glyn was walking as if her heart pained her. Kinkaid swept her along with him, pelting into the bushy field, splashing, stumbling through the growth. It seemed a long way to where the nearest of the three spans jutted from the heights and inclined down to the water.

They reached it at last, stopped for breath and looked back. Just then, they heard a muffled hail from below them on the barrier. Kinkaid turned and saw the broken bridge span descending in a straight, rain-shiny slope for about fifty paces, like a wide, canted plank, to where its end was lost in the heaps and tangles below. There was Haven, just at the lower end, waving them forward.

The risk here was that they might slide, and Kinkaid took a grip on Glyn's arm and moved carefully. Beyond Haven's shaggy head he could see the water, and for the first time, he realized that it had become a swollen, thrusting flood.

At the last ten paces, they began to skid. Haven spread his big arms, laughing, and enfolded them both in a hug. 'Steady! I'm glad to see you, but don't knock me over. So you brought the hornets on your trail?' Then he was at the lip of the incline, motioning for them to follow. There was a twisting channel through a mass of broken stone and iron beams that led to his nest beside the water. He made them squat down behind the breastwork of mud and rubble.

'How soon before they're here?'

'A hundred counts or so,' Kinkaid said. 'They're roweling their horses.'

Haven shook his head. 'And so we must rowel ourselves.'

Glyn, panting began, 'Father, I have to tell you—'

'Stories later, words later. We'll be moving.' He rose.

'Cross in the rain?' Kinkaid asked. He was remembering the slips and near-mishaps he'd had on a sunny and windless day.

'Twisty and risky, I admit. But can you think of another way?' He was already tying a light rope from his waist to Glyn's. He handed Kinkaid another coil of it. 'We'll go first because there're places where only two can go at a time. Follow us about twenty paces back.' He put his hand into a recess of the breastwork, drew out one of the Armalite rifles and handed it to Kinkaid. 'You know how to use it. If they get too close, give 'em a few barks.'

Kinkaid watched them start out down the hilly path through the branches, jagged chunks of stone and beam ends of metal. Then they were at the water's edge, navigating a teetering strip of planks and logs out toward the first barrier gap. With a start, he noticed that the water had already overlapped the footway by a few inches and they were wading. The river looked like a thick, waxy gravy.

They moved carefully, clinging to the strung rope like two wind-troubled leaves. But Haven appeared to know every step and he moved agilely; behind him, Glyn seemed to gain a little confidence. The wet rope shivered in the wind.

The rain had borne off to the north, leaving swirls of mist, and now it was pocking a wide sheet of the river upstream. A little breeze came from the southwest; with luck, it would hold and the traverse would be that jot less treacherous. But Kinkaid looked to the western sky and saw clouds like a flock of huge black storm birds coming from far off and he knew he would have more weather before he could rest on the other side.

He took a long look at the bluff, saw nothing changed, could not help turning to watch as Haven and Glyn reached the first gap. Two ropes spanned it, and from one dangled the short loop that rode on a pulley—Piet's device. He saw Haven grasp the loop, seize the second span rope and, with four great clutches, haul himself over the channel. He'd scarcely planted his feet when he sent the loop sliding back to Glyn. She was just hooking her arm in the loop and drawing her legs up when Kinkaid heard the first shot.

It had the hollow crack of a branch breaking far off in the forest and then a dull echo. Two horsemen sat their mounts above on the bluff edge, black cutouts against the cindery sky; two beards, two down-curled hat brims, two rifles cradled.

The taller one raised his arm and silently the high shore grew serrated with a line of black riders, more than a dozen. For the moment, they seemed blind to Kinkaid as he crouched behind the breastwork, and they studied the movements of Haven and Glyn. Evidently at an order, one of them swung off his horse, knelt, brought up his rifle and began to sight.

Kinkaid stroked the Armalite, felt gently to see if the bullet holder was snug in place, breathed a wish to his omens, raised the barrel slowly to rest across the breastwork, aimed, caught the line-end silhouette lodged at the tip of his sight.

The sound burst. Kinkaid felt only the pressure of his muscles working from left to right and the strain to hold down the rearing, live thing in his arms. He was deafened.

Up there, he could see horses' bodies as they climbed the air and twisted; hoofs pedaled wildly, riders jerked backward and vanished. Then the thunderous cracking under his hands was cut off, trailing behind it a long, thin clamor of neigh and scream.

The sound died away. Kinkaid laid the rifle on the parapet, stunned and grateful for silence, and stared at what he had wrought. The power of his own destruction astonished him. The line on the bluffs had been scythed away and only some dark heaps remained along the rim. A little farther back, a few horsemen seemed to be riding furiously in circles, struggling for control of their beasts. A breeze-borne mist swept over Kinkaid and obscured the shore. When it cleared a little, he could see only the heaps and the sky. Somewhere in the distance, he heard the halloo of a rider.

Then it came to Kinkaid that, just now, the rifle had jerked to a stop before he had released his pressure; either the bullets were all fired or there had been some snag. He examined it, tinkered with it for a moment, and decided that it was beyond quick repair. He started to sling it, with his own, across his shoulder, and knew immediately that it would be too cumbersome to carry. And there was something else: just the touch of it gave him a kind of horror now. He cast it into the river and, with his own rifle slung across his back, started down the path along the barrier.

Haven and Glyn were out of sight by this time; all he could see were the waters to his right and the looming brier mass of the barrier to his left. It was like a steep cliff, with all the dead things of the world collected by the river brought and stored here over countless years. He waded cautiously along the pieced-out path of logs, going as quickly as prudence let him, feeling forward with his foot before he planted it. Among the banks of dead branches he could see old bottles, chairs, floorboards, animal pens, rusted buckets, broken wheels, basketwork, festoons of rags. A log end bobbed and swung outward under his step and he had to jump quickly. Luckily, the next plank was firmly grounded.

As he worked his way along to the first barrier gap, the path became a muddy ledge. Piet had stretched a rope here and so, sliding his hands along the rough, wet line and pulling himself forward, he reached the crossing. He took his knife and sawed the path line down to its last strand.

The next move, which had seemed so dangerous the first day, now seemed the easiest. He took one look at the rushing water at his feet, hooked his arm in the hanging loop, grasped the first knot in the span rope and, knot by knot, swayed himself across. Then he cut both ropes and looped them well back over a branch on his side. The next man would have a trickier crossing.

He was sure that there would be a next, probably more than one. Every sign he knew showed them as hard, tenacious men, and slippery footing would not hold them up for long. As he went on, he wondered what was happening behind him. Absorbed in the separate problem of each step, he had no notion of how much time had passed since the tumult on the riverbank. Just now there was the feat of twisting his body through a narrow alley of sharp points—metal and stone from the wreck of the bridge. Ahead, there were the tactics of climbing a mound of rubble and branches and sliding down the other side, sliding just to the right spot on the water-covered ribbon of path. A hand's span wrong and he'd be in the river.

Had they gathered themselves, tended to their wounded and sent back for more riders? Had they picked a few scouts to attack the barrier, even now working their way down cautiously toward the nook from which had come that astounding eruption of bullets? Did they imagine there had been a hundred men there, all firing at once?

Several times, he looked back along what he could see of the path and upward to the bluffs, but the drizzle obscured all details.

The trouble ahead was clear enough, though. There was a bulky outcrop of debris that jutted about ten paces into the water. The top and sides were covered with such a jumble of old ironwork and stone that they had found it impossible to run the path over it. And so Piet had improvised a kind of crazy skirt of stone and timber, lashed with rope and old wire. It was still just clear of the lapping water, but the river had cast up on it a foamy brown scum that made every step treacherous. Looking at it, Kinkaid thought of some greasy discharge from the belly of the great stream.

He began to maneuver his way along. To make the stretch even worse, Piet's guide rope was strung in zigs and zags among the wild lacery of brush and branch. Each new clutching place had to be sighted ahead and the step and the grasp coordinated. It was literally hand over hand. Kinkaid knew that he was edging out into deadly exposure to any riflemen on the bluff or on the trail behind him, and he tried to hurry.

He was getting close to the point and reaching out for another handhold when he felt a length of timber roll beneath his foot. He lunged for the line and caught it just with his fingertips, but it was too slippery to hold. As he spun helplessly, sidewise toward the water, a man who had come along the path to his rear shot him.

Over the noise of the river, Kinkaid heard the report, startlingly close, felt a burn in his side, felt grains and slivers sting his cheek as he fell. Then he was under the cold darkness.

He was fighting the current, staying submerged, thinking. He had felt the flying grit on his face, so the bullet had either passed through him or had grazed him—only grazed, he thought. Up there on the bank there might be one man or several. But if there had been several, there would have been more than one shot because he had made such an easy target. He was tempted to take his chance in the current and to feel his way underwater along the shore, but the strong pull of the current made him fearful. He surfaced and, as he did so, he felt the force of the river pinning him against the shore between two rocky spurs. His right arm was prisoned and he thrust desperately with his left to make a half turn against the shelf.

A man stood reloading his rifle at a crook in the path about fifty paces behind Kinkaid. The rain had died away for the time being and Kinkaid could see him very clearly—the bloody rag bound around his head, the eyebrows like black wings above a whittled, bone-white face, the black clump of beard on his chin. He seemed very deliberate and dispassionate, as if he were hunting squirrels on a morning stroll in the woods.

He had finished and now he was raising the short, horseman's rifle to take aim. Kinkaid was looking at his eyes to watch them narrow as the barrel rose.

Kinkaid thought: I have walked all the length of this land, worked and sweated in the sun, to come to this narrow place where a stranger will kill me in the flood? The spell held him for a moment. He knew it was not true. He got ready for a great thrust outward; let the river take him instead.

Before he could make his lunge, a shot sounded. He ducked his head, but there was no splash, no spray of pebbles, no stunning blow.

And Kinkaid saw the second man then. He was perhaps a hundred paces back on the barrier path, partly hidden by brush and crouched on one knee. He wore the sag-brimmed horseman's hat and all that Kinkaid could see of his face was a mop of wet beard that was strangely split in the middle.

The lead man stared in a puzzled way at Kinkaid and then slowly brought his rifle close to his chest as if he was weary of the weight of it. One knee began to buckle. Then he turned his head slowly, looking toward the man behind him, letting the rifle slip from his hands. He turned back toward Kinkaid then and spread his arms wide, almost as if imploring, and fell silently forward, his face in the water.

It seemed to make no sense at all. But there was no time to wonder. Kinkaid guessed that he would have about twenty counts while the man in the bushes reloaded and got him in his sights.

Getting a purchase with one knee, Kinkaid heaved and so managed to twist his body and get one arm free. He reached and caught a branch and then, with painful slowness, he was able to half drag, half claw his way ashore. Winded and exhausted, he waited for the second shot.

It did not come. Instead, when he'd shaken the water from his eyes, he saw the horseman walk slowly forward to where the body lay. He squatted down next to it, took the head by the back hair and looked into the face. Kinkaid was on his feet now, catching the rope and pulling himself forward. The blunt end of the outcrop was only a few paces away, but he felt the rifleman's aim behind him and knew that he would not miss.

He reached the point. With a last tug, he pulled himself beyond it and into shelter. Then, amazed to find himself safe, he risked a backward look. The second horseman had been paying no attention to him at all. He had evidently just picked the body up and cast it into the river, because it was lying there, arms still outstretched like the wings of a fallen hawk, as the water played with the bandage and unrolled it. Then the current tumbled the body over and rushed it along.

The man turned his back, cupped his hands to his mouth and gave a long halloo. He did not appear to be in any great hurry to pursue and Kinkaid assumed that he must be waiting for others to catch up with him.

Kinkaid made a quick survey of his troubles. His right side was shiny with dark blood and it felt numb to his hip. But wiping the blood away with his shirttail, he found that the bullet had done no more than cut a deep furrow in his side and, he thought, broken his lowest rib. The pain was beginning to come.

He tore a strip from his shirt. He had been carrying the light line that Haven had given him wrapped around his waist, and now he rewound it higher up. He rose, took the rope and staggered forward. Then something in the river current caught his eye and he stopped.

It was nothing more than a half-submerged log with a few branches projecting above the water, but Kinkaid watched it intently as it rounded the point of the outcrop and was carried strongly past him by the current. Then he remembered that while he had been in the water, there had been a constant pressure drawing him outward along the barrier toward the middle of the river. And this fathered an improbable idea in his mind.

Time was what he needed most of all, enough to let Glyn and Haven reach the boat, enough to let him limp his way to the end of this fearsome crossing. He set out, moving as quickly as the pain and the dubious footing would let him. Through a bristling stand of vine-covered branches he could already see the open place where the next channel would be.

The horsemen, he guessed, would work along slowly, two in advance to string again the ropes he had cut, and a few more would follow the path to the rear, to cover them with their rifles. They knew that he was hurt and that his rifle was waterlogged, and so all that they needed was persistence. He had a sudden picture of those men, concealed in the bushes or rock crannies of the barrier, firing on the open boat.

Kinkaid came to the next gap, a wider one than any before. He tested the loop and noticed that this one had no pulley—but Piet had greased the span rope well enough and the slide would not be too troublesome, unless he lost consciousness. However, he was not yet ready to cross.

He turned around and, with his knife, sliced the guide rope; that would give him a little time but not much, because it was tied in sections to whatever firm supports Piet had found in the tortuous semicircle that rounded the point. Then, knowing that he was about to stretch his luck to its last inch, Kinkaid squatted on his heels and waited, staring into the water where the current ran along his small gravelly apron and joined the powerful rush of water pouring through the gap.

Nothing happened. There was no sound except the drone of the flood. They would be noting the bloodstains he had left behind, taking up their positions to edge forward along the trail. He wondered how the man with the split beard would explain the loss of the leader. Most likely, he would let the others assume that the man was still in advance, out of their sight.

The rain had come back again in a very fine fall, almost like the damp breath of the river. Kinkaid had long ago lost the sheet of covering he'd taken from the house and, sitting still like this, he shivered in the cold air. He wondered how long he dared wait. He would give himself fifty counts more. At the count eleven, he saw it.

A hand appeared above a dark mass in the water and slowly sank back. Kinkaid was ready with a long branch, and struggling and slipping, he managed to hook the body. Then, using the current to help him, he drew it slowly alongside the shore and wrestled it onto the apron.

He spent no time examining it. He simply tied one end of his line around the chest under the armpits and the other end around his own waist. Moving quickly, he grasped the span rope, stuck his arm through the loop and jumped outward. At once, his whole torso blazed with pain. The sky and the barrier whirled dizzily before his eyes, but some willful force kept stretching his arm toward the next knot, one, two, three. He looked down for a moment and saw the violent flume of yellow water an inch beneath his heels. And then he was over. And then he could squat down and let the pain have its way for a few moments.

Kinkaid did not cut the span rope this time. He found a thick branch where he could tie his line. He braced himself, took four deep breaths and put all his strength into the pull.

When the body was caught by the full force of the current, Kinkaid was almost dragged off his feet, but in the next moment, he had a little luck. Some quirk of the flood threw the body up to the very surface and he gave a great haul with all his strength until he felt the form grate on the little shore.

It was about ten paces back from the gap line where Kinkaid arranged the body. He propped it on a piece of a log and, with the help of sticks under the clothes, he was able to put it in a fairly lifelike position. The head still drooped, but he cut a thin strip of cloth from the coat and, binding it to a stick, made the head stand as upright as possible. The hair was sticky with blood. The belly was a gruesome hole where the bullet had made its exit; Kinkaid buttoned the coat over that.

He stepped back for one brief look. The man seemed to be sitting there either very tired or very pensive and his bloodless face seemed no paler than it had a little while ago in the last minutes of his life. Looking at his sharp and bony features, Kinkaid thought to see a harsh cruelty in them, but he did not. He could not tell whether the man had been harsh or mild, good or bad. Whatever spirit of this or that, he decided, vanishes from the face with death.

It was not very far, about twenty paces ahead on the path, where stood one of the great stone slabs of the old bridge supports. Kinkaid had just settled behind it and had begun to watch the far shore of the gap when two of his hunters cautiously emerged from the path.

When they saw the figure on the opposite side, they hurried ahead to the gap. One of them was the man with the cleft beard and the other was a taller, rangy man. They stared for a moment. Then one of them called out and Kinkaid could hear the voice in the background of the waters: 'Cunel! Yawl raht? Cunel?'

So it was the leader Glyn had spoken of. Kinkaid, crouching, slipped away and took the path again, up the stripped bole of a large dead pine, from there a drop of a few feet to the ground, again along a thin ledge that bordered the water.

Those men, if they were anything like the settlement people he knew, would be disconcerted by a sight so strange and unexplained. Especially, he thought, the killer. Then, going a little closer, they would find that their cunel had been shot in the back. Thus it would seem—not to the killer, but to the others—that Kinkaid must have got behind him. And they would begin to look over their shoulders. With that, they would have to assume that Kinkaid now had a rifle that could fire.

They would not go back; he knew that. They would listen to the bearded man trying to encourage them. But now they would take twice as long over every step, take cover at the least disturbance, spend long moments studying every obstacle ahead of them and at their flank on the barrier's wild hillside.

Still, the bearded man, he had a feeling, was a stubborn hunter. He could not capture Kinkaid now, only kill him. No dangerous trail or cut ropes would hold up that hunter very long. But there was one thing he could not know about—the second Armalite.

Kinkaid moved on, cutting ropes methodically and destroying the path wherever stones had been cleared or timbers had been staked end to end. The pain, which had let up for a short time, was with him again and he found himself pausing to rest every dozen paces or so. He scrabbled up a small, stony mound, trying to keep as low as possible, and then limped down the reverse slope to pursue the snaking path through another dead, uprooted forest and again arrive at a precarious shelf where the river chuted through a barrier break with a humpbacked surge that made the earlier gaps seem puny.

Since long ago this morning, when he had first walked down the bridge slope into the narrow country of the barrier, he'd had the feeling of being in some phantom place. It was a territory all negative. The signals of the world—settlement or forest—had always come first through his hearing, but in this place, there was one steady sound alone. And so he was deaf. Around him there was a nightmare imitation of a forest, a forest of dead, uprooted trees. And the stone was not real stone but the grainy, molded stuff of the forefathers. Mixed in it all were the ancient glass, metal, wooden objects of the gone world, scavenged by the river and dumped here. He felt cut off from real ground, real sight, real hearing and—hunted when he could not fight—any real way of action.

He had lost all sense of how far he'd come, how many barrier gaps he'd swung himself over, how many thin edges of the trail he'd traversed, when at last he arrived at a tiny spit of land that faced another gap. The rain had stopped and the dull light shone on the coursing water. He was worn out. He raised his eyes to the double rope that swayed in the air, wondering if his body coud stand one more haul on them, and at that moment a burst of sunlight lit the riverscape in front of him. Through a ragged aperture in the brush the boat magically appeared, riding at its tethers by the barrier shore, its yellow planking bright in the sun. He could make out the figures of the men aboard. He thought he saw Haven standing at the prow. They had come through!

Haven seemed to look directly at him, but Kinkaid was sure he could not be seen. The boat was in motion, tugging outward at its lines and then drawing in to shore. He had only to get across the next short stretch to the last channel before he could signal.

He looked backward, scrutinizing, but he could see no sign of the hunters. They were still piecing lines together, he hoped, still trying to make one carry across that biggest channel of all.

The familiar air dance was even more agonizing this time than before and he strode dizzily—a flash of the boat bucking against its moorings, a flash of mottled sky, a flash of his ragged legs kicking out. He did not remember falling on the other side.

He opened his eyes and felt tenderly under his torn shirt. His side was a cracked shell of blood. Almost every breath now was a stab in his ribs. He leg muscles jerked with fatigue. He waited while the pain burned down to an ache.

Compared with the barrier he had traveled, this stretch was lower—no more than three times his own height—and shelving off. Here Piet had been able to lay a path almost solid and nearly straight. Twenty counts, he told himself. But when he had at last, with agony, risen to his feet, his body had no more to give than a slow limp.

He did not know how long it took him; he left off at seventy counts, but all at once, there was a quick glare of sunlight on his face and he looked up, to be startled by the boat, no more than a hundred paces away, on the other side of the last trench in the barrier.

Haven and most of the men were busy trying to shorten the

mooring ropes to keep the boat from sliding out into the full force of the current. But Glyn was at the prow, on one knee, raising her arm to him. He could see her smile, saw her turn her head to speak to the others. He was surprised that he had never seen her before; had looked at her, but had not seen her. She was beautiful. Haven turned to wave to him.

Winning positions, Kinkaid thought.

The ropes had been spliced, the channel had been bridged, the dark tunnel through the branches scouted painfully by a man crawling. It might be that the split-beard man had already sighted the boat from his place on the trail.

Kinkaid wanted Piet and a rifleman or two to come to the head of the boat and cover him while he made this last crossing. He tried to signal that, raising his arm and, with a sweeping motion, pointing behind him.

But they were trying to manage the boat and they were distracted. Haven looked up a moment, simply beckoned, and went back to the work.

Kinkaid saw himself with great weariness raising his arms to the last ropes, kicking out from the shore, numbly seizing, reaching, grasping until he seemed to be swinging at the halfway point. And, in a double vision, he saw some distance at his back a bush move, the brim of a hat show, a black rifle barrel rise slowly to point. He was hit as he dangled and he fell into the black water to be rolled far out into the deeps and shallows of the river, dreaming a dead man's dream of a black hand moving endlessly across a white page.

Kinkaid opened his eyes. He had not moved at all and he was still standing next to the loop of rope as if ready to take it in his hand.

The boat was in trouble now. In spite of the men hauling, the stern ropes seemed to have loosened and it began to swing in a slow arc into the fierce-running current. Haven and some of the other men were now at the tiller, struggling to turn the boat back shoreward. Glyn alone was at the prow, looking toward him still, and he suddenly saw her face change; a great fright came into it. She raised her arm and Kinkaid knew what she was pointing at.

He dropped to his hands and knees and crawled to what cover he could find, a thing that looked like a big door, partly buried in debris. Lying behind it, he looked back for another signal from Glyn.

She had half turned; she seemed to have called and Haven seemed to have heard. He left the tiller and came running to the front of the boat. Kinkaid saw him squint and move his head sidewise to look where Glyn was pointing.

Somehow, Kinkaid did not hear the shot from behind him, but one of the men at the ropes suddenly straightened up, his head thrown back for an instant as if he were contemplating the sky, and then slumped over the side into the water. Haven was bracing himself on the unsteady deck as the boat slowly revolved outward into the river. In his arms he cradled the Armalite. And then he raised it.

Kindaid felt a compulsion to see this ending. He turned his head and edged cautiously to where he could look back at the trail. In the sunlight, every mound of broken branches, every pebble, every shard of broken bottle, was sharply distinct.

Haven began to fire. Above the river's low thunder, it was a sound like the breaking of mountains.

Kinkaid saw a clump of bushes and dead boughs boil up into dust and cloud the air. Then, a little to the right and farther back, a pile of rubble began to splinter. A brimmed hat spun up and then disappeared. The noise of the firing halted sharply. And then, after a long moment, a bearded figure of dust and blood rose up from the wreckage, still holding a short rifle in his hands. But, Kinkaid saw, the face was a smear of red. One hand kept trying to wipe the blood from the eyes and everything stood still for an instant as the fingers passed across the face. Then the man dropped limply forward, the rifle fell on the ground, and the last of the dust began to settle on him.

Kinkaid turned his eyes back toward the boat; it had swiveled so far in the last few moments that it was nearly broadside on to the current. The knot of men still struggled with the ropes, but suddenly one line rose snaking into the air. The boat switched and jogged sidewise, like a wild horse freeing itself of its hobble, and turned in a faster and faster glide moving toward the chute.

He could no longer make out Haven or Glyn. A man with a terrified face—Kinkaid thought he was Kip, the skeptical one—stood at the side of the boat for a moment. Kinkaid was astonished to see him put his hand to his face and hold his nose before he jumped in. As soon as he hit the water, he was sucked under, and he did not reappear. The boat was bearing down toward the channel mouth now, caught in the current's full surge.

Kinkaid stood up and ran limpingly to the edge of the water. He knew that there was one poor chance left and he knew he would take it.

He reached up and gripped both the span ropes and hung all his weight from them. Piet had long ago removed the stub of mast, after the sail had proved useless, but the stout plank lean-to was about high enough to catch the span ropes. If he could hold the boat in midstream just a little time . . .

The boat bore down, only a few paces away from him now. He

could see mouths open, but he heard only the faint echo of their shouts. Piet, who had seen what he was trying to do, stumbled forward on the rushing deck. Kinkaid pulled downward with all his strength.

The ropes caught the edge of the lean-to and, for a moment, held. The ropes bowed outward and the boat shuddered, slowed, came to a halt. Piet grasped one of the span ropes and tried to tug it downward.

Then slowly the boat began to hitch forward and the bow in the rope increased. Kinkaid cast a glance behind him and saw the reason—the high branch to which the rope had been lashed was being torn from the body of the dead tree. Kinkaid looked back at the boat and stared in grief at their faces.

He saw Piet's, scowling and stubborn as he tried to hold on; he saw Glyn's, lost and beautiful; he saw Haven's with its strange, sad, serene smile.

The branch snapped and Kinkaid was suddenly pitched forward. The rope flew into the air over the lean-to and the boat bucked, nose down in the current, and shot away.

Kinkaid remembered nothing clearly after that. He knew that he was in the water, trying to thrash against it, being pulled under, still holding the rope in the crook of his arm and his hands. He was rolled over, dragged along rough stone underwater, beaten and suffocated.

He came to himself on an unfamiliar shore, washed up in the lee of a big log. He managed to sit up and to vomit a good deal of river water. He looked around. Strangely, he seemed to be on the landward side of the barrier, across the final gap. But the mass of the barrier now rose on his right. Somehow, he had grounded on its southern edge.

His eyes were bleary from the water, and when he tried to look downstream, he could not see if the boat was still above water. He thought that he saw some darker shape on the vast sunlit surface, but he could not be sure.

22

Kinkaid, dead-alive, slept and the season changed. He could not calculate how long he had lain under the lean-to in the improvised camp, but in whatever morning, he woke to find white clawprints of frost on the ground and the grass silvery. With pain, he got up to feed and water his horses and found three scrawny wild ones tethered with them, and he let these go.

Kinkaid rode the downstream bank for two days, hoping. The last he had seen of the boat, it had been rolling crazily as it shot into the river beyond the gap, awash but not engulfed. If it had survived, Haven would bring it to shore somewhere.

To the west of the camp, he found the small forefather settlement where he and Piet had done their salvaging, and he followed the S-bend of the river to a big island. It was a logical place for a landing, but though he scrutinized it for a long time, he found no signs.

One evening, he stood at a high place on the bank and lost hope as he watched it flow on into the distant haze. His mind could not conceive of a river, or anything else, without an earthly ending point, but Haven had come to be entranced with the idea of a distance beyond imagining. 'At least, longer than any man's life,' he'd said. 'And can there be an end unless it can be reached?' It was strange how Haven, during their long river trip, had become absorbed with the idea of journeying on into twilights, almost as if he had forgotten the sense of turning home again.

In the morning, Kinkaid turned back. Now the frost was a heavier brush on the land and the air pinched. Near the camp, he shot a deer, smoked and dried strips of the flesh, then loaded whatever was useful in the camp onto his horses, and struck north.

By the logic of forefather building, there should be a road from the ruined settlement leading far northward. And it was there—a broad, smooth way that had not suffered so much as the others from time and flood and the ever-working roots. It lay flat and straight as a knife blade to the line between earth and sky.

His wound was still painful but beginning to heal. Day after day, he walked or rode. At the first shading of the light, he would look for some standing building for shelter, and at the first shading of dark into day, he would eat his meager breakfast and begin again. The country he passed through at first was desolate, flat and abandoned from antiquity. There were no remains of high-towered settlements here; just the villages gone to decay and the farms gone to brush.

On the fourth day, he saw, some distance from the road, a cluster of buildings that gave thin chimney trails into the air. They huddled in the circle of a poor trench and earthen mound. Kinkaid approached slowly, his hands in the air, and saw three ragged men with rifles kneeling on the mound, ready to release a pair of growling dogs. He stopped and called in a friendly voice, saying he was alone and asking to trade something for food. But no voice came, only a pitched stone for an answer.

It was always the same in the rare patches of farm or tiny settlement he came across. Once, he was fired on from a tree lookout. In other places, the dogs were loosed and he had to discourage them with his whip. Spots of human faces far off. A roof and a hearth, a few animals, a little field of pasture and tilled ground, all in the midst of great solitude. They had a right to fear him, not because he was harmful but because he came out of unknown spaces and moved on to farther spaces, an apparition on the road one day.

The land grew more hilly, and after many days, he arrived in sight of a great ruined settlement on the banks of a river—the same river, he thought—but he bypassed it along a roadway that ran west of it. He did spend part of one morning foraging in some outlying buildings and he came away with a fork, a comb, a cook pan, an extra water bottle and two lengths of the slick-surfaced cover stuff, one for a second blanket, one for a kind of cape against the wind and rain.

All this time, he had been possessed by the idea that one day he would return to the country of Esso and would be able to find his way by the map again. The map had left off when they had embarked on the big river. One night, studying it again by the light of his fire, he found the true name of the river and tried to repeat the slippery sound aloud. He peered at the shaded place marked 'St. Louis' in the lower left corner and decided that it was the big settlement ruin he'd just passed. He looked for lines that seemed to cut the blue meander of the river because he thought these might be the sites of old bridges. He would try them, one by one, get across some way, and head north to the blue water Michigan, the sea that Haven had described to him. Then he would follow the curve of the shore north and west to the place he now knew to be the end of his night journeys, the cliff city, the place called Chicago.

The next morning early, he found his bridge sooner than he'd expected. Coming along the road of approach, he saw that only one of the center supports had given way, leaving a long slope and a V-shaped gap in the middle. He started out; the hollow sound was a firm sound under his horses' hoofs. When he came to the broken span, he saw that someone had moored a raft there and had rigged ropes from either end to the two shores. A few pulls would get him across.

And someone had employed the raft that morning—Kinkaid found fresh horse-droppings on it—and his own horses stamped impatiently and neighed. But, once on the far side, he saw no one in the streets of the old settlement beyond. He looked again at his map for correspondences. 'Alton,' he decided.

From there, the countryside was level and the marching easy on broad roads that led northeast. It gave Kinkaid a renewed pleasure to contemplate the idea of a man and his horses walking on a road in exact relation to an invisible dot moving along a line on the paper, and he made a habit of pronouncing the names of old places aloud as he came to them—Carpenter, Farmersville, Springfield.

But before he reached that last name, the snow began. All day, the sky had been the color of slate and there was the kind of cold that cut to the bone. He had seen some habitations—they were a little more frequent now—but had resisted the temptation to approach again for a little warmth and food. He was lucky enough to find a still-roofed brick building for the night. When he woke the next morning, the fields were salted with white and the air hazy with falling snow. Oddly, it cheered him. He liked the freshness it gave to the contours of the land. He realized that he had been anxious for it to come—his old enemy out of ambush at last.

From then on, he tried to make his pace faster and his marches longer, walking even after the last twilight. At first, that was not hard. But in a few days, the true iron season came on the winds from the west and Kinkaid paused more frequently to make small fires and found himself sheltering earlier.

In the days that followed, winter fell on him with a fierceness he could not remember from all years past. It was worse than the great snow winter when he was a small boy; then there had been such days and nights of constant fall that the roof creaked under the weight and his father had had to make an ice tunnel below the drifts so that they could reach the barn to feed the animals.

The days were meager now. The road was often hidden under the drifted snow and walking became so laborious that he would look for any hiding hole to wait until the winds scoured the stone way. The wind itself was fanged, and it fatigued him and froze him. When he could, he scavenged for more layers to wrap himself in. He cut a slit in his blanket and used it for a kind of cloak. In time, he became a moving rag bag. But still, his hands were frostbitten and his feet felt like stumps.

The worst omen now was the nearly empty food bags. On the first days of the march, he had found plenty of wild corn in the fields and he had shelled enough, he thought, to last the journey. His own jerky meat was nearly gone as well and half a day wasted in hunting brought him no game.

One dark morning, with a new blizzard blowing in, his packhorse slipped on ice and fell with a broken leg. Kinkaid stared at it morosely as it struggled feebly in the snow. At last, he forced himself to shoot it. That day, he had blood to drink and meat to roast for the first time in weeks. But now his riding horse became his pack bearer and all the long way ahead he must take on foot. The days and nights blurred into one struggle to move forward through the white wall without crossing the inch that divided life from death.

And did he die? It is possible that, in this worst of all winters, his horse foundered at the end of a weary day. It is possible that, as he stood and watched the down-swirling flakes begin to cover it, the ice finally bit through the bone to the last candle flicker of his determination. And so it is reasonable to believe that he laid himself down beside the horse to rest for a moment and that moment became forever. It is possible that some settlement man or wandering trader, walking that road the next spring, came across the bodies of a horse and a blanket-covered man lying by the roadside and wondered who he had been, from where he had come, and what disaster had befallen him.

But there exists an alternative way that is just as likely. It is quite possible to think that Kinkaid found a nook in some building to wait a few days until the storm relented—as it will in even the worst seasons in those parts—and he was again able to push himself along the level roads until in the course of time he found himself entering among the endless streets of the forefather place he thought he had once created in his dream—the many-towered city by the great lake—drawn toward his dream rendezvous.

As he would walk through the snow-covered streets, looking at the empty face of the city, it is likely that he made some conjecture in regard to the people who built it and to the time and means of its depopulation, by what dire calamity of the sword or famine or pestilence it became a desolation and a ruin. And, on the path of possibility, it seems that Kinkaid must have come at last to a broad avenue choked with wreckage and a great building that still displayed fragments of strangely intricate stone carving on its façade. And here he entered into a dark chamber and called out as if there were someone listening through all the years for his arrival, but heard nothing except the draft and rustle of the wind through vacant rooms. Lighting a fire and finding a makeshift torch, he would have walked on instinctively, descending stairs, coming to an unfamiliar but remembered door, opening it, going into the musty room still furnished with the things of a man who had lived there, looking about, being drawn to a certain place in a certain corner, investigating and finding a stone that could be shifted to reveal a hiding place and, as he had known he would since his journey began, putting his hand inside and drawing out a dusty book. And opening it, began to read. Day of portents, day when the skin crawls suddenly, day of soundless thunder enough to deafen you . . .

THE END

A CANTICLE FOR LEIBOWITZ
by Walter M. Miller Jr.

A Canticle For Leibowitz is one of the great legendary novels of SF. It begins twelve hundred years after the Fallout. The darkest of dark ages has passed and human intelligence has been reborn. And in a monastery cell the monks and novices of the Blessed Order of Leibowitz pore over the records left by the Saint – then, fearfully, tentatively, they begin to experiment with electric light. . . . . .

0 552 11178 3   £1.25

THE DEVIL'S ALTERNATIVE
by Frederick Forsyth

"Whichever option I choose, men are going to die." This is the Devil's Alternative, the appalling choice facing the President of the USA and other statesmen throughout the world.

As the gripping story gathers momentum, the reader is transported from Moscow to London, from Rotterdam to Washington, from a country house in Ireland to the world's biggest oil tanker which threatens to pollute the whole of the North Sea. The climax is the most exciting that even this master story-teller has contrived, and the last-minute surprises in the concluding chapters take the breath away.

0 552 11495 2   £1.95

CATCH-22
by Joseph Heller

CATCH-22 has become a byword in its own time. It is a novel of enormous richness and art. It is deeply serious, yet at the same time, brilliantly funny. It is mentally gymnastic. It is without question one of the great novels of the century.

"Remarkable, mind-spinning, rave of a novel. Uniquely funny." *Daily Mail*

"Comic, macabre, knockabout, nightmarish, ironic, bawdy, illogical, formless, Shavian." *Books and Bookmen*

"Blessedly, monstrously, bloatedly, cynically funnily, and fantastically unique. No one has ever written a book like this." *Financial Times*

"Wildly original, brutally gruesome, a dazzling performance that will outrage as many readers as it delights. Vulgarly, bitterly, savagely funny, it will not be forgotten by those who can take it." *New York Times*

0 552 09755 1   £1.95

GREEN BEACH
by James Leasor

THIS HAS GOT TO BE ONE OF THE GREATEST
PERSONAL STORIES OF WORLD WAR II

19 August 1942 . . . Six thousand Canadian and British
Commandos strike at Hitler's Europe. With them is one
young man – a man whose mission is so vital that he cannot
possibly be allowed to fall into enemy hands . . . alive.

This is Jack Nissenthall's brave and gripping story – the
story told in GREEN BEACH.

"If I had been aware of the orders given to the escort to
shoot him rather than let him be captured, I would have
cancelled immediately." *Lord Mountbatten*

"Makes excellent reading." *Daily Telegraph*

"GREEN BEACH is a vivid, moving and at times nerve-
racking reconstruction of an act of outstanding but horrific
heroism."

0 552 11922 9   £1.75